Featherweight Heart

JILLIAN SNYDER

Published by

DREAMSPINNER PRESS

5032 Capital Circle SW, Suite 2, PMB# 279, Tallahassee, FL 32305-7886 USA
www.dreamspinnerpress.com

Featherweight Heart
© 2016 Jillian Snyder.

Cover Art
© 2016 Aaron Anderson.
aaronbydesign55@gmail.com
Cover content is for illustrative purposes only and any person depicted on the cover is a model.

ISBN: 978-1-63476-918-1
Digital ISBN: 978-1-63476-919-8
Library of Congress Control Number: 2015952964
Published February 2016
v. 1.0
Printed in the United States of America
∞

This paper meets the requirements of
ANSI/NISO Z39.48-1992 (Permanence of Paper).

For Dad, who never stopped believing in this story.

Acknowledgments

THANK YOU to Jen for the consistent and outstanding feedback as I worked through this story. Thank you to J, my longtime prereader, for her valuable comments. Also, thank you to my wife, Camilla, who makes me possible from day to day.

MYTHOLOGY

THE GODDESS Ma'at was the ancient Egyptian goddess of the underworld, truth, and justice. In the underworld, Ma'at awaited each soul, which the Egyptians believed resided in the heart. When a deceased soul passed into the Hall of Ma'at, the heart was placed on a scale and weighed against a feather. If the soul weighed less than the feather of Ma'at, it was deemed to have lived a good life, unburdened and free of sin, and so was allowed to pass into paradise. A heart heavy with sin for having lived an unbalanced or untruthful life was thrown to the Lake of Fire or consumed by the menacing deity Ammit.

CHAPTER 1

THIN TRAILS of smoke snaked upward from the burning bundle of sage and wound their way toward the ceiling of the small shop, filling it with a bitter, woodsy aroma. A single lamp, perched on an antique desk in the corner, burned with a low-watt bulb and suffused the room with dim light that compounded the aura of evening that had settled outside with the waning autumn day. The haunting sound of harmonious female voices chanting Celtic hymns drifted out from an old portable stereo on a shelf above the desk.

With a smooth arcing movement, Jake Parker pushed his hand through the gathering cloud of smoke, dispersing it throughout the room. He walked around the space, holding the smudging stick in one hand and an abalone shell in the other hand underneath it, careful not to let any bits of burning herb come in contact with anything flammable. The store, which he had christened the Witching Well, had an impressive stock of books that covered a wide range of spiritual, metaphysical, and pagan topics. As he wove his way through the aisles, his hand swaying back and forth through the sage smoke as he spread it to the far corners of the shop, he passed by shelves assigned to life after death, spirit communication, Wicca, and Egyptian myth until he reached the back and came to a stop.

He stood between the display of crystals and a rack of cloaks and allowed the sage to burn for a moment undisturbed, his eyes following the gray plumes as they wafted upward. When he felt the area was sufficiently infused with the protective herb, he turned back down the aisle and made his way around the perimeter of the store. Under his breath he repeated the words of the ritual:

> *I call upon the elements to cleanse this space;*
> *This herb of earth and water offered with grace.*
> *As air turns it to fire, in the smoke I shall see*
> *The return of peace and balance, so mote it be.*

As he uttered the final word, he stopped in front of the glass counter of the display case and set down his tools, the sage bundle placed carefully inside its shell. He glanced around and sighed contentedly as he felt the familiar calm that always settled within him after completing a cleansing ritual. He reached for the damp cloth he had left on the counter and wrapped it loosely around the sage to make sure the smoldering herbs were truly out.

He left it to sit inside the shell and glanced at the clock: seven thirty. Only half an hour left before it was time to close up for the day and head home, which for Jake meant locking the front door and climbing the interior stairs to his cozy one-bedroom apartment above the store. He wandered over to the desk and absently flipped open his appointment book to check his schedule for tomorrow; he wrinkled his nose in displeasure when he saw that he had a reading scheduled bright and early at nine. Most days he didn't open the shop until eleven o'clock to allow for time to schedule readings, but he still wasn't a fan of early morning work. That meant he would need to be up by seven thirty so he had time to center himself and prepare.

Jake's second-in-command at the shop was Jessie Hall. She was a part-time grad student on the verge of graduation, and though her hours were usually afternoon or evenings, her schedule was fairly flexible. She gave her own readings, and if Jake couldn't be there to mind the shop, Jessie usually had it covered. He contemplated locking up right then and heading upstairs to compensate for his early start the next day when the tarnished brass bell over the entryway announced the arrival of a customer.

Jake had his back to the door, and he rolled his eyes. He knew any plans for calling it quits early had just been scrapped. He turned around slowly, expecting to see some teenagers clad in black making their way to the display of herbs used for spells and rituals, or a young thirtysomething woman heading toward the kitchen witchery section in the hope of turning her spaghetti sauce into a potion that would make Mr. Right materialize in front of her electric range. Had he bet on either of those possibilities, though, he would've lost.

The heavy door whooshed shut, and a lone man, over six feet tall from the look of him and toeing the line between slender and skinny, skulked into the shop. He hunched his shoulders as he walked, as if he were trying to fold in on himself to disguise his height, or maybe even his very existence. Jake watched as he stopped a few feet inside the door, raised his head, and sniffed the air, no doubt smelling the sage, before he let out a sneeze that sounded like it came from somewhere down around his ankles.

Jake couldn't help but smile at the man's scrunched-up face as he wiped his nose across the sleeve of his gray woolen coat. "Sage," Jake offered.

The man jerked his head up, his eyes wide as though he was surprised to find someone actually staffing the shop. "Hmm?" It was more of a grunt than a word.

"The smell. It's sage. I had some burning just a few minutes ago."

The man stared at him blankly for a moment and then barely nodded as he shifted his gaze to the floor and started up the nearest aisle. Jake shrugged, scooped up a pile of mail still waiting to be sorted, and set to work, determined to at least be productive if he was going to stay open for the remainder of the evening. He flipped through the envelopes and separated them into three piles: junk, might read, and must read. When he reached the last piece of mail, he looked down at the piles and frowned at the height of the must-read stack. While paperwork and bills came with the territory of running your own business, it was his absolute least favorite part, and he had no trouble deciding that the pile could wait until tomorrow. Or the next day.

He sighed and glanced up at his solitary customer. From the looks of it, the guy either wasn't finding what he was looking for or didn't know what it was, because he was wandering aimlessly through the shop, steps slow and deliberate, barely stopping in front of any one thing for more than a few seconds. The clock now read seven forty-five and Jake had no intention of staying open even one minute past eight o'clock so he walked casually over to where the man stood. He stopped in front of an endcap display entitled "Life After Death?" with an array of books on the subject lined up neatly on the shelves below.

"Is there something I can help you find?" Jake asked, his friendly customer-service smile in place.

The man cut his eyes to Jake only briefly before looking back down at the shelf. "Uh, not really" came the mumbled response. Up close, Jake could see that despite the hunched, shadowy way the man carried himself, he was really quite handsome. His slightly overgrown blond hair hung down in loose waves and framed a strong jaw. His light brown eyes reminded Jake of the caramel apples he loved so much this time of year. A smattering of freckles across his nose added youth to his appearance, though Jake guessed he was probably in his early thirties, give or take a few years.

Not easily deterred, Jake stuck out his hand in a greeting. "My name's Jake Parker. I own the place."

After a moment's hesitation, the man reached out to grasp Jake's hand. "Eric."

"Nice to meet you, Eric." Jake shook his hand, holding on just a bit longer than necessary. Eric's hand felt warm and surprisingly smooth despite his weathered appearance. There was something strangely familiar about the feel of Eric's grip and the energy that passed between them with the contact. Jake released him finally and plowed ahead, as was his usual style. "Are you sure there's nothing I can help you find? I know where everything is in this place, and if I don't have it, I can probably get it."

Eric shifted his weight from one foot to the other, awkward and uncomfortable. "Mmm. No, I uh… don't think so. I just, uh…."

Jake wasn't sure if it was his sixth sense kicking in or a simple process of elimination, but he knew at once why this shy, towering man was standing before him. "Did you come in for a reading?" As soon as he said it, he felt the vibration in the room ratchet up a notch or two, and he knew he'd hit the nail on the head.

"A reading? I, uh—you really do that?" Eric asked, holding Jake's gaze this time.

Jake opted to keep the conversation moving forward and decided against mentioning the ten or so signs in the store windows that advertised readings via Tarot, palm, mediumship, and psychometry.

"Yes, I do." He smiled reassuringly. His previous thoughts of rushing the man out and closing up shop had vanished; if there was a force strong enough to lure this unwilling customer into Jake's shop, he knew he had to do it. "What did you have in mind?"

"Umm, I don't really know. Never did anything like that before."

"Well, do you have specific questions, or were you thinking about a more general look at your life? Work, goals, love, finances—that kind of stuff?"

"Uh, general, I guess," Eric replied, obviously unsure.

"Okay," Jake said with a nod, "we'll start there. Follow me." Jake flipped the sign on the door to "Closed" and led the way to the small room off the main store where he conducted his readings. He grabbed his well-used Rider Waite Tarot deck as he passed his desk. He pushed the curtain in the doorway aside and let his new client enter. The room was sparsely furnished, with only a table and a few chairs in the center. Jake kept the lights dim to create a calm atmosphere conducive to relaxation for both his client and himself. The table, covered in a black velvet cloth that hung nearly to the floor, stood next to a small stand that held a variety of crystals, along with two white candles.

"Have a seat." Jake gestured to the side of the table that had two chairs, and Eric settled himself in one of them. Jake lit the candles, took the seat across from Eric, and shook the Tarot cards free from their velvet pouch. He was quiet for a moment as he took a few deep breaths and sifted through the cards. He looked up when he was ready and saw Eric was watching him intently. "Okay, first, I need you to try to clear your mind. But if there's a specific area of your life you want information about, focus on that." Eric nodded. "I'm going to shuffle the cards, and I need you to tell me when to stop."

"How do I know when?"

"It's just a sense you'll have. Whenever you feel they've been shuffled enough." That was the standard answer he gave to customers who often asked that question. People seemed to understand what he meant without requiring an in-depth explanation on the inner workings of the Tarot deck. Eric nodded again, and Jake began to shuffle the cards.

After the deck had been reordered several times, Eric said quietly, "Okay, stop."

Jake stopped shuffling and set the deck in front of Eric. "Now I need you to cut the deck."

Eric complied wordlessly and divided the deck in two. Jake placed one pile on top of the other and fanned the deck out facedown across the table. "Pick ten cards." Eric looked over at him and he nodded in encouragement. Slowly Eric drew ten cards from the deck. When he was done, Jake scooped the remaining cards into a pile and set them aside. He took the ten chosen cards and began to lay them out in a traditional Celtic Cross spread. "Now I don't want you to give me any information as I'm reading. Just let me know if what I'm saying makes sense to you or not, okay?"

"Okay."

When the spread was complete, Jake took a moment to study the cards. One area jumped out at him right away: Pentacles paired with Wands. "Looks like you've had some real success with your work." He looked up at Eric, who nodded in confirmation. "It's not just regular success either. This is something pretty big... big, like, widespread. Reaching a lot of people." Eric nodded again. So far, so good.

Jake was about to move on to the card that represented past events from Eric's life when he stopped short. The hair on the back of his neck stood up, and he felt a chill, telltale signs that they were no longer alone in the room. He dropped his hands to his lap and closed his eyes, trying to focus on whoever was trying to get through to him. He relaxed his posture and tried to open himself to the energy, and with no further effort on his part, his mind filled with images that were not his own. He saw Eric, smiling big and holding somebody close. Phantom laughter echoed in his ears as he saw Eric raising a wineglass in a toast with someone, and then the image changed abruptly to a broken and crumpled Eric, sobbing on the floor of an unknown room.

"Who are you?" Jake asked quietly, trying to make sense of what he was seeing. "What's your name?" Letters flashed in his mind, and he went with his first instinct—a woman. "Do you know someone named... Ann? Or Andrea, maybe?" It didn't feel right, so he opened his eyes and looked at Eric who shook his head, his expression confused. "Give me a second," Jake said and closed his eyes. Again, the letters "AN" flashed before his eyes. As he racked his brain for other "An" names, he saw the image of a man. The face was blurred, but it was a distinctly male form and he understood where he'd made his error. He focused on male names beginning with those letters and he knew the correct one instantly. His eyes flew open, and he looked straight at Eric. "Do you know an Andrew? Someone who's passed over?"

The color drained from Eric's face until he was as white as the candles that flickered beside them. "How do you—" His voice was choked and hoarse. "It... it says that in those cards?"

"No." Jake shook his head emphatically. "This is something else. It's someone in spirit form. He comes through very strong, almost... panicked, like he *has* to talk to you." Eric had gone from looking pale to downright unwell, but Jake couldn't hold the energy back. He closed his eyes again to let it come. "He's showing me a—no, wait." The images and sounds came too quickly to hold on to without context, but Jake picked up what he could. "He says... over and over...'I'm sorry, I'm so sorry.' Do you know wha—" Jake opened his eyes just in time to see Eric's retreating back as he bolted from the room. Jake looked down at the table and saw a crisp fifty-dollar bill tossed carelessly across the spread of cards in the hasty exit.

As soon as Eric was gone, the spirit energy retreated, and Jake was left alone. "What the hell was that?" Jake asked out loud. As much as he'd have liked to just chalk the whole experience up to a reading gone bad, he knew that wasn't the case. The connection between this Eric character and the spirit who tried to come through was way too strong, and Jake had a sneaking suspicion that wasn't the last he'd see of either of them. He got up and went back out to the main store to lock the door, dropping the fifty dollars on the desk. He felt slow and heavy as he made his way up the interior stairs to his apartment, exhausted by the energy he had expended. A short ten minutes later, as he was climbing into bed, he silently prayed for restful sleep; he had a feeling he'd be needing it.

CHAPTER 2

JAKE PULLED back the reading room curtain and moved aside to let the petite, red-haired woman he'd just read for pass through the door. She dabbed at her eyes with a balled-up tissue one last time and reentered the store. She took a few steps in the direction of the door, and then turned back around and flung herself at Jake, enveloping him in an embrace tighter than he would have thought possible judging by her stature.

"Thank you so much," she whispered as she choked back a sob. "You have no idea what it means to me to know she's all right."

He squeezed her back. "You're welcome." He pulled away to look down at her, and she gave him a shaky smile. "And I do know what it means. She wants you to be happy, to live your life. Give it a try, okay?" He disentangled himself from her arms and gave her shoulder a final pat. She nodded bravely, and he followed her to the front of the store. He unlocked the door and she left, heading down the sidewalk with a final wave. He flipped the sign on the door to "Open" and stepped back inside, the overhead bell jingling as he closed the door. Thankful for a few minutes of solitude, he walked over to his desk and collapsed in the timeworn chair that squeaked and groaned under his weight. The reading had been especially draining, and he leaned forward, his elbows on the desk and his head in his hands.

He never knew what he was going to get when someone walked through the door to ask for a look into the future or the past, and Jake did his best to keep himself centered and ready to handle whatever might present itself. Every once in a while, though, he would have a session that really took a toll on him. The woman who had just left had lost her young daughter to an inoperable brain tumor two years earlier and had not been able to get past her grief. She was racked with guilt that she'd somehow failed her child and had slipped into a depression. While Jake had never experienced the loss of a child, he knew the difference it could make just knowing that a loved one was safe and happy and not harboring any ill will on the Other Side. He had just finished his third reading for her, and he hoped she was getting closer to making peace with what had happened.

He'd had a series of trying readings this week that began with the Eric episode several nights ago. That energy had come through so strong, and he'd honestly expected to hear from either Eric or the spirit who identified himself as Andrew, but neither had returned. He'd kept his eyes open, both physically and spiritually, for a day or two afterward, but when no more came of it, the encounter drifted to the back of his mind. Perhaps Eric just hadn't been ready for the reading, and Jake was making more of it than there actually was because of the connection he'd felt with Eric and the way Andrew had hijacked the reading. He didn't doubt that if there was more he needed to do, it would be made clear to him one way or another.

He sighed and stood up to switch off the stereo, afraid that the quiet meditative music might send him to sleep right there. He scooped up a box from the floor and set it on the desk as he brushed a lock of dark brown hair from his eyes. He started to unpack the shipment, laying out pendulums and crystals in front of him. As he contemplated where best to display them, the bell rang again. This time, instead of a customer, a whirlwind of preteen boy barreled through the door, careened down an aisle, and came to a stop in front of his desk, backpack slung over his shoulder and a couple of books cradled in his arm.

"Hey, Uncle Jake!" Bobby gasped, left breathless by his attempt to break the land-speed record as he entered the store.

"Whoa, kid. Where's the fire? I didn't know you were coming by today. Your mom didn't say anything."

"She got stuck at work. She left a message for me at school and said I should come here."

"I see. Lucky me, then. Why don't you run upstairs for a snack, then come back down and get started on your homework, okay?"

Bobby nodded, his shaggy brown hair bouncing with the movement. "What's there to eat?"

"Umm, I'm pretty sure there's a microwave pizza in the freezer, or there's stuff to make a sandwich."

"Okay." Bobby let his backpack fall to the floor and unceremoniously dropped his books on the desk. "Be back in a few."

"There's also a bowl of fruit on the table if you want to make your mom really happy."

"Yeah, right!" Bobby's voice echoed as he bounded up the stairway to Jake's apartment.

Jake chuckled to himself. The kid never seemed to run out of energy or room for more food. While he wasn't Bobby's uncle by blood, he loved that he had a place in the boy's life. Jake and Laney, Bobby's mother, had known each other for over fifteen years. Once upon a time, when they were young and Jake was just figuring out that girls might not be what did it for him, they'd tried to be more than friends. The attempt had fizzled and died, though, as Jake's definite preference for men became an undeniable fact. Luckily, they had been able to weather that storm and had become closer than ever. Several years later, when Laney found herself pregnant by a man who wanted nothing to do with a child, Jake had stepped in and become "Uncle Jake," and he'd been a permanent fixture in Bobby's life since the day he was born.

Bobby was now eleven years old, soon to be twelve, and while he was probably at an age where he'd be able to stay home alone, Laney was overprotective and hesitant to leave him unsupervised. She worked long days as a nurse at Boston Children's Hospital, but most days she started early enough so she was home by the time Bobby got out of school. On the days when she couldn't be there for whatever reason, Bobby came to the store after school and spent time with Jake.

Jake smiled at the crashing and banging coming from overhead as Bobby tore through his kitchen. He picked up the pendulums and crystals and stood, ready to set them up in the main display case. As he rounded the corner of the desk, his eyes lit on the pile of books Bobby had left on his desk, and he saw something that made him suck in a sharp breath. There, on the back of the hardcover book that rested facedown on top of the pile, was Eric's face. The same Eric who'd wandered into his shop the other night and then had taken off without a word, two sentences into his reading. Jake slowly set the merchandise down and picked up the book. It was definitely the same man; the soft brown eyes, freckled nose, and sandy blond hair were etched into Jake's memory. He looked as somber in his photograph as he had the night he was in the shop, and Jake paused to wonder if the man ever smiled at all.

His eyes traveled to the blocks of text beneath the picture; they were snippets of reviews from well-known sources, all claiming the triumphant success of this latest work.

"Austin delivers spine-tingling suspense in this can't-miss thriller!"

"Delving into the occult, Austin weaves a chilling tale of murder and madness as he takes readers with him to 'the other side.'"

"*Trial by Fire* is so masterfully crafted, it will leave readers wondering if, perhaps, witches and demons really do exist."

Jake chuckled at the last blurb; there was no wondering about that in *his* life. He confirmed it every day he got up and came to work. He flipped the book over to look at the cover: *Trial by Fire*, by Eric Austin. The letters were scripted in blood red, and the cover art depicted the silhouette of a large, sprawling house surrounded by a decrepit metal fence. The full moon shone brightly in the night sky above and cast an eerie blue glow over the image. He turned the book back over to stare at the photograph again as Bobby launched himself down the stairs, taking them two at a time judging by the sound.

"Hey, Bobby, what's this?" Jake held up the book and waved it in the air.

Bobby looked over from where he stood by the incense rack. "A book," he said through a mouthful of pizza.

Jake rolled his eyes. "Don't be a smartass. Where'd you get it?"

"Mom."

"Your mom lets you read this? Isn't it a little old for you?"

It was Bobby's turn to roll his eyes as he swallowed his last bite of pizza. "Jeez, Uncle Jake, I'm not, like, a *little* kid! Mom read it and when I asked her about it, she said it was by some famous author guy who lives right around here. It's about spirits and stuff, but not like what you do here. Demons, I think. I asked and she said I could read it as long as I didn't get scared. You know how she is about reading."

Jake did know. Early on in school, Bobby had struggled mightily with dyslexia, and it had always been a chore to get him to read, even when he had to for school. With Bobby offering to read something voluntarily, he imagined Laney would've said yes to just about anything short of *Playboy* or *The Satanic Bible*.

"Okay," Jake said doubtfully. "So, you say the author lives around here?"

"Uh-huh. Somewhere nearby, maybe Boston. That's, like, his brand-new book or something. He's having this thing at the Barnes and Noble in Boston on Saturday where he signs books and reads out loud from it. Why would he read out loud from his own book? Anyway, I wanted to go get an autograph, but Mom has to work."

"Are you supposed to go to your grandparents' house?"

"Yeah."

Jake paused for only a few seconds before he spoke. He knew then he'd seen the book for a reason, and he knew better than to let signs like that go unheeded. "I've got an idea. Why don't I talk to your mom and see if you can come here instead, and then I'll take you to the book signing?"

"Really? Awesome!"

"Well, let me ask her first, and we'll see what she says." Jake added the last part to make sure Laney retained the role of decision-maker in Bobby's eyes, though he knew she'd say yes in a heartbeat. She didn't like Bobby spending any more time around her overbearing father than was absolutely necessary. Still, she sent Bobby there regularly in her constant worry about being a burden to Jake or cramping his social life. Where she got that idea from he had no clue, because it had been a couple of months since he'd had so much as an interested glance from an eligible man. He put that thought aside as mental fodder for another time and focused his attention back on Bobby. "All right, kiddo, let's start your homework."

Bobby sighed liked a doomed man and dragged his feet over to the desk. He grabbed his backpack as he passed it and flopped down into Jake's chair.

He unloaded his books, muttering under his breath, "Homework sucks."

"Yeah, yeah, I've heard it all before. Get busy!" Jake picked up the crystals and pendulums again and headed for the display case. He stood at the counter and sorted them by stone, thinking about the upcoming book signing. His mind drifted back to the almost-reading with Eric, and how close he'd come in describing Eric's work. As he wondered what else would have come out in the cards if he'd had the chance to keep going, a familiar feeling came over him. Hairs stood on end and he shivered as an icy chill breezed across his skin. Unbidden, the same images from the reading flickered through his mind like a silent movie, only this time there was a new one as well. He saw Eric grinning big as he held someone, then Eric raising a glass in a toast, then Eric crumpled on the floor in a heap of despair. At the very end, just before the energy he now recognized as Andrew faded out, he saw a ring, a plain gold band, falling, falling, falling, until it hit a hardwood floor and rolled away.

Jake shook his head and took a deep breath, frustrated with his inability to find meaning in what he was shown. He returned to his work, and despite his confusion, he felt certain of two things: he was meant to be at that book signing on Saturday, and Andrew, whoever he was, would be there right beside him.

CHAPTER 3

SATURDAY CAME around, and as Jake had suspected, Laney was more than happy to have Bobby spend the day with Jake instead of with her parents. The book signing was scheduled to start at two o'clock at the Barnes and Noble in the Prudential Center in downtown Boston. It took about twenty minutes on the subway—known as the T to locals—to get from Brookline Village, where Jake lived, into the city, and then another fifteen minutes or so on foot to the Prudential. He'd told Bobby to be at the store by noon, and at five minutes till twelve, the bell jangled and he came charging into the store, carrying the book that had set the whole day's adventure in motion.

"Uncle Jake! I'm here!"

Jake grinned and stood up from where he knelt behind the glass display case, rearranging merchandise to make room for some newly arrived scrying mirrors.

"Thanks for telling me. I'd have never known."

Bobby made a face and flopped down in the chair behind Jake's desk, which squeaked in protest. "Are you ready to go?"

"In a few minutes. Let me just finish up with this." He returned to his position on the floor to put the last two mirrors in their places.

Bobby sighed dramatically. "I don't wanna be late. What if the trains are crowded, or we get there and there's no seats in the bookstore, or—"

"Bobby! It'll be fine. We won't be late, and they won't run out of seats—I'm sure."

"You mean 'you're sure' 'cause we have plenty of time, or 'you're sure' 'cause the spirits told you?"

Jake chuckled. He'd always been particularly proud of the way Bobby took some of the weird things that were part of his life in stride. "Which one would make you feel better?" he joked. As he rose and slid the case door shut, he caught the tail end of Bobby's eye roll. "You want to grab a snack to bring on the train? There's bags of Doritos up in the kitchen, and some packs of...." He let his words trail off since Bobby was already out of the room and halfway up the stairs to his apartment.

Bobby had tossed his copy of *Trial by Fire* on the desk in his haste to get upstairs, and Jake walked over and flipped it facedown so the picture of Eric was staring up at him. As he studied the serious brown eyes, he could feel Andrew's energy pressing, trying to come through. He'd thought something like that might happen, so that morning he'd made a special point of going through a short ritual to close his Third Eye chakra, otherwise he feared he'd see and hear nothing but Andrew all day. While the block was effective, Andrew was strong and persistent enough that Jake was still aware of him, and he suspected that the closer he got to Eric, the harder it would be to hold the energy at bay. It was unusual, even for him, for a spirit to distinguish itself so unmistakably after only a short encounter. He could only guess Andrew had something major to say, and he'd been waiting a while to do it. Jake stood, so lost in thought, hypnotized by the face staring up at him, that he didn't hear Bobby come back downstairs. He sucked in a surprised breath and jerked his hand away from the book when Bobby spoke.

"Do you like him, Uncle Jake?"

Jake stared at Bobby blankly, a hand splayed open on his chest over his hammering heart. "Huh? Why would I like him? I don't even know him," Jake sputtered.

Bobby shot him a look like he'd just channeled an alien. "*It*, Uncle Jake. I said 'Do you like it?' Ya know, the *book*."

Jake shook his head. "Oh, the book. Yeah, I don't know. Haven't read it."

Bobby rolled his eyes again. "Okay, whatever. You should. Or you can just *like* the guy," he added with adolescent emphasis on "like," then wrinkled his nose and stuck out his tongue.

Jake dropped his hand to his side and shook his head, laughing. Another thing he was proud of Bobby for, though this made him a little nervous at times, was the way Bobby accepted Jake's preference for men without question. It was a good thing, and he and Laney had worked hard to be honest with Bobby about it from a young age, but there were definitely times he wished the kid wasn't so observant. Jake had been on his own for a while, and as Bobby got older, he began to worry about Jake being alone. He'd taken it upon himself, on occasion, to play matchmaker for Jake (though *troublemaker* might be a more apt word), pointing out a guy here or there, often at inopportune moments, whom he thought might be acceptable candidates for Jake.

"No, Bobby. I mean, yes, I'll read the book, but *that's* not why I was looking at the picture. And besides, I seriously doubt he's gay." He felt a surge of energy roll through him with those words, followed by the word "*Yes*" that Jake heard so clearly Andrew might as well have been standing there in the flesh. Jake knew then what he'd just said was false. The knowledge Eric was gay and that Andrew knew it gave him more information to fit into the puzzle that was missing so many pieces at the moment, but it wasn't something he was inclined to share with Bobby. It was better for everyone if Bobby went without that seed planted in his head.

Bobby shrugged. "Whatever."

"Okay, you ready to go?"

"Yeah, for like ten minutes."

"Put the 'Closed for Spiritual Emergency' sign in the window, and I'll meet you out front." Bobby nodded, grabbed his book, and headed for the door. The sign was meant in a tongue-in-cheek way, and Jake used it only on the rare occasions when he had to close unexpectedly. But this time he felt it wasn't that far from the truth. He picked up his cell phone from the desk, slipped it into his pocket, and lifted his coat from a peg on the ancient coatrack that stood in the corner behind the counter. He made his way to the front of the store and stepped out into the unseasonably warm fall air. He locked up the store and turned to Bobby. "Let's go!" Side by side they headed down Harvard Street toward the train station.

AN HOUR and a half later, Jake and Bobby stepped through the main entrance of Barnes and Noble at the Prudential Center. Jake scanned the store and located a sign labeled "Author's Corner" with a big picture of the cover of *Trial by Fire* and an arrow pointing the way down an aisle. They walked in the direction the sign indicated and came to a separate common area where folding chairs were set up in rows, the same layout you might see for a small wedding or concert: two sections of folding chairs divided by a wide aisle in the middle. A long table with a podium and a microphone atop it stood ready and waiting for the guest of honor. The room was already quite full, with only single vacant seats here and there. Bobby tugged on Jake's coat sleeve and led him up near the front.

"Aw, man! I wanted to be up close," Bobby whined.

Jake had a sneaking suspicion it would be a bad idea for him to sit front and center, certain that it would throw Eric for a loop after the way things had gone in the shop. He spied a single empty seat in the third row and offered it to Bobby.

"Why don't you grab that spot right there, and I'll hang out in the back till it's over. I'd rather stand anyway after sitting on the train all that time."

Bobby looked moderately appeased. "Really?"

"Sure. Go sit down and I'll be over there against the wall, okay?"

"Yeah!" Jake was happy to see that Bobby minded his manners and excused himself as he worked his way past the other people who were already seated to the empty spot in the middle of the row. Once he was sure Bobby was set, Jake headed for the back of the room to find a spot where he could blend into the crowd. The last thing he wanted to do was cause any upset for Eric in public. Once he found a corner where he felt sufficiently inconspicuous, he leaned against the wall to wait.

He barely had time to get comfortable, though, and the wait was over. The same long, lean figure he recognized from the night in the shop strode confidently down the middle aisle toward the front of the room. Excited whispers and nervous giggles from female voices rippled through the room as Eric set his worn army-issue shoulder bag down on the table, ran a hand through his wavy blond hair, and shot the crowd a disarming smile. Jake couldn't help the smirk that spread across his face at this, knowing what he now did about Eric's sexual inclinations.

Eric stepped over to the microphone, his deep, rumbling voice bouncing off the walls of the room as he spoke. "Thank you all for coming. Just give me a minute and we'll get started." Eric had been so reticent and had said so little the night he showed up in Jake's store that Jake hadn't had any real recollection of what the man sounded like. A shiver raced up his spine now as the sound hit his ears like the first swallow of a good whiskey after a long day, dark and rich, leaving a warm glow behind in his core. He studied Eric's fluid movements as he pulled papers, his laptop, and finally a copy of *Trial by Fire* from his bag. Jake was taken aback by the sharp contrast between the poised, self-assured man before him now and the lost and lonely creature who had shown up in his shop.

Once all his materials were laid out to his liking, Eric returned to the mic. "Okay, I think we're ready to go ahead now. I'm Eric Austin, and I'll start by reading a few of my favorite passages from *Trial by Fire*. Then I'll take a few questions, followed by the book signing." He paused for a moment as though he were waiting for agreement from the audience. Met with silence from the crowd, he reached down to grab the reading glasses that were hooked on the V-neck of his navy-blue sweater. He slipped the glasses on and riffled through his book until he found the right page. "The first excerpt begins on page forty-eight, for anyone who'd like to follow along." He turned his head away from the mic and cleared his throat, then turned back and began to read. "'As I sat huddled in the low-lying bushes, I struggled to make sense of what I saw before me. The flames leapt high and sinister into the black backdrop of the night sky, and the cloaked figures congregated around the roaring fire, every movement purposeful and deliberate. Their voices rose up in an eerie chorus that sent a chill through my body and soul, far colder than the autumn breeze that dared disturb the surrounding trees. I watched as....'"

Eric read on, and while Jake had no doubt that the story was spellbinding, he barely took in a single word. With Eric so close by, his voice filling the room, Andrew's energy surged up, and it took every ounce of concentration Jake had to keep it at a manageable level. He knew Andrew wanted to communicate, to show him more pictures, to give more information that might help Jake solve this minimystery that had fallen into his lap. And as much as he wanted to do that, he knew this wasn't the time or place. He focused so hard on keeping all the images and sounds at bay that he had one hell of a headache by the time Eric finished reading through three passages and had moved on to taking questions. Jake glanced at the seated crowd and saw Bobby listening with rapt attention, so he decided to step outside of the room for a moment, if for no other reason than to preserve his own sanity. He hoped that, with any luck, Andrew would remain as close to Eric as possible and leave him be for a moment.

As soon as Jake put some distance between himself and Eric, he felt the pressure in his head decrease. Able to breathe a little easier, he paced the floor not far from the entrance to the common area so he could keep tabs on what was happening. After about twenty minutes, Eric wrapped up the questions from the audience and announced that anyone who'd like their book signed should line up and he'd be happy to do it.

Jake knew that Bobby would want his copy signed so he slipped back in the room just as Bobby rushed up the aisle looking for him.

"Uncle Jake! Did you hear all that? Wasn't it awesome?" Bobby's whole body vibrated with excitement as he spoke, and Jake grinned down at him.

"Sure did. That was pretty cool. He's a really good writer."

"I know! I wanna get my book signed. Will you get in line with me? I don't wanna go up there by myself."

"Sure. Let's just wait a while until some of these people go through the line. We won't have to stand there as long." The reasoning sounded vaguely ridiculous to Jake, but Bobby seemed to accept it without question. He nodded, went to sit in a nearby chair and started flipping through the pages of the book. In truth, Jake wanted to be as close to the end of the line as possible, hoping he might have a chance to speak with Eric. After about thirty minutes, the crowd had thinned considerably and Jake didn't see any more people joining the back of the line, so he called Bobby over and they took their places at the end. After another fifteen minutes of painfully slow forward movement, Jake and Bobby were next to approach the table at the front.

When the woman ahead of them moved aside with a giggle and a shy wave at Eric, the two of them stepped up to the table. Eric was obviously functioning on autopilot at this point because he didn't even glance up at the two fans in front of him.

He took the book as Bobby slid it across the table toward him, opened it to the title page, and asked, "Who should I sign it to?" When Bobby gave his name, Jake assumed it was the young voice that caused Eric to look up in surprise. He glanced at Bobby first before his eyes moved upward and fixed on Jake. A spark of recognition smoldered in Eric's gaze as Jake nodded and gave a friendly smile. Eric seemed unsure of what to do for a moment, but he collected himself and turned back to Bobby. "Bobby, huh? I think you might be my youngest fan yet."

Bobby beamed with pride. "I got the book from my mom. She read it, and then I wanted to, and she said I could."

"What about your dad?" Eric nodded in Jake's direction as he wrote.

"Oh, he's my uncle, not my dad. Well, not really my uncle. But anyway, he doesn't have any kids. He's single."

Jake sighed and dropped his chin to his chest. He looked up just in time to catch the funny half smile on Eric's lips as he asked, "Is that so?"

Bobby nodded emphatically and opened his mouth to speak again, but Jake beat him to it. "All right, Bobby, thank Mr. Austin and let's move along. We don't want to take up all his time."

Bobby agreed reluctantly. "Thanks, Mr. Austin. I really like your book."

"Thank you, Bobby. Glad to hear it."

As Bobby stepped aside, Jake caught him by the coat sleeve. "Bob, can you do me a favor? Go over to the magazine section and see if they have this month's copy of *Fate*. I've been thinking about stocking it in the store, and I want to have a look, okay?"

"'Kay." Bobby waved to Eric and then took off up the aisle, leaving the two men alone except for the few stragglers who were clustered in pairs and small groups around the room, chatting.

"Cute kid," Eric offered.

"Yeah, he's great. When he's not running his mouth, that is." Jake smiled, but his expression quickly turned serious. "Look, I don't want to keep you. I just wanted to say sorry for the other night. I didn't mean...."

Eric held up his hand to stop Jake. "No, I'm the one who should say sorry. I shouldn't have taken off like that, without a word. I just...."

"It's okay, really. You weren't prepared for me to go that way and... hell, *I* wasn't prepared. It was strong, though—this guy...." He stopped short when Eric swallowed and shifted his gaze to the floor. "Anyway, I just wanted to let you know that if you ever think you want to try the reading again, I'd like to help. Or if you just want a friendly ear, you know?" Jake paused, not sure if he'd said too much. He felt Andrew's presence building around him again as he stood in such close proximity to Eric, but he did his best to ignore it. He was treading on unfamiliar terrain with Eric, and he needed to go slow.

Eric twirled his pen between his fingers. Finally, he sighed and looked up at Jake through dark brown lashes. "You'll be there later tonight?"

Jake nodded, beyond relieved that Eric was at least open to talking with him. "The shop closes at eight, but my apartment is right above it. If I'm closed, just go around the side of the building and there's an entrance with a doorbell. Give me a buzz."

Eric was quiet for another moment and then finally acquiesced, his voice tinged with resignation. "Okay. It'll be after eight, but I'll come by." A series of emotions passed over Eric's features, too quick for Jake to identify, but he could sense the turmoil churning inside Eric nonetheless.

"See you then." Jake smiled, then turned and headed up the aisle just as Bobby came back into the room, magazine in hand. As he and Bobby stood in line for the cashier, he hoped Eric wouldn't change his mind between now and this evening, though Jake knew there was really nothing he could do about it. He'd made the offer, and now it was out of his hands.

CHAPTER 4

AFTER THE trip back to Brookline Village, Jake saw Bobby home, stayed for a bit to catch up with Laney, and then headed back to his place. There were only a couple hours of the workday left, but he opened the shop anyway, just on the off chance that somebody might need his services or some final complement to a carefully crafted spell. And it was with no small hope that Eric would come striding through the doors, exuding the same quiet confidence he had shown this afternoon, that Jake waited through two long hours before it was time to close up for the night.

He headed up the interior stairs to his apartment, his body humming with nervous energy. He straightened up the place, assuming that if Eric showed up, he would invite him upstairs instead of fumbling around to reopen the shop. He had rearranged the throw pillows on the couch for the third time when his actions registered in his brain and he slowly sat down, perched on the edge of the couch, and closed his eyes. He quieted his mind and tried to figure out where these feelings were coming from. He didn't sense Andrew around, or any spirits. He was pretty adept at closing off the channels of communication when he wasn't working so he wasn't constantly bombarded with incoming information. Really, no good could come from him knowing that the Stop & Shop cashier's husband was cheating on her as he paid for his things. He had smudged the apartment only two days ago, as was his weekly ritual, to keep the energy in balance and get rid of any negativity.

He realized that to *most* people, lots of things that were everyday parts of his life would seem like something straight out of a teen supernatural novel at best, and complete delusion at worst. He'd learned how it all worked early on from the woman who had raised him and was still far superior to him when it came to dealing with the Other Side: his grandmother. Rebecca Parker—Gram to him—still lived in Salem, Massachusetts, in the house Jake had grown up in, and although she was in her seventies, she was still a well-respected member of the psychic community. Jake's situation was unusual; the gifts he possessed were most often passed down from mothers to daughters within families, skipping a generation here and there. In his case, as an only child, he'd gotten it from both his grandmother *and* mother, though his mom had taken off early on, distancing herself from the weird world of readings and ghosts she'd grown up in and dulling her natural talents with alcohol and drugs. He still couldn't say where exactly his mother was at any given moment—she sporadically popped in and out of his life—but he always knew exactly where to find Gram.

He'd only been five years old when his grandmother had known for sure he could follow in her footsteps, and they had their first talk about what went on in her "workroom." From as early as he could remember, he'd been warned about leaving Gram alone while she worked, seeing her clients. He grew curious, like any kid would, and one day got brave and spied on one of her readings. He tucked himself away in a closet with a shuttered door and peered out at Gram doing her very important work. An older woman sat at the table across from Gram, and an older man in a suit stood behind the woman. He watched as Gram lit candles, took out some colorful stones and cards, and set them in front of the woman. The rest of the scene didn't make much sense to Jake; he saw the woman cry and ask Gram questions, which the man *answered, and then Gram would repeat what he had said (mostly—some things she skipped over), and that made the woman cry even harder.*

When it was all over, Gram saw her clients out and then came back into the room, looked straight at the closet, and said, "C'mon out, Jakey." He remembered feeling momentarily terrified, but she didn't sound angry, so he slowly opened the door to reveal his hiding space. She studied him silently for a moment and then said, "Let's go to the kitchen. Snack time." Once he was settled at the kitchen table, she sat across from him and asked, "So, what did you think?"

"Of what?" he asked, his five-year-old brain already on ten other subjects.

"Of my work. What you saw in my workroom," she answered.

Jake shrugged and took a bite of cookie. "I don't know. It was okay. I don't know why she didn't just talk to him."

Gram's eyes lit up. "Talk to who?" she asked.

"The suit man. He was right behind her!" he said with exasperation.

Gram nodded and spoke her next words carefully. "So you saw him? The suit man?"

Jake looked at her like she was a few cookies short of a batch. "Yeah."

"I see," she said. "Did he look the same? Like me and you and the woman?"

Jake rolled his eyes upward and thought. "Hmm… kind of. But no."

"What do you mean? How was he different?" Gram prodded.

Jake took a swallow of milk. "He looked the same, but he was… shinier," *he said with a wave of his hands.*

Gram laughed. "Yes. Yes, he was." She went on to explain, as much as she could for his age, that the woman couldn't see the man, which was why she'd come to Gram. He was the woman's husband, who'd gotten sick and passed away, and Gram could see him and help them talk. And so, apparently, could Jake. "We're like bright lights to people on the Other Side, like lighthouses," she explained. "They see us and know we're a safe place where they can come and talk." Jake thought about it for a second and nodded. "But," she added, holding his hand for emphasis, "if anyone comes to talk to you and they're mean or they make you feel bad, you just close your eyes and send them away. They have to go. And make sure you tell me, okay?"

"Okay," he agreed and swallowed the last bit of his cookie.

She'd been his go-to person on all things supernatural ever since. He picked up a framed photo of the two of them from the end table and smiled. It had been taken at a psychic fair the previous summer. As he put it back on the table, he realized that even his trip down memory lane hadn't done much to settle his jittery mind. Again, he did a quick inventory of possible sources of his keyed-up feelings and he was soon left with only one conclusion: they were his own. He puzzled over this for a moment; he'd always prided himself on his ability to remain objective and uninvolved with his clients, despite their sometimes vulnerable or emotional circumstances. He viewed his role as a conduit for information, and he couldn't do that job very well if he let himself be overwhelmed by the feelings a reading could evoke. He did the best he could for each person who came into his shop, and when his day was done, he was careful not to bring any "work" home with him. So why now? What was it about this Austin guy that had him running around arranging pillows and wiping down counters that were already spotless?

Always up for some introspection and good advice from a willing spirit guide, Jake sat down in his favorite chair and tried to relax. The quickest way to reach a guide was by way of an open Third Eye chakra, so he shut his eyes and went through a meditative exercise he'd done countless times before. Mind quiet, breathing steady, and a soothing indigo color swirling before his closed eyes, he opened himself to communicate with his guides and offered up his questions regarding Eric for interpretation. What he got wasn't what he expected, though. As soon as he opened the channels, he felt a familiar chill wash over him and the hair on his arms stood on end: Andrew was ready and waiting. Jake took this as a positive sign that Eric was coming. Andrew was so tightly bound to Eric that Jake knew the spirit wouldn't stray far from him, which must mean Eric was in the vicinity or would be shortly.

Instead of trying to force things to go the way he wanted, Jake decided to sit back and let Andrew have his say. He spoke out loud to the spirit, as he often did when he was alone. Experience had taught him that by talking with them the way he would with any other person—and as so few people did—he had a better shot at getting the information he wanted. Only this time, he had no idea what he was after.

"Okay, I'm listening. Go ahead—what've you got?" No sooner had he spoken the words when Andrew began his usual way of sharing information by showing Jake images and snippets of scenes, presumably from the past. Jake had no doubt that Andrew believed he was being quite clear, unaware that quite a bit was often lost in translation from one side to the other. Jake saw the same images Andrew had shown him before, until the gold band fell and rolled away and Jake knew they had reached the end. Or so he thought. He didn't see anything new immediately, but he suddenly felt a wave of calm and warmth wash over him, the likes of which he'd never felt before. He sighed contentedly and settled back farther into his chair to bask in the good feelings.

"Wish you guys could all do this," Jake joked. "I'd never leave work."

But along with the warm and fuzzy feelings, he had more to show Jake. A close-up image of two faces pressed together, lips joined in an affectionate kiss. Jake could tell by the two stubbled cheeks he saw that both participants were male. A golden wave hung loosely at the side of one of the men's faces, which Jake used to identify Eric. He let the image float in his mind for a moment. It was a touching and tender scene, and the picture it painted, coupled with the warm feeling of the rightness of it all, made it a place Jake knew he could stay for a long time. He tried to focus, though, because there had to be a reason he was seeing this.

"I know you loved him. As far as I can tell, he loved you too. But what am I supposed to do with it?" The picture disappeared as soon as the words were out of his mouth, but the feelings stayed. "Okay, I got that one wrong. Try again?"

After a few seconds of nothing, the same image filled Jake's mind, only from a different perspective; this time he saw the men from farther away. He got a full view of Eric, and he looked... happy. The serious, pinched look he seemed to have permanently etched on his face was gone, and there was a serenity to his features Jake had not yet seen in actual life. Jake smiled slightly as he watched Eric slowly lift his hand and run his long fingers through the thick, dark hair of the other man. He shifted his focus to the other half of this equation and what he saw made his heart stick in his throat. He expelled all the air in his lungs in one harsh gasp.

It was him.

Jake was the other man, kissing Eric as though he'd spent a lifetime perfecting the art, smiling against Eric's lips as his hand combed through Jake's hair. Now Jake's eyes flew open, and he leapt from the couch.

"What the fuck?" The exclamation rang out in the room that was now devoid of any presence but his own. Hands on his hips, he looked from side to side as though Andrew might suddenly materialize and offer a perfectly reasonable explanation for what he'd just shown Jake. No such explanation seemed to be forthcoming, though, and Jake had a full ten seconds to collect himself before the sound of the buzzer echoed through the apartment, signaling someone waiting downstairs.

Eric.

Jake took a deep breath and headed out the door and down the stairs to let Eric in. He had no intention of sharing what he had seen with Eric, but he hoped like hell that he'd be able to make some sense of it before the night was over.

CHAPTER 5

JAKE REACHED the bottom of the stairs and flipped on the light for the entryway. He turned the lock and pulled open the door to reveal a nervous-looking Eric on his doorstep, sucking on the dregs of a cigarette.

"Hey," Jake said with a smile, much happier than he should have been that he was essentially working late.

Eric took a last puff on the cigarette and then ground it into the pavement under an edgy-looking black Oxford. He was still dressed the way he had been earlier, sleek and professional in a navy V-neck sweater with a white T-shirt underneath and dark gray dress pants. His expression was a sharp contrast to his overall look, though, his forehead wrinkled and his eyes brimming with unease.

"Hi." His one word response gave way to a series of coughs. "Sorry."

"Didn't figure you for a smoker."

"I'm not, usually."

"I see." Jake decided to leave it at that. He realized it must have been hard for Eric to agree to see him and then to actually show up, knowing he was taking a step toward facing whatever it was that had sent him running the first night in the shop. "Well, c'mon in. Is it okay with you if we head upstairs? The shop's already closed up for the night."

"Sure. Fine."

Jake stepped aside to let Eric into the entryway, shut and locked the door, and led the way upstairs. They entered Jake's apartment through the upstairs door that opened into the living room and Jake gestured toward the space.

"Have a seat. Make yourself comfortable. Can I get you something to drink? Coffee, water, beer?"

"Water's good. Thanks."

Jake went into the kitchen and pulled two bottles of water from the fridge and returned to the living room, where he found Eric seated on the couch. He handed Eric a bottle and took a seat in the armchair nearest the couch. He watched as Eric's eyes roamed all over his apartment, a vaguely surprised look on his face.

"You like it?" Jake asked in an amused tone.

"Huh?" Eric flicked his eyes to Jake. "Oh, yeah. It's nice. Just… not what I expected."

"No shrunken heads, coffins, or skeletons?" Jake teased.

Eric chuckled. "Yeah, something like that."

"So how long have you been in the city?"

"Mmm, close to ten years now. I grew up in the suburbs, but I did my master's degree in English at Boston University, then stayed after I finished. Picked up freelance writing jobs wherever I could while I worked on my first novel."

"And the first one was a success?" Jake didn't know much about Eric's field, but he thought the chances of that were unlikely.

"Not really. I got an agent and a small publisher picked it up after a while. It did okay, but nothing great. Then the second one did better, with a bigger publishing house. *Trial by Fire*'s my third and it's doing real well." Eric gave him a tense smile.

"I figured as much with the crowd you had this afternoon. That's great," Jake said sincerely.

Eric shrugged. "It is and it's not. I mean, I'm lucky to be able to do what I do for a living, but I hate the readings and signings and things that are part of the deal now. All I can think of is how much I'd rather be home working on my next project."

"I can understand that. Must take up a lot of time."

Eric nodded.

"Well, I can tell you one thing: you sure made Bobby's day. He'd probably 'totally freak,'" Jake said with air quotes, "if he knew you were sitting here in my apartment."

Eric laughed quietly. "He seems like a nice kid."

"He is," Jake said. "I like having him around."

Eric nodded again, and they fell into silence for a short time until Eric spoke up.

"So, uh, what about you? How long have you been doing… what you do?" he asked.

Jake laughed at his choice of words. People often had a hard time trying to figure out what to call him. He'd heard everything from gypsy to warlock. "Well, I've had the store for a few years now. It's nice to have a kind of home base to operate from. Before, I used to go to people's houses mostly, and do readings or parties. It's easier now that they come to me, instead of me having to go to them all the time."

Eric looked at him directly. "Seems like you came to me this afternoon."

"I did," Jake said, meeting his gaze.

"Why?"

"I…"—visions of what Jake had seen just before Eric had arrived danced in his head—"don't know," he finished, aware of how lame he sounded.

"I see." Eric shifted nervously in his seat, sipped his water, and eyed Jake with a piercing gaze. "Are you doing it right now?" His tone bore a hint of accusation.

"Huh? Doing what?" Jake was still lingering on the kissing scene in his head, and he was quite sure he wasn't doing that at the moment.

"You know… what you do." Eric flailed his hand in Jake's general direction as though that clarified his meaning.

"What I…. Oh! Oh, you mean reading, or channeling? No, I'm not. Not right this second."

"So, it's something you can turn off, then?"

"Shit, yes! I'd have been locked up long ago if all that stuff came through 24-7 for every person I met." Jake shuddered at the thought, which got him a quiet chuckle from Eric. The deep rumbling sound brought a smile to Jake's face. "I let it in—open myself up—while I'm working, and then I 'turn it off,' like you said, when I leave. I try not to bring it home with me. Though sometimes that works better than others," he added under his breath.

"What is it that you *do*, exactly? If you don't mind me asking." Jake heard nothing but curiosity this time, so he took his best shot at explaining himself.

"Not at all. I'm a clairvoyant and a medium."

Eric stared at him with raised eyebrows, awaiting further explanation.

"Clairvoyant is kind of a general term—seeing or knowing things beyond the usual five senses. People use it to mean all kinds of things nowadays, though: ESP, telepathy, psychic dreams, or visions."

Eric nodded for Jake to continue, his brow furrowed in concentration as he listened.

"I use tools like Tarot cards and runes to help me interpret what I see, either through that sixth sense or through mediumship."

"Medium—that's like one of those 'I see dead people' things, isn't it?"

Jake laughed. "Yeah, I guess so. I don't usually 'see' them, but sometimes I do. For me, it's kind of connected to the clairvoyance. I can sense them—their energy—when they're around, and they show me pictures, or sometimes give me words or feelings."

"Pictures?" Eric looked at Jake doubtfully.

"Images. It's like… having thoughts that aren't your own, if that makes any sense. They show me things from the past, or about the person I'm reading for. Sometimes it's clear and I get the meaning right away, and sometimes it's like a puzzle to figure out. Most of the time, if I describe what I see, it means something to the person getting the reading, and we can go from there."

Eric leaned forward and set his water on the coffee table, then rested his elbows on his knees, locking his fingers together. He glanced up at Jake, his mouth set in a thin, hard line.

"Is, uh… is that what happened the other night?"

Eric's agitation was plain, and Jake knew he needed to tread lightly or he risked losing the fragile trust they'd started to build.

"Yes. I wasn't expecting it. I'd planned on doing just a regular reading with the cards but…. When I'm working, I'm 'open,' so to speak, and energies can sometimes just come barreling through if they're determined enough."

"Energies?" Eric questioned.

"Spirits. Those who've passed on."

"And you saw… or heard or whatever… someone wanting to talk to me?"

"Andrew." Jake felt familiar enough with Andrew that he replied without thinking, as though Andrew was someone they both knew. He realized it might have been a mistake when Eric jerked his head around to look at Jake through narrowed eyes.

"How can you possibly…?" Eric spoke quietly, and his words trailed off as he shook his head. "I guess you just explained the 'how' of it. It's just strange to hear his name like that, like he's still here."

Jake got up from the armchair and joined Eric on the couch. He was used to working with people in closer proximity when dealing with these things, across the small table in his reading room. The closeness allowed him to better focus on the person he was reading for, their emotions and the energy coming off them. Jake positioned himself with one knee bent underneath him, facing Eric.

"Eric." Jake paused for a beat, hoping for some kind of sign that this was the right direction to go with this subject. When he got nothing, he forged ahead. "He *is* still here. Not like he was before, but he's still around you. A lot, I think."

Eric stared, his eyes awash in confusion. "But... why? I mean, he never... we weren't.... God! I just don't get it." His chin dropped against his chest.

During a reading, Jake avoided asking direct questions to his client at all costs. That's how some psychics operated, some legitimately and some not. It could easily be mistaken for fishing for information, so he always did his best to work with what he had. This wasn't a typical reading, though, and Eric was obviously struggling.

"Who is Andrew? Who was he to you?" Jake asked softly.

Eric raised his head and met Jake's gaze, a half smirk on his lips. "Why don't you tell me?" Although his tone was teasing, Jake read the underlying challenge in his words.

"Okay, well, I certainly don't know everything, but I'll tell you what I've got. You and Andrew were... together. You were lovers." It was really just an assumption on Jake's part, based on what he'd seen and the attachment Andrew seemed to have to Eric, but Eric's startled reaction confirmed it as fact. "I think it ended badly, and he passed on before the two of you had a chance to set things right." That was the CliffsNotes version, taken from the little bit Andrew had shown him, but Jake felt it best to continue with the slow and steady approach.

Eric's mouth opened slightly in surprise, though Jake felt he'd hardly revealed anything earth-shattering. "So, you know that he and I were together, and you're not surprised?"

It seemed to Jake the question was asked more in confirmation than out of shock or concern, and he laughed quietly. Maybe Bobby was more subtle than Jake gave him credit for.

"Yes, I know that." Jake sighed but followed the guiding voice in his head that told him to keep talking. "It's not my practice to share much about myself with my clients, but I think we've already gone well outside the scope of an average reading here. I'm gay, Eric, so I'd be the last person to have anything to say about it."

"You are? I thought, maybe, but I wasn't sure…." Jake watched as Eric's eyes skimmed over his form from head to toe, as though seeing a whole new person. Eric's eyes lingered for a moment at what Jake chose to think of as his belt, and he cleared his throat to bring Eric back to the discussion.

"So, I guess I was pretty close, then?" Jake asked.

Eric moved his eyes back up to Jake's face and nodded. "Yeah. That's the gist of it. I still don't get why he's around me now, though. I mean, he never would've… he wasn't out when he was alive. We fought about it all the time."

"Well, sometimes, when someone passes on, there are still things they need to make right—for themselves and for people they've left behind—before they can move on. How long ago did he pass?"

"A little over a year ago."

"And would you say you're still affected by it?"

Eric shrugged and picked some invisible lint from his pant leg. "I don't know. Maybe."

Jake had a sudden urge to do something he knew would give him a little insight. "Can I hold your hands?"

Eric looked up at Jake, surprised. "What?"

Jake raised his hand and shook his head. "I'm sorry. That sounds weird, I know. Sometimes if I can touch a person, it helps me get a better handle on where they're at, their energy and emotions. I can only take what they give me from the Other Side, but there are two participants in these situations, and you're right here in front of me. You've got something to tell me too." When Eric still looked doubtful, to lighten the mood he added, "I promise not to steal any future novels from your brain or anything. Strictly business, I swear."

Eric snickered and relented. "All right. What do I do?"

"Just turn to face me and hold out your hands."

Eric mimicked Jake's position and faced him on the couch, hands open and outstretched. Jake took Eric's hands in his own and let them settle together. He let his thumb run up and down the smooth skin alongside Eric's index finger, a tactic he used often to help his clients relax. He felt Eric's hands go slack.

"I'm just going to close my eyes and be quiet for a minute so I can focus on your chakras, okay?" Jake was always careful to ask permission, reminding his clients that they were in control of the process.

"My what?" Eric asked.

"Chakras. They're energy centers in the body. They're each responsible for different things—communication, creativity, feelings—so reading them gives me a better overall picture."

Eric shrugged. "Okay," he agreed.

Jake shut his eyes and cleared his mind. He read chakras similar to how one might read auras. He saw the different colors of varying intensities as he tuned into Eric's energy and emotions, looking for any colors that jumped out at him as either dim or overly intense, indicating possible trouble spots. He started at the bottom and worked his way up: the root and sacral chakras passed easily with their strong red and orange colors. Jake noted a dimness in the yellow of Eric's solar plexus, which could indicate some insecurity brewing. While that was mildly concerning, Jake couldn't help but suck in a breath when he moved on to the heart chakra—a muted, barely-there green darkened further by a black shadow he couldn't recall having seen in other readings. Based on that, Jake concluded that Eric wasn't feeling much love for himself or anyone else these days.

The bitter, unhappy feelings started to seep over into Jake and he took a cleansing breath to expel them before he continued. Moving up, he saw the healthy, vibrant blue of the throat chakra, which made sense since Eric communicated for a living. He wasn't the least bit surprised by Eric's closed Third Eye chakra—barely a pinpoint of indigo, which explained why Andrew likely couldn't get through to Eric at all on his own. Finally, and again no surprise, Eric's crown chakra glowed an almost sacred white, healthy and strong and no doubt providing him with endless inspiration for his writing.

Jake took a deep breath, opened his eyes, and saw Eric staring at him intently.

"Well? What's the damage?" Eric asked with a forced smile.

Jake tried to smile back, but he was overcome with a sad sympathy for the man before him. He couldn't even imagine carrying that kind of heaviness around with him on a daily basis. That wasn't something he wanted to tell Eric, though, so he tried to make his words as neutral as possible.

"Well, your brain and creativity are firing on all eight cylinders. You've got at least another dozen or so bestsellers in there." He smiled and Eric laughed. "As for the emotional part… I think you're in a tough spot. It's not the end of the world, but you've got to work through some stuff, kind of clear out the cobwebs. I think that losing Andrew, whatever happened between the two of you, has been really hard." Eric turned his head to the side and nodded almost imperceptibly. "But you *could* be happy again," Jake added after a few seconds of silence. "I'd like to help if I can."

Eric turned back and met his gaze, then nodded more confidently. His voice was rough when he spoke. "Okay. I'd like to try. Thank you, Jake." Jake felt a gentle pressure between his fingers as Eric squeezed his hands. His eyes darted to the space between them and he was shocked to see that not only were they still holding hands, but at some point the fingers of his left hand and Eric's right had become entwined.

He began to extricate himself gently while he apologized. "I'm sorry. I don't know why… I didn't even realize…." he stammered.

His fingers weren't easily freed, though, because Eric didn't let go right away. They lingered there for a brief moment, and he felt another squeeze before Eric finally separated from him.

"It's okay. No need to apologize." Eric fidgeted in his seat and Jake waited, knowing he had something else he wanted to say. After a deep sigh, he asked, "Is he—Andrew—here now?"

"Well, like I said before, I'm closed off right now, so I can't say for sure. I think it's a pretty safe bet, though. Did you want me to try to—?"

"No." Eric's answer was immediate and emphatic, and Jake felt inwardly grateful. Truth be told, he was bone-tired and he didn't think he'd make a top-notch medium at that point in the day. "Not tonight, anyway. This is a lot to take in. I just need some time to process it all."

"I understand completely," Jake said with a smile.

"Do you think we could talk again? I mean, I'd like to, if you're willing."

"Just say when."

"Damn, I don't have my calendar with me. Do you have a card or something? Can I give you a call? I think the end of the week should be good, but I'll have to double-check."

Jake reached into his back pocket, took out his wallet, and handed Eric a business card. "I'm pretty accommodating, so just let me know when's good for you."

"Okay." Eric stood up and tucked the card away in his wallet. "Jake… I don't know what made you come to that book signing, or come talk to me afterward, but thanks. Really." Eric extended his hand and Jake took it, giving him a firm shake.

"Don't thank me. I think there's something a little bigger at work here." He grinned as he walked Eric to the door and back down the stairs. He unlocked the outside door and held it open as Eric stepped outside.

Eric looked back and returned the smile. "Well, then I'm glad at least one of us is listening." He gave a wave and headed out into the night. Jake stood in the doorway, watching until he was gone.

CHAPTER 6

"SO THE book signing was fun?" Laney asked as she reached across the table and stole a tortilla chip from Bobby's plate. Laney, Bobby, and Jake were seated in a booth at Baja Betty's in Brookline Village. It was Wednesday, and Bobby had come to the shop after school. Laney met them after work, and they'd walked down the street for dinner at their favorite neighborhood Tex-Mex place.

Bobby just nodded, all his attention focused on his Nintendo 3DS and the occasional wedge of quesadilla he grabbed off his plate and crammed into his mouth. Jake nodded too, and Laney raised her eyebrows in a request for more information.

"Yeah, it was interesting," Jake said. "There was a pretty good crowd, he read from the book, and then we got Bobby's book signed."

"Wow, that's pretty cool," Laney said, nudging Bobby with her elbow. "So you even got to talk to him?"

Bobby nodded again. "Yeah, he said I was his youngest fan." He still kept his eyes on his game. Jake smiled and took another bite of his burrito. "But he talked to Uncle Jake way longer," Bobby added. Jake's eyes grew wide, and he froze midchew. He had no idea Bobby had seen him speaking with Eric after the book signing. He should've known better, though; not much got by the kid.

"Really?" Laney drawled, giving Jake a totally different kind of eyebrow raise.

Jake rolled his eyes and swallowed his food. "Oh, yeah," he said casually. "We just talked about the book for a bit… you know."

"You didn't read it," Bobby said.

Jake pressed his lips together and shot a narrow-eyed glance at Bobby who *still* hadn't looked up. "Right," Jake said. "It was more about… I mean, considering my work, we were just talking about how that might coincide with him. And his writing."

"You mean, like, consulting?" Laney asked with a furrowed brow. "Is he going to write a sequel to *Trial by Fire* and use you for some supernatural research or something?"

Jake sighed and put his burrito down. He needed to answer carefully. Though he wasn't sure he would call Eric his client, he still knew some fairly personal information he felt obligated to keep private. "Not exactly," Jake said. "He has some issues with…. Well, he has some *company*, and I think I might be able to—"

Bobby's 3DS hit the table with a thud. "Oh, my gosh, you mean you're going to *read*? For *him*? When? Is he coming to the shop? Can I be there? Does he have a demon following him and that's why he writes such weird, scary stuff?" The questions flew from Bobby at lightning speed.

Jake sputtered out a laugh at the last question. "No, he does not have a demon attached to him. Not that I've seen so far, at least."

"So you've already read for him?" Laney asked.

Jake groaned. "No, not exactly. He came by and we talked some. I'm not sure if he's ready for that yet. You know how it is. You can only tell a person something when they're ready to hear it. And," he added, looking pointedly at both of them, "even if I had read for him and knew his entire life story and ten past lives, I couldn't talk about it."

Now it was Laney and Bobby's turn to groan. "You and your ethics," Laney said with a fond touch of sarcasm. "Is he as hot in person as he is on his book jacket?" she asked, switching gears.

Jake glanced down and felt his face flush as he recalled again the image of him and Eric kissing he'd been shown just before Eric arrived at his apartment. He glanced over and saw that Bobby had returned to his video game. "He's a good-looking guy, yeah," Jake answered noncommittally.

Laney looked over at Bobby, checking that he was no longer paying attention. She shifted her gaze back to Jake and soundlessly mouthed, "*Gay?*"

Jake chewed on his lower lip, then gave her a quick nod. He had no idea how out Eric was, but he knew at least that wouldn't go any further than Laney. A grin spread across her face. "Well," she said, "I'm sure you'll be a big help to him. You know, in lots of ways."

Jake turned even redder, and she pursed her lips to stifle a giggle. He scratched the side of his nose with his middle finger and Laney burst out laughing.

"What's funny?" Bobby asked, glancing up from his game.

"Nothing," Jake said. "Trust me. How about dessert?"

THAT NIGHT, Jake had a dream. He believed the mind was capable of a number of different kinds of dreams: the type where it just seemed to be piecing together random bits of information from your day, the kind that sometimes helped you solve a problem you'd been thinking about, and the plain old drawn-out story type. This one, however, was different. It was the kind he classified as a visit. Sometimes a visit meant exactly what it sounded like: an interaction with a person who had passed on, or a guide who had some information to share. Sometimes a visit was a story a spirit wanted to tell, past, present, or future.

He knew from his work over the years that it could be easier for a spirit to pass on longer, more detailed bits of information in dreams because generally all guards were down in a sleeping mind. It required less energy, so they had a chance to say or show a little bit more. For reasons he would never understand, these sleeping visits always happened for him without sound, like watching a movie on TV with the volume on zero. He found that immensely frustrating, but at the same time, he couldn't complain. It was an attempt to communicate from the Other Side, and usually he was grateful for whatever information they wanted to pass on.

That night he got his first clear picture of Andrew: average height and strong build with straight, light brown hair that fell across his forehead and sometimes into his eyes. He had quirky green eyes and a warm, genuine smile—the kind that made you want to smile back. As Andrew seemed to favor in waking hours, he shared what he had to show film-clip style in a string of isolated scenes. Jake saw Andrew sitting at a desk, a stern look of concentration on his face as he stared at his laptop until Eric came up behind him and wrapped his arms around his neck. Jake saw Eric's mouth move as he spoke, and Andrew threw his head back and laughed. He looked up at Eric, who spoke again, and then they exchanged a backward kiss.

Next, Eric and Andrew were poolside somewhere, probably a house because they were the only two there. They lay side by side, stretched out on chaise lounges, their fingers hanging loosely entwined between them.

Then they were in a car—a shiny black BMW, Jake noted from the badge on the steering wheel and the gleaming hood—with Eric behind the wheel. Eric glanced from the road over to the passenger seat where Andrew sat, sound asleep, a sweater bunched under his head against the window.

There was a pause and then a final image filled Jake's sleeping mind, though this one was less clear, like an over-the-air television picture at war with static. But he was able to make out that same BMW crushed like an accordion against a tree on a nameless dark road. The deployed airbag filled the space on the driver's side, and all he could see was the shoulder of the driver, slumped motionless toward the passenger seat.

Jake jerked awake, tangled in the sheets and sweating, a panicked cry rising in his throat. He huffed out a shaky breath and looked around frantically, slowly realizing he was in his own bedroom. He closed his eyes, blew out a long breath, and flopped back down on his pillow, his heart still hammering.

"Fuck," he whispered. He felt absolutely sure of what had just happened: a visit from Andrew. He was unsure, however, about what he'd been shown in the last image—something that had already happened, or something that hadn't happened yet? A third option remained as well, although it was rare. Had he been shown something—a horrible something, in this case—at the *same time* it happened, as a sort of out-of-body witness? Andrew was glued to Eric and could certainly show Jake a glimpse of the present if he wanted or needed to. But even if that had been a supernatural SOS, what could Jake do about a totaled car on some unknown road?

"Shit, shit, shit," Jake muttered. He turned on the lamp beside the bed and reached for his cell phone, ready to call Eric and make sure he was okay regardless of the fact that it was three thirty in the morning. He grabbed his phone, sat up, and clicked on his contacts, and then dropped his chin to his chest with a mournful groan. He'd given Eric his business card but hadn't gotten one in return. He had no way to contact the man. With a sigh, he set the phone down and turned off the light. He lay back down in bed, first on his side and then on his back, unable to get comfortable and, every time he closed his eyes, unable to rid himself of the image of the crushed car and lifeless driver. When the first light of morning peeked through his window, he officially abandoned any hope of sleep and got up. He padded down the hall to the kitchen where he fired up the coffeemaker, sending out feelers and prayers to every spirit and guide on the wire that Eric would call him today.

WHILE JAKE wouldn't swear to it, he felt fairly certain that there had been more than twenty-four hours in Thursday and at least double that for Friday. With no word from Eric, he couldn't rid himself of the knot that had formed in his stomach the second his mind's eye had seen the totaled car. A car, based on what little information he had, he assumed was Eric's. Eric had said he thought he was free at the end of the week, and Jake had expected to hear from him before that to make plans for… whatever came next.

"Not if he's dead," he mumbled to himself as he looked over a vendor form for an upcoming psychic fair somewhere out on the Cape. When he'd looked it over the week before, he hadn't been able to decide if he wanted to travel that far for a fair, and he sure as hell couldn't think about it now.

He tossed the paperwork back into his inbox and ran a hand through his hair. His rational mind tried to break through the muddle of worry and fear and reason his way to calming down. Surely if Eric had been killed in an accident, he would have heard about it on the news, right? Maybe he wasn't a literary lion who would warrant national coverage, but there would have been some local coverage. If one of Boston's own, an up-and-comer currently working his way up the best-seller lists, had died, he would've seen *something* about it. Or heard something. Right?

No answer was forthcoming from any of his channels. *Where the fuck was Andrew now*, he wondered. *With Eric, one way or another*, he thought in answer to his own question. He picked up his cards and tried to concentrate on Eric's status among the living or the dead. He threw down a quick yes-no spread, which told him absolutely nothing. He wasn't really surprised; his mind was too clouded to be able to elicit anything helpful or informative. He drew the cards up and set them aside in a stack. He'd need them for his Beginner Tarot class the next morning.

He glanced at the clock on the wall and, with twenty minutes still technically left in his workday, he decided to close up shop. Fridays tended to be slow, and he probably wouldn't be much good to anyone who showed up anyway. He locked up, shut off the lights, and then made his way slowly upstairs to his apartment, his mind cycling endlessly on the same questions he'd had since the dream. He stretched out on his couch, pushing his fingers to his eyes.

"Where the hell are you?" he called out to the empty apartment. "Are you at least all right?"

The hair on his arms stood on end, and he sensed a shift in the energy in the room. He thought it might be Andrew, but far less intense than he usually felt, which could mean he was either drained for some reason or coming across from far away. What he presented Jake with, however, was not an answer but another question.

Like a whisper breathed through his mind, Jake heard, *"Why do you care?"*

He waited a minute or two more, but as quickly as the energy had come, it left. He sat up and pondered what had just happened. It wasn't a totally new question; it had popped into his mind more than once over the past two days of hand-wringing. He'd let it slide right by, though, because truthfully he didn't know why he was so concerned. Yes, he'd met with Eric and had been able to make a fairly easy connection, especially considering Eric's hesitance. But he wouldn't say they were friends; Eric wasn't even really a formal client. So why had he spent the past two days fretting over a dream and a phone call he might never receive? Eric could be perfectly fine, could have simply decided Jake was a whackjob and he wasn't going to call again.

Jake didn't have a good answer other than to acknowledge the fact that somehow, Eric had gotten under his skin. Even in his fuzzy state, he knew better than to question that; people came into your life for a reason, and he knew there was a greater purpose for this too. Eric, Andrew—all of it. He'd just have to be patient and know the answer would reveal itself in time. But that brought him little comfort as he stripped down to his boxers and slid into bed for another sleepless night.

"TODAY, WE'LL be discussing the Major Arcana," Jake said to his eight eager students in Beginning Tarot. "Go ahead and separate those out from your deck." As the class began shuffling through cards, Jake turned and tried to stifle a yawn.

"Are those the ones with the coins on them?" a blonde-haired woman seated a little too close to him asked.

"No," Jake answered patiently. "Those are Pentacles. That's a suit in the deck. Your Major Arcana are the first cards in the deck. They have Roman numerals at the top from zero to twenty-one. Zero is The Fool."

He waited while they sorted through their decks, sighing inwardly that only fifteen minutes of the two-hour class had passed. He let his tired mind wander over the past couple days until the same blonde woman put her hand on his arm and said, "Jake, are you okay? I think we're all ready."

Jake removed her hand and stood. "Now," he began, "it's important to remember that the cards are not always iconic. They don't always mean what you might think at first glance. The Fool doesn't necessarily refer to an idiot, and Death rarely refers to an actual physical death."

He had a vague notion of himself droning on and his students taking feverish notes until his concentration was broken by the vibration of his phone in his pocket. He usually left it in his desk for class, but he hadn't been able to part with it that morning. He slid the phone out of his pocket to check the caller ID and, although he didn't recognize the number, he knew at once he had to take it. His answer was on the other end of the line.

"All right," he said briskly, "I want you to look carefully at card number ten, the Wheel of Fortune, and jot down what you see in the artwork of the card that might help you interpret its meaning. I'll be right back."

He headed to the front of the store, nodding at Jessie and holding up his phone as he passed the register. She smiled and nodded, and he opened the door and stepped out onto the sidewalk.

"Hello?" he said breathlessly into the phone.

"Jake? Hi, it's Eric. Austin," he added, as though Jake had a sea of Erics floating through his life.

"Hi," Jake said. He stopped there, unsure where to begin, or if he should even begin at all.

"Is this a bad time? I can try to give you a call later on—"

"No!" Jake interjected. "I mean, no, now's good. Now's fine. I just… I know it's a weird question but are you all right?" he asked quickly before he chickened out.

"Yes, I think so," Eric replied carefully. "What do you mean, exactly?"

"Are you okay? Like, physically?"

Eric coughed. "Uh, yeah. I'm fine. I had a bit of a cold earlier in the week, but—"

"No, not like that," Jake interrupted, frustrated with his own inept communication. "You've been okay this week? Nothing major happened? No… car accidents?"

Eric stayed silent for longer than Jake was comfortable with. Finally, he cleared his throat and said quietly, "No. No accidents. Why would you ask that?"

Jake sighed and scrubbed a hand over his face. "It was just something I saw," he said tiredly. "And I hadn't heard from you so I wasn't sure what it meant, and I thought maybe…." He trailed off, not wanting to voice aloud what he'd been fearing. "Anyway, you're fine. That's good." He felt some of the tension he'd been carrying dissipate with the words.

"Yes, I'm fine," Eric said. "Sorry, I… I didn't mean to worry you."

"It's okay—it wasn't you. I mean, I was worried, but it wasn't your fault." He tried to focus, ignore the warm feeling brewing in his belly. "So, what's up?"

"Right," Eric said. "Well, I had said I'd give you a call. I thought maybe we could meet up, talk some more about things."

"Sure," Jake said, "that sounds great. Do you want to come by the shop?"

Eric paused. "I was thinking of something a little different," he said. Jake heard him take a deep breath on the other end of the line, and then he asked, "Will you have dinner with me?"

CHAPTER 7

"DINNER?" JAKE repeated, caught off guard.

"I'm sorry," Eric said quickly. "I don't mean to put you on the spot. I've been thinking about seeing you… I mean, we had said we'd meet up, talk a bit more. I thought it might be good to relax, have a nice evening. I don't know about you, but I've had a hell of a week."

"Dinner?" Jake said again, willing his neurons to start firing and get him past single-word responses.

"If you don't want to, that's fine," Eric began. "I just thought—"

"No," Jake said. "I mean, yes. Dinner would be great. When?"

"Well…." Eric hesitated. "I know it's short notice, but are you free tonight? I'm sure you have an actual life and everything, so it's fine if you're not. We can pick another day. I should be around for at least the next week or so."

Jake chuckled. "Not as much of a life as you might think," he said. "Tonight's fine. Where should I meet you?"

Eric cleared his throat. "Well, I kind of had a place in mind, but it's a bit of a drive. Can I pick you up at seven o'clock?"

"Seven?" Jake repeated, again unprepared for Eric's suggestion. "Sure, seven's fine," he said, hoping he sounded if not smooth at least sane.

"Great," Eric said, and Jake could hear the smile in his voice. "I'll see you tonight, then. And, uh, I'm sorry you were worried."

Jake smiled into the phone. "No problem—occupational hazard. I'll see you tonight."

They disconnected and Jake stood on the sidewalk outside the shop, still smiling to himself. He glanced through the window at his class and saw that Jessie had gone over to the group. They were all busily comparing cards and firing questions at her. That bought him a few more minutes, and on autopilot he clicked the first speed dial in his phone. On the third ring, a familiar voice picked up.

"Hi, Gram—it's Jake," he said.

"Hello, sweetie. Shouldn't you be in your class right now?" she asked.

He could visualize her checking her watch as she spoke. "Yes," he said. "I should. I am, actually. I just stepped out for a second."

"Okay. What's up?" she asked. The expression and her tone sounded too forced-casual to Jake, which told him she'd likely been expecting his call.

"Will you be around this afternoon? I was going to catch the one-thirty train from North Station and come by to see you."

"Sure, dear," she said. "I'll be here. Is everything all right?"

He laughed. "You'd know before me if it weren't," he joked. "Yes, everything's fine. I just have this client—I'm having trouble. I've hit a bit of a blind spot or something. I'm not sure."

"Hmm. All right, then, I'll see you this afternoon," she said.

"Okay. Thanks, Gram. See you about two fifteen."

They hung up and he turned to go back in the store but paused with his fingers around the door handle. He heard the echo of his own words—*blind spot*—and puzzled over them. It was oftentimes one of the negatives of his gift. Good psychics could read, channel, and answer questions about life, love, loss, and everything in between for their clients most of the time. When it came to their own lives, however, most hit exactly that—a blind spot. Gifts didn't always work the same way—sometimes not at all—when you used them to try to divine information for yourself. The logic behind it, or so Gram had taught him, was that they were really no different from any other people. What they had was a gift like any other—musical talent, the guy who's first in his class at Harvard Med—and they were here to live, learn, love, sometimes lose, and make mistakes just like everyone else. Their extrasensory abilities were not a free pass from learning life's lessons or a ticket to easy street by beating the house in Vegas.

Jake thought about it. If he were truly hitting a blind spot, that would mean the puzzle of Eric and Andrew had something to do with him too. He shook his head, doubting the likelihood of that. However, if there were any chance that was the case, there was one person who would know, and he'd be seeing her in a few hours. He reentered the shop, ready to give the rest of the class his full attention.

JAKE WALKED briskly up Essex Street from the train station and glanced at his watch as he approached Gram's house: just after two fifteen. He always tried to be on time, but he never worried about it too much with Gram. It was like she'd had a psychic LoJack installed in him as a child and always seemed to know where he was, especially when he was on his way to her. He jogged up the side steps of the pea-soup-colored house and gave a quick knock. The house dated back to the 1800s, and although Gram had made improvements and modernizations over the years since it came into her possession from her parents, he'd never been able to convince her to part with the god-awful color. Even as a teenager when he'd nagged her to repaint it something less embarrassing, she'd refused. The house had been that color as far back as she could trace and it would stay that way, she'd insisted.

He opened the door into the kitchen and smiled when he saw Gram standing at the stove, moving the steaming tea kettle from a hot burner.

"There's my boy," she said as she turned and opened her arms to him.

"Hi, Gram," Jake said, crossing the kitchen and enfolding her small frame in a hug. "Good to see you."

She pulled back and patted his cheek. "Good to see you too. Have a seat," she said, gesturing toward the small cherrywood kitchen table, which matched all the cherrywood cabinets. When Gram got fixed on a color, she didn't let go, but at least the dark wood gave the kitchen a warm, homey feel. He pulled out a chair and sat just as Gram set down a mug of tea in front of him. He wafted the steam toward his nose, trying to identify which leaves and herbs made up this week's concoction. He picked out the licorice scent of anise right away, along with a touch of mint and a third scent he couldn't name. He knew the first two were used in a variety of ways to enhance psychic vision.

"I see you're trying to help me out already," he said appreciatively.

She sat down across from him with her own mug and tucked a lock of short silver hair behind her ear. "Every little bit helps," she said with a smile. "So, how are you?"

He talked about the shop for a bit, told her about a new psychic development class he was thinking of offering, and gave her an update on Laney and Bobby. She listened quietly, nodding her head and sipping her tea until he ran out of words.

She reached across the table and patted his hand. "That's good, dear. Very good. Now, why don't you tell me why you're really here?"

Jake sighed and dropped his chin to his chest. "Where do I start?"

"At the beginning, of course," she answered, and so he did just that. He began with the night Eric wandered into the shop and ended with the phone conversation that had taken place just a few hours earlier. "Well, that's quite a story," she said when he'd finished. She picked up their now-empty mugs and carried them over to the sink.

"I know," Jake said. "It's driving me nuts. I haven't gotten things in such bits and pieces since I don't know when."

"Hmm," Gram murmured as she rinsed the mugs.

"What's 'hmm'?" Jake asked.

"Nothing, sweetie," she said as she sat down again. "Just... have you tried stepping back and looking at the full picture? Not just the individual incidents?"

Jake furrowed his brow, the phrase "full picture" calling to mind the vision of him and Eric kissing. He shook his head and put that aside. "I think so. I feel like I've looked at it from every angle. But there are still holes—information I haven't seen, or haven't been given. Or maybe I just missed it."

"Yes, I see. Well, the universe seems rather determined to put this Eric character in your path."

He looked at her quizzically, a half smile on his face. "Yeah. I guess you could say that. It's the guy on the Other Side I'm more worried about."

"They're *both* important," she reminded him, emphasizing her point with a tap of her fingernails on the table. Jake nodded; Gram had emphasized the importance of giving each side equal time since he began learning about his gifts. They sat in silence for a moment and then Gram leapt out of her chair. "I need to read for you," she said—a statement, not a question.

Jake groaned and covered his eyes with his hand. Whenever Gram read for him, he usually ended up finding out something he'd rather not know. "Now? Really? I'm supposed to meet with this guy in a few hours."

"Yes," she said, determined. "It won't take long. I only have a couple questions."

"Oh, so this is for you, not for me?" he asked with a laugh.

"In a way," she answered vaguely. Jake knew better than to press for answers—he wouldn't get them. One of Gram's greatest gifts was knowing what to tell people and when to tell them. "I just need to know how I can help you best."

Jake shrugged his consent. She was already on her way out of the kitchen, no doubt headed to her reading room to grab her tools of choice. She returned with her Tarot deck and a velvet pouch of crystals. She shuffled the deck a few times and then passed it to Jake. He shuffled it for a good minute and then passed it back to her. She fanned the cards expertly across the table.

"Pick one," she instructed. He closed his eyes and passed his hand slowly over the cards until he felt the energy jump under his hand. He set his fingers on a card and slid it out from the others. Gram positioned it in the middle of the table, rolled the crystals in her hands, and let them scatter across the table around the card. She studied the layout silently, tilting her head every so often as though she were listening to something. Jake wasn't picking up anything, so he sat patiently until she nodded and turned the card over. Ten of Swords.

He knew the deck well so he knew the meaning of the card. It usually represented someone who'd changed in some way—moved on or often passed on—and was happier now for having done so. "That's Andrew," he said. "It's got to be."

Gram pressed her lips together and studied it for a second longer. "Pick one more card, honey," she said. Jake repeated the process of selecting a card and she flipped it over beside the first one. The Lovers—a card in the deck that needed no further explanation. Jake looked up at her, and she wore a faint smile, doing her funny head-tilt thing again.

"Well?" he asked expectantly. "Did you get your answers?"

She met his gaze still wearing a half smile. "Yes. I did," she said with satisfaction. "But more importantly, so will you. Soon."

Jake blew out a long breath. He knew better than to try to coax further information from her. If it were hers to tell or his to know, she'd have already shared it.

"Well, that's something," he said.

"Yes, it is." She smiled wider and glanced up at the clock. "Oh, my! Look at the time! It's nearly four o'clock, and you need to be on your way."

In a very un-Gram-like way, she rushed him to the door. "Are you trying to get rid of me?" he asked, only half joking.

"Of course not!" she exclaimed as she led him to the door. "But you need to get back—you've got someplace to be!"

"Uh, okay," he said, confused about why his dinner meeting had suddenly taken on such importance. "Well, it was good to see you, Gram."

"Good to see you too, sweetie," she said as she opened the door. She reached up and gave him a tight squeeze. "Wear your blue jacket. Your eyes are just breathtaking in that," she whispered in his ear. Before he could respond, she turned him bodily and shuffled him out the door. "I love you!" she sang. "Call soon!"

He stood on her porch and gave a halfhearted wave to the closed door. He couldn't be sure if he picked it up with his actual ears or the ones inside his head, but as he headed slowly back down the stairs he heard Gram's soft chuckle from somewhere. Shaking his head, he did the only thing he could at the moment and turned his feet back toward the train station.

AT FIVE after seven, Jake popped up from the couch and zipped down the hall to his bedroom to check his reflection in the full-length mirror for the tenth time. He tugged at the sleeves of his dark blue sport coat (even without explanation he wasn't about to ignore orders from Gram and her Other Side army) and ran his hands down the front of his dress shirt. He felt unusually giddy, though he couldn't pinpoint the exact reason why. He chalked it up to a long time without a nice, grown-up evening out, even if this one was business.

He glanced at his watch again and, just as he did, the buzzer to his apartment rang. He ran a hand through his hair and, after one last check, he headed back down the hall and downstairs to meet Eric. Before he opened the door, he opened up his mind's eye, doing a quick sweep for any spirit hangers-on. He'd gone through a quick ritual earlier to close himself down—like hanging the "Closed" sign in the shop window for the night—but it wasn't ironclad. He could bring his walls down without much effort should the need arise; he just wasn't sure what to expect from the Eric-Andrew connection. Satisfied by the supernatural silence, he opened the door and stepped out.

"Hey," he said with a smile as Eric turned quickly from stubbing out a cigarette. "Good to see you."

Eric stared at him, mouth slightly ajar. After a few seconds of silence, Jake furrowed his brow and Eric said, "Uh... hi."

"Hi," Jake repeated with a laugh.

Eric shook his head like he was trying to clear away a fog. "Sorry. I just…." He blew out a breath and looked Jake over from head to toe. "Wow. You look great."

Jake felt his cheeks flush. *Dammit, Gram*, he thought. "Thanks," he said softly.

Eric laughed nervously and studied his shoes. "Sorry. Not exactly *New York Times* best-selling prose. You just…I mean, I didn't expect— you know what? I'm going to shut up now. I do a lot better with words on paper."

"You're doing just fine," Jake said steadily and without a thought, surprised when the words left his mouth.

Eric raised his eyes to meet Jake's, and Jake felt the electricity crackle in the air around them. He was acutely aware, however, that this electricity, the prickling of his skin, the hitch in his breath were entirely of *this* world. Unused to the sensations, he cleared his throat and looked away.

Eric stepped toward his car, which was parked along the curb. He opened the passenger door and gestured toward Jake. "Shall we?"

Relieved to move on from the moment that had passed between them, Jake smiled and said, "Absolutely." He reached the vehicle in two long strides and slid into the passenger seat of Eric's white SUV.

CHAPTER 8

THEY DROVE for a few minutes in silence, Jake aware of Eric sneaking sideways glances at him only because Jake was doing the exact same thing. He had known from the beginning—well, maybe not the beginning but at least since he'd seen the jacket on Bobby's book—that Eric was a good-looking guy. It was a whole different kind of knowing, though, when the guy was sitting a foot away in a quiet vehicle on the way to a dinner that Jake no longer felt was entirely business.

Eric looked just right in black dress pants and a deep purple dress shirt, and Jake spotted a black jacket laid out neatly over the back seat. Eric's hair looked a little different—the waves more noticeable—and Jake's hand tingled with the unexpected desire to run his fingers through them. He pressed his lips together and exhaled soundlessly in an effort to quell the spark he felt buzzing between them like fireflies on a warm summer night.

"So, you had a busy week?" Jake asked, conversation a sensible diversion.

Eric glanced over at him and nodded. "You have no idea," he said and launched into an account of his week, which had taken him down to New York City for a few days of readings and book signings, followed by an overnight in Providence, Rhode Island, before returning home to Boston.

Jake listened attentively and kept his ears open for any mention of a totaled BMW in the course of Eric's travels. There was none, and he assumed an event like that would rate a comment at the very least if it had occurred. So he assumed it hadn't—not recently, anyway—and focused on what Eric *did* tell him. He soon found himself relaxed and genuinely interested in the unique life Eric described, laughing out loud as Eric detailed an encounter with an overly enthusiastic female fan.

"She actually cornered you in the *children's* section when you were leaving?" Jake asked.

Eric nodded with a grim smile. "Yep. Reached around to slip her number in my back pocket and pinched my ass. Jesus."

"So did you call her?" Jake asked, deadpan.

Eric whipped his head around to look at Jake, but caught on in a second. "Ha-ha. No, I did *not* call her."

"That's got to be some kind of harassment," Jake said.

Eric shrugged. "Probably. It's not worth making a big deal of it. There're a lot of whackjobs walking around, as you probably know. If I come home and find her camped out in front of my condo, then I'll worry."

Jake chuckled as Eric made a right and navigated the car up a short driveway and into a semicircle for valet parking. Jake glanced up at the restaurant name, scripted along a deep blue awning: "Blue Ginger." He wasn't familiar with it, but he was also starving and not picky.

They exited the car and Eric handed off the keys to the valet. As they neared the entrance, Eric jogged a few steps ahead, grabbed the handle, and pulled the door open for Jake. Jake paused a moment and locked his eyes on Eric's, the same electric feeling from the car buzzing around him again.

Eric winked and smiled. "After you," he said quietly, gesturing at the entrance.

"Thanks," Jake said, returning the smile and stepping through the door. They approached the hostess station, and an attractive dark-haired woman in a formfitting black dress glanced up at them.

"Mr. Austin," she said with a smile.

"Hi, Andie," Eric replied with a nod, returning the smile.

Her eyes skimmed over the computer in front of her, and she slid out a couple of menus from under her station. "Right this way, gentlemen," she said as she directed them through the dining room and seated them at a secluded corner table. Jake sat down and took in the dim lighting, minimalist décor, and crisp white tablecloths.

"Nice," he said, meeting Eric's gaze across the table.

"I'm kind of a regular," Eric said with a sheepish shrug.

"Pretty high-end regular," Jake said, eyebrow cocked.

Eric sighed. "I know. I live nearby—a ten-minute walk—and the food is amazing. Carryout most times. It's laziness, I guess. Habit, maybe." Jake nodded. "Besides, it's usually just me. I haven't had many hot dates that warrant a trip here," he added with a mischievous smile.

"Is that what I am?" Jake asked, his tone playful but his mind genuinely curious. Eric had been sending out pretty clear date-like vibes that Jake didn't need to be psychic to pick up.

Eric slid his hand forward from where it rested on the table like he might reach across and touch Jake's hand, but diverted the move at the last minute. He lifted his hand and traced the rim of his water glass with a long finger.

"I'd hoped," he said softly, flicking his eyes up to Jake's face.

"Oh," Jake said ineloquently. What he had suspected had become fact, and as much as he understood his ethical responsibility to his client, he couldn't deny the attraction between them. "I don't usually date clients," he explained, only half believing his own words.

Eric nodded slowly. "Well," he said, "the argument could be made that I'm not actually a client."

"Really? How's that?" Jake asked.

At that moment, their waitress appeared to take their drink orders. "Is white wine all right with you?" Eric asked and Jake nodded. Eric ordered a bottle of a Reserve Riesling and returned to the study of his water glass as the waitress departed.

"So?" Jake prompted.

"It's not even much of a stretch, really," Eric said, propping his elbows on the table and clasping his hands. "I mean, you haven't actually read for me yet. I didn't stick around long enough the first time, and the second time we didn't talk much about my... situation. I haven't confided any inviolable secrets so as to invoke the medium-client privilege yet." Jake laughed. "So, the way I see it, you could most definitely be my hot date."

Jake felt his face get warm. "All very good points," he said, still smiling. "Although I don't think it's only up to us, unfortunately. At least not for me. There's someone who wants to talk to you, and he wants me to help."

A momentary shadow passed over Eric's features before his smile returned. "Yes, well... how about humoring me, then?"

Jake grinned. "Gladly."

ABOUT FORTY-FIVE minutes later, they had polished off two appetizers and consumed most of the bottle of wine. Eric refilled their glasses, leaving the bottle nearly empty as they waited for their entrees to arrive.

"Do you have family around here?" Eric asked.

Jake nodded. "Well, you met Bobby at the book signing. He's not a blood relative, but I've been close with his mom, Laney, for a long time. Since he was born I've been Uncle Jake. And, of course, there's my grandma."

Jake paused as their dinners arrived and the server got everything situated.

"So, your grandma," Eric asked as he picked up his fork, "is she retired? A lady of leisure?"

Jake laughed. "Not quite. Gram does what I do. Readings, mediumship, Reiki—that's a kind of energy-based healing. She's over in Salem, still working out of the same house where I grew up. And she makes me look like I don't know a Tarot card from a birthday card," Jake said with a shake of his head as he started in on his meal. "Our family name, Parker, can be traced back in the Salem area to the time of the witch trials."

"Wow. That's fascinating," Eric said.

As they ate, Eric fired off question after question, but it didn't feel nosy or pushy to Jake. Eric seemed genuinely curious about his life and his work, so dinner passed with Jake recounting stories of his childhood, Gram, and how they'd come to do the kind of work they did.

"Wow, I don't usually talk that much about myself," Jake said, folding his napkin in his lap and pushing his cleaned plate a few inches away.

"Why not?" Eric asked.

"Well, it depends," Jake said. "My clients shouldn't really know that much about me. There are all kinds of ways people can feel you're not neutral, or influencing their reading somehow. Not to mention that when they come to see me, they're there to hear about themselves." Eric nodded. "From the 'hot date' perspective, however, I've learned from experience that oftentimes people ask but they don't really want to *know*. The reality of it gets them all freaked out, wondering if I'm seeing their dead aunt behind them or reading all the dirty secrets in their head, and they bolt."

Eric casually let his fingers brush over Jake's as he reached for his wineglass and drained the last drop. "I'm still here," he said, setting the glass aside and holding Jake's gaze.

Jake gave him a small smile. "Yes. You are."

They fell into silence for a few moments until the server reappeared to clear the table.

"Can I interest you in any coffee or dessert?" she asked brightly.

"Coffee, please," Eric said.

"Hot tea for me," added Jake.

Eric reached across the table and this time he did briefly rest his hand over Jake's and said, "If you've got any room, they have a vanilla crème brûlée that's not to be missed."

Jake glanced down at their hands as Eric pulled his back.

"It's *very* good," the server added.

"Well, with those reviews, how can I say no?" Jake said with a smile.

Eric excused himself to the restroom and returned just as the coffee and tea arrived. While they waited for their desserts to arrive, Jake reciprocated a bit with background questions and listened intently as Eric described what he called an "unremarkable upbringing" in the suburbs of Boston.

"So, regular parents, regular schools, regular friends, regular college... and best-selling author?" Jake concluded.

"Yeah, that's pretty much the size of it. I wrote a lot... I mean, *a lot* before I got to the best-selling author part. But I love it. I love what I do."

Jake smiled. "I totally understand."

Dessert arrived and Eric waited, watching Jake expectantly as he picked up his spoon, cracked the hard topping of cooked sugar, and scooped up some of the dense crème. He tasted it and his eyes closed involuntarily.

"Wow," he said, nodding. "That's good."

Eric grinned and dug into his own dessert. "I told you."

They ate in silence for a few minutes until Eric paused and set his spoon down.

"Can I ask you a question?" he asked.

Jake met his gaze, lifting another delicate spoonful to his lips. "Sure."

"Why did you worry?" Eric asked.

Jake furrowed his brow. "Worry? About what?" They had covered so much ground in their conversation he couldn't put a finger on what Eric meant.

"When I called you earlier," Eric explained. "You sounded worried. You asked if I was all right." He took a breath. "You asked if I'd had a car accident."

Jake swallowed and set down his spoon. "Right. I'm sorry about that. Sometimes when I connect with someone, I get information from unexpected places with no context. I don't know if it's past, present, future—a warning, even."

"So, what was this?" Eric asked quietly.

Jake sighed. "It was a dream. I saw you driving a black BMW. Then I saw the same car wrapped around a tree and the driver…. Well, it didn't end well. I knew you were traveling, so I thought maybe something had happened. I know; it sounds completely insane now."

Eric shook his head. "It doesn't."

Jake's eyes grew wide. "You *were* in an accident?" he asked, simultaneously panicked and puzzled.

"No," Eric said. "Not me. It was Andrew." He sighed. "It was his car. And that's how he died."

"Shit," Jake whispered and just stared for a moment as another piece of the puzzle snapped into place. Then his attention focused on Eric's averted eyes, shining in the glow of the light above their table. He reached across and covered Eric's hand with his own. "I'm sorry," he said softly.

Eric gave Jake's fingers a quick squeeze. He pressed his lips together and ran his other hand through his hair. "Thank you," he said, flicking his eyes up to meet Jake's. "It was a while ago."

"You may have mentioned it before, but can I ask how long?" Jake prodded cautiously.

"A bit over a year now," Eric said. "But we weren't in the best place when he passed away."

"I gathered as much," Jake said and took a sip from his water glass.

"Did he tell you that?" Eric whispered, his face etched with confusion.

Jake shook his head. "He doesn't *tell* me much, actually. He prefers… images. And dreams, I guess."

"Is he here now?" Eric asked, glancing around them.

Jake suppressed a sigh. *Here comes the bolt*, he thought. "I don't know, honestly. I haven't been—"

"I'm sorry," Eric interrupted, raising a hand. "I knew that." He tapped a finger at the side of his head. "The radio's off, right?"

Jake smiled. "Yes, it is. Has been all night." He allowed himself a moment of internal debate before saying, "If you want, I can try to…." He tapped the side of his head as Eric had done.

Eric stared at him for a second before shaking his head vehemently. "No. Absolutely not."

"Okay," Jake said, nodding. "But why?"

Eric huffed out a breath and smiled. "First of all, look where we are," he said, waving vaguely at the full restaurant. "I doubt these are ideal working conditions." Jake nodded. "Secondly, I don't know if I'm ready. I don't even know if I *want* to hear what he has to say."

Jake shifted in his chair as the hair on his neck stood on end and a muted buzzing began in his head. Without a doubt, he knew Andrew was there and he hadn't liked what he just heard. Jake decided to try to nip it in the bud before he found himself playing Ghost Whisperer in the middle of the restaurant. He lowered his internal walls and opened himself just enough to communicate clearly. *It's his choice too*, he reminded Andrew, projecting the thought in the direction of the energy. *He still has to live with it. He* gets *a say.*

Eric looked lost in thought, and Jake's blood pressure dropped a few points when, after thirty seconds or so, the buzzing receded and the energy dissipated. He slammed his Third Eye shut and tapped the table gently to get Eric's attention.

"Hey," he said.

Eric blinked at him and ran a hand over his face. "I'm sorry."

"It's all right," Jake assured him but Eric shook his head.

"No, it's not. Because, last and most important, that's not why I asked you here."

"Why did you ask me?"

"Well, it sure as hell wasn't to have a threesome with my dead ex," he said with a roll of his eyes and Jake laughed. "No, I asked you because I like you. I wanted to get to know you, talk to you, spend some time with you." He paused. "And you make one hell of a hot date," he added with a grin.

Jake silently cursed his cheeks for heating up for what felt like the hundredth time that night. "Well," he said, tracing condensation lines down his water glass, "I hope I didn't disappoint."

Eric ducked his head to catch Jake's gaze. "Not a chance," he said. "We should probably head out. It's a bit of a drive back to your place."

Jake agreed and Eric hailed their server. She brought the check, which Eric picked up without a second thought, and they were on their way.

THEY CHATTED quietly on the drive back, Jake commenting on how much he'd liked the restaurant, and Eric launching into a list of all his favorites there.

"I almost went with the flat-iron steak," Jake said. "But the curry pasta was too interesting to pass up."

"Well, you'll have to try the steak next time," Eric said casually, taking his eyes from the road to glance over at Jake.

Jake smiled. "Okay, then. Next time." They drove silently for a few minutes until Jake asked, "So, is your schedule still crazy this week?"

Eric rattled off a list of meetings he had scheduled, but they were all via conference call since he was staying in town for the week. "And writing, of course," he added and Jake nodded.

Eric made a left and pulled up next to the side entrance of Jake's building. He shut the car off and started to get out. Jake froze for a moment, puzzled because nothing had been said about Eric coming up to Jake's place after dinner.

Eric slid back into his seat and gave Jake's arm a squeeze. "Relax," Eric said, smiling. "I'm a proper date, and I'm going to see you to the door."

"Oh," Jake said. "You don't have to—" but Eric raised his hand, letting Jake know there was no use in protesting.

They got out of the car and walked up to the door of Jake's apartment where they stood facing each other, silent for a few long seconds.

"Well," Eric said. "I had a really nice time tonight. The best in a long time."

Jake smiled. "Same here," he said. He fumbled with words in his head, wanting to say something more and realizing in that moment he was far more accustomed to passing on the words of others than expressing himself. He took a deep breath and gave it his best shot. "I know this is… unusual—for me, anyway—because of how we met and your situation. But I want you to know I like you, too. A lot. I can't even really explain it, but…." He looked at the ground and shook his head. "I think I'm going to stop talking now because I sound like I'm in junior high," he concluded with a nervous laugh.

Eric shook his head. "Not at all. Assuming I remember the rules right, if you like me and I like you, then it's okay for me to do this." In a heartbeat Eric closed the gap between them and pressed a warm hand along Jake's jaw as he brought their lips together in a soft kiss.

Jake closed his eyes, and the moment their mouths met, it felt as though something physically changed in him. It was a first kiss, and he got dizzy and lightheaded and turned on—all the things he would have expected. But the other part of him, his sixth sense, which was always running in the background, sent off such intense signals of familiarity and belonging and rightness that he didn't have to think when he slid an arm around Eric's waist and drew him closer.

He parted his lips and deepened the kiss, letting his tongue slide languidly against Eric's, drawing a deep rumble from Eric's chest. Eric put a hand on Jake's shoulder and turned him just enough so they were pressed up against the ragged brick of the building, hands in hair, bodies fused together, making out like they were in a suite at the Four Seasons instead of on a street corner. Jake was completely lost in the act until he noted his hand sliding down Eric's side and heading for the hard ridge pressing at his zipper. He focused himself and slowed down, logic at war with the part of him that wanted to stay this close to Eric forever, the part that, in some strange way, felt he *had* been this close to Eric forever.

His hand came to rest on Eric's waist and their kisses slowed until they were nose to nose, sharing each other's breath. Eric pulled back enough to look at him, and Jake saw a dazed look on Eric's face he felt certain mirrored his own.

"Wow," Eric said softly, running his fingers lightly over his lips. "That was… I mean, did you…?"

Jake smiled as Eric took his turn searching for words and nodded. "Yeah," he said. "Wow is right."

Eric smiled but then his brow furrowed. "But did it feel… I mean, I felt like… I don't know…."

Jake silenced him with a brush of his lips over Eric's. "Shhh. I know," he said.

Eric, still looking slightly off-kilter, nodded and smiled. He took Jake's hand and laced their fingers together. "So, can I call you? Like, from the car on the way home?"

Jake laughed and bumped his forehead lightly against Eric's. "Hmm. How about tomorrow? I'm pretty beat."

Eric nodded, most of his usual composure regained. "All right— tomorrow. I think I can hold off."

"Thank you," Jake said. "For tonight, dinner… everything."

"You're welcome." Eric leaned in for one more chaste kiss before he let go of Jake's hand and stepped toward the car.

Jake smiled, then unlocked the door and slipped inside. He waited, listening for the sound of Eric's departing vehicle before heading up the stairs to his apartment, all the while shaking his head at the new layer that had just been added to their relationship.

"Where the hell did that come from?" he murmured aloud as he wandered into his bedroom. He stripped down to his boxers and slid under the covers. In that moment, he couldn't answer that question, but he didn't really care. He fell asleep with a smile on his face.

CHAPTER 9

THE NEXT morning, Jake awoke with a comforting warmth at his back. As he floated to consciousness, he smiled as he replayed the kiss by the door in his mind and rolled over toward the steady heat beside him. He reached his arm out, patting the other side of the bed for Eric's solid form and found… nothing. Nothing but the morning sun streaming through the window, warming his back and the empty other half of the bed.

He furrowed his brow; when he'd rolled over, he'd been sure someone was there. He'd thought Eric, but now that he was more fully awake, he recalled the end of their evening the night before and Eric's promise to call. He flopped back onto his pillow and ran a hand over his face. Though it was likely just his imagination or the remnants of a dream, he made a mental note to do a thorough cleansing of his bedroom. The last thing he needed was spirits hopping into bed with him for an early-morning snuggle.

He reached over to his bedside table and grabbed his phone, an informal morning ritual to check the weather, his e-mail, and whatever other apps caught his attention. This time he got distracted by the small number "2" next to the telephone icon. Puzzled as to who would've called him before nine, he tapped the icon to open up his recent calls and messages. He smiled when he saw one missed call and one message from Eric. He clicked on the message and put the phone to his ear.

"Hey, Jake, it's me. Uh, Eric, I mean. It's seven thirty in the morning and you're probably thinking I'm a total freak, but I only promised to wait until tomorrow to call. Well, today, now. Anyway, I had a great time last night… which you already know. I'm heading out to the gym and I just… well, I wanted to call and say good morning and see if maybe you had any room in your schedule this evening. So, I'll be around on and off today—give me a call when you have a chance. Bye."

Jake wanted to smile at Eric's eagerness, and because he'd had a great time the night before too, but something nagged at him. Despite the undeniable attraction between them, he couldn't get past the fact that he had a job to do and, unfortunately, Eric was part of it. He couldn't claim to know the reasons why his and Eric's paths had crossed, but he knew Andrew was probably responsible and Jake was there to bridge the gap between Andrew and Eric.

He'd never encountered a client with whom he felt such a connection as he did with Eric. The selfish part of him wanted to say, "Screw it!" and just go for it with Eric; Jake wasn't a martyr for the Other Side. He couldn't shake the feeling, though, that this was something he *had* to do. Andrew and whatever energies he had working with him had managed to get Eric into Jake's shop and that was no small feat. And that nagging voice in Jake's head—a spirit guide, Gram, his conscience—told him the more time he spent with Eric in the "hot date" category, the less he'd be able to do his job.

His stomach dropped a little at the thought of drawing a strictly business line with Eric. Jake genuinely liked him, the attraction was obvious, and that *kiss*.... That had been one for the books. He closed his eyes and took a long breath in and slowly let it out. It was a brief exercise in meditation that often helped him clear his head. He sat still, slowing his thoughts until he was left with nothing but quiet. Just as he was about to open his eyes, he heard a heavy *thump* from across the room. His eyes flew open and he saw the amethyst obelisk that stood on a shelf knocked on its side.

He sighed and got up and walked over to the shelf so he was eye-level with the toppled crystal. He shook his head; that, too, was no small feat. The first order of business was now definitely a smudging for his bedroom. He zipped down the hall to the living room and opened up a drawer in one of the end tables. He grabbed the sage wand, the smudging fan, and a small packet of spelled sea salt. Back down the hall and into his bedroom, he got to work cleansing the space. He sprinkled the sea salt along the windowsill and the threshold of the door to set a clear boundary where spirits couldn't enter. He felt better as he stepped out of the bedroom. While he was almost always open to communication from the Other Side, he did not want it crawling into bed with him.

He knew Jessie would be in shortly to open up the shop, so Jake was in no rush. He put some coffee on and headed back to the living room where he flopped into his favorite chair. Since someone obviously wanted to get his attention, he decided to try to have a chat. He closed his eyes, ran through his chakras, opening each one and balancing the colors. He surrounded himself with white light in his mind's eye just to be safe, and then he waited. It wasn't long before he felt a presence close by—too close, almost oppressive. The hair on his neck stood on end, and he felt a distinct rush of cold air, which sent an army of goosebumps marching up his arms. The scent of cigars filled his nostrils, and he wrinkled his forehead.

"All right," Jake said quietly, "you've got my attention. Now who are you?"

The movie reel in his head kicked on, and he knew instantly what he was dealing with: a pissed-off Andrew. The images proceeded in the same way they had previous times, except before the ring fell and rolled away, he got some additional footage. He saw Eric sitting close to Andrew—maybe on his lap—as Andrew puffed on a cigar. Eric made a face and fanned the smoke away from him. Andrew took the cigar from his lips and offered it to Eric, who took it and stubbed it out in a nearby ashtray.

Jake laughed out loud, and he felt the energy push closer. "Okay, I'm sorry," he said. "Sorry he didn't like your cigars." That obviously wasn't the problem, though, because Andrew persisted, moving in close enough that Jake began to feel claustrophobic. He put his hands up, as though he could put physical space between himself and the energy. "What?" he asked loudly, annoyed by the spirit bullying. "What the hell's your problem?"

He waited a few seconds and then a voice vibrated through the apartment, low and quick but clear and distinct enough that Jake knew it was not heard in his head. Anyone who'd been standing in the room would have heard it.

"Stop."

And with that, all the energy, the pressure, the cold in the room receded and Jake was alone. "Fuck," he muttered and ran a hand through his hair. He'd known Andrew was with them last night when Eric's comment about not wanting to talk to Andrew had sparked such a strong reaction. Jake had been able to quash that quickly, but that didn't mean Andrew had left. It followed logically—in Jake's world—that Andrew had been there as Eric walked him to the door and kissed him like… *like he'd never kissed Andrew*, a soft inner voice finished.

"Shit," Jake said as he stood up from the chair. He knew Andrew wasn't dangerous; he just wanted to communicate with someone he'd left behind. Jake also knew spirits that got angry and *stayed* angry were a lot harder to deal with and a lot more likely to hang around, lingering in their attachment to a person or place when they needed to move on. He certainly didn't want that for Eric, and he only knew one way to make sure it didn't happen. Jake needed to keep his distance until Eric was ready to work with him to resolve whatever had gone on with Andrew.

JAKE THREW himself into his work that day, purposely leaving his cell phone in his desk drawer in the shop. He rearranged displays, updated the website with upcoming classes, and did readings for a few walk-in customers.

When Bobby burst through the door at three thirty, Jake left the shop to Jessie and followed Bobby upstairs—which earned him raised eyebrows and a "What the heck?" from Bobby—and asked him about school as he fussed in the kitchen making Bobby a snack. Not long after, Jake was summarily dismissed when Bobby said, "Umm, thanks, Uncle Jake, but I have to start my homework. Got a lot of it tonight," as he pulled his laptop out of his school bag.

Jake sighed and made his way back downstairs and to the shop. He hopped onto the edge of the desk where Jessie sat.

"Anything going on?" he asked.

She glanced up from the palmistry book she was reading and gave him a quizzical look. "No. Why? Are you expecting something?"

Jake shook his head. "Nope. Just checking in."

She studied him for a moment. "What's your deal?" she asked as she set down her book.

"My *deal*?" Jake repeated, brows furrowed.

Jessie tucked a curly blonde strand behind her ear. "Yeah, what's up with you? All day you've been all over the place, all fidgety. And you feel… off."

Jake hitched a leg up onto the desk to face her. "What do you mean 'off'?"

"Your energy… your aura…. They're all messed up."

Jake rolled his eyes. "I sincerely hope you don't say that to clients."

Jessie swatted his knee. "No! Just my mentor," she said with a laugh.

"Good," Jake said. "And besides, you've never even read for me. How do you know my 'energy'?"

"Are you serious? You taught me, worked with me one-on-one, and now I work here. Do you really think I never get *anything* off you?"

Jake nodded. She was a good reader, especially with auras. "Okay, fair point."

"Let me do you now!" Jessie said excitedly, reaching for her bag.

"Do—*what*?" Jake asked.

"Read for you! You just said I've never read for you, so let me do it now. I know there's something weird going on."

She set her deck of Tarot cards on the desk, and Jake immediately started shaking his head. Jessie might trump him at auras, but the cards were his thing, and no way did he want to see what they had to say just then.

"No, thank you. I'll deal with the 'weirdness' on my own."

"Oh, c'mon. Please? Just one. I won't do a full reading, but just let me pull a card for you, okay?" she pleaded.

Even Jake couldn't pretend he wasn't a little curious. What could one card hurt? "All right. Just *one*," he emphasized as she removed the deck from its velvet pouch and began to shuffle.

"Deal," she said and handed him the cards. "All right. Shuffle till you feel like it's enough."

Jake knew the drill; he closed his eyes and shuffled, the cards sliding expertly up and down and around each other until his gut told him to stop. He opened his eyes and set the deck on the desk.

"Cut the deck," Jessie instructed, and Jake did. She gathered the cards in her hands and looked him in the eye. "Ready?"

Jake smiled. "Have at it."

She nodded and flipped the top card onto the table. "Oh, nice!" she exclaimed, her voice covering Jake's sharp intake of breath as he stared down at the card he'd seen not that long ago in Gram's kitchen: The Lovers.

Jessie looked at him, puzzled. "Hey," she said and tapped his knee. "What's with the weird vibes again? That's a good one! You're going to meet someone," she said in a singsong voice.

Jake shook his head. "No. No, it's not about me. It's for—"

"It sure as hell is!" she interrupted.

"What? No, I've already seen this. It's hard to explain but it's—"

He stopped as she sat back, hands fisted on her hips. "And how often is it you can read for yourself?" Jake just stared at her. "That's what I thought. Nine times out of ten you can't. *I can.* Here, let me see something." She held out her hands, palms up and Jake slowly placed his hands in hers. She grasped lightly and closed her eyes. After a moment, a smile spread across her face and she opened her eyes. "Oh, yes. It's definitely you. You've met someone—or you will soon."

Jake took his hands back and slid off the desk. "Well, I'll uh… I'll keep my eyes open. Thanks," he replied, flustered. His eyes searched for a task to occupy him. He scooped a handful of mail out of his inbox and Jessie reached over and laid a hand on his wrist.

"Jake," she said, her expression now all seriousness. "You really should. Keep your eyes open, I mean. Whoever he is, he's important. Like life-partner important."

Dumbfounded, Jake just nodded at her for a few seconds until they both jumped at the vibrating sound coming from his desk drawer.

"Sorry," Jake said. "My phone's in there."

"Oh, I'll grab it," Jessie said and reached for the drawer.

"No, no, just leave it," Jake said quickly, fairly certain who was on the other end. "I'll check it later. I've got…" He held up the fistful of non-urgent mail and headed for the stairs up to his apartment.

SEVERAL HOURS later, Jessie already gone and shortly before closing time, Jake sat at the desk in the shop listening to the second voice mail Eric had left for the third time in a row, losing himself in the warm, deep rumbling in his ear.

"Hi, Jake. It's me again. Umm, I guess you had a full day since I didn't hear back from you. It's okay. No problem. Maybe tomorrow? I don't mean to be pushy or anything. It's just… I'd really like to see you again (audible sigh). I have tomorrow set aside for writing, mostly. Though I have to admit, I'm pretty distracted right now, so I don't know how productive I'll be (forced laugh). If something's wrong, or you don't want to… pursue this any further, please let me know. Call, text, send a smoke signal… whatever. It's all right, just… I'd like to know, because all I really want to do is to kiss you again. (Pause, then *shit*, muttered) So, hope to hear from you soon. Bye."

Thump! "So how was your day? 'Cause mine sucked. Where's Bobby—upstairs? Hey, are you okay?"

Jake had been so involved in obsessing over the voice mail, he hadn't even heard the bell over the door chime when Laney came in until she dropped her shoulder bag onto the desk and nearly scared the life out of him.

He dropped his hand from where he had spread it over his chest and took a deep breath. "Shit! Sorry, I didn't hear you come in."

"Obviously," she said with a laugh. "Everything okay?"

"Yeah, fine," Jake began, but stopped when she cocked an eyebrow at him. "Okay. Not so fine."

He got Laney caught up on the latest Jake/Eric and Jake/Andrew happenings and she listened in silence, eyes growing wider.

"Wow," she said when he finished. "Well, it sounds like a good date!" She ducked down a little and looked over her shoulders. "Is he here now?" she whispered. "The other one?"

Jake shook his head. "I don't think so. He tends to stay pretty close to 'his man.' Unless he's busy chasing others away, I guess."

"You have to tell Eric," Laney said. "He's obviously into you—just let him know what's going on."

Jake dropped his head into his hands. "I can't. It may just piss him off and make him even less likely to deal with Andrew. And I *really* need him to deal."

Laney blew out a long breath. "I'm sorry, sweetie," she said as she patted his hand. "It's a tough one."

"Yeah, well, I'll live. I may stay single, but I'll live. So, what happened to you? Your day sucked?"

Laney waved a dismissive hand. "Oh, the usual—understaffed, overworked, not enough time with my kid. Speaking of which, I need to get him and get going—it's late."

Jake helped her gather up Bobby and his things and walked them to the door.

Laney hugged him and he ruffled Bobby's hair. "Night, you two," he said.

"Good night. So, you'll be okay with everything?" she asked.

He smiled. "Yep. I'll handle it."

Laney nodded and they left, and Jake closed and locked the shop behind them. He trudged upstairs, with no idea where to begin handling things.

CHAPTER 10

ERIC CALLED only once the next day, and he didn't leave a message. Jake couldn't decide if that was a good thing or a bad thing in the grand scheme, but he took the day for what it was: a break from what-if-ing, second-guessing, and overanalyzing. He was on his own in the shop that day, but there were enough customers to keep him busy, along with a delivery of some new inventory that had to be logged and entered into the shop's computer system.

He took a break around dinner time, when things usually got quiet anyway, flipped the sign on the door to "Closed" and locked the door behind him. He breathed deep and the crisp, late-October air filled his lungs and cleared his head. He made his way toward the café a block up the street, nodding and smiling at a couple of familiar faces as they passed. Once inside, he ordered a sandwich and a pumpkin spice latte to go. He started back toward the shop, but a few steps into the trip his phone rang from his coat pocket.

"Shit," he muttered as he juggled the hot drink and sandwich bag. He grabbed the phone and pulled it out of his pocket. A smile spread across his face when the caller ID showed a name he'd never dodge. Almost never.

"Hi, Gram," he said, his smile clear in his voice.

"Hello, sweetie!" she said. "Is this a bad time? Are you busy?"

"No, it's all good. I just grabbed some dinner, and now I'm heading back to the shop."

"I hope you're having a real dinner and not just one of those fancy coffees," she said.

Jake glanced at his latte and shook his head. "You're right about the 'fancy coffee,' but I've got a sandwich to go with it."

"Good. You need to eat better, you know. Speaking of eating, didn't you have a dinner... meeting the other day? How did that go?" she asked, voice brimming with curiosity.

Jake sighed. "Fine. Good, even, I guess," Jake answered.

"You don't sound happy. What is it?" she asked.

"Well, hindsight being twenty-twenty and all, I probably don't need to tell you this, but it didn't really turn out to be a meeting. It was more like… a date."

"Hmm. You don't say." Jake could hear her smile.

"Now, wait a minute—don't go there. It's not like that," Jake said.

"So, it wasn't a date?" Gram asked sounding puzzled.

"No, it was. It's just not anymore. I mean, it can't be. It's complicated," Jake finished with a sigh.

"I know things have changed since my time, but it can't be all *that* complicated. I know it's not," she said, laughing.

"But, Gram, it's just that—"

"Did you have a good time?" she interrupted.

Jake paused for a moment. "Well, yes, but that's—"

"Did he have a good time?" she continued.

Jake huffed out a frustrated breath. "Yes, judging by the messages he's left."

Gram snickered. "So when will you see him again?"

"I don't know. I haven't called him back."

Gram was quiet for a few long seconds and then cleared her throat. "And why is that?" she asked, forced lightness in her voice.

"I was trying to tell you! It's complicated. He's got this spirit attached to him, and he—"

"Jake, listen to me." She cut him off, and the no-nonsense tone in her voice shut him up. "Call him back."

"What? But, why? I mean, why are you calling to talk about my love life like it's a matter of life and death?" he asked.

"It's not that, sweetie," she said. "But you know how sometimes, you and I, we just *know* things, right?"

"Yes," Jake said.

"And sometimes, when it's something in our own lives, we can't see it for ourselves," she continued.

"Yeah," he said. He stopped walking and leaned back against the brick façade of the shop.

"Well, I *know* this, dear. Call him. I know there's a 'complication,' as you call him. Call anyway, okay? You'll see… you'll figure it out. And I'll help. Heck, I'm already helping!"

Jake laughed quietly. "So you are. All right, Gram. I'll call him. I promise."

"Good boy," she said, the smile back in her voice. "Now get inside and eat! It's too cold to stand around outside."

Jake chuckled as he unlocked the door and let himself in. "Yes, ma'am," he said, marveling again at her uncanny ability to know where he was.

"Have a good night, sweetie. I'll be in touch," she said.

"I'm sure you will. Night, Gram."

Jake hung up the phone and tossed it on his desk. He glanced at it and thought about carrying out Gram's witchy order right then, but couldn't quite gear himself up to do it. *Tomorrow*, he told himself. He'd get it all sorted out tomorrow. He sat down at the desk and took a sip of his latte. He left the sandwich untouched; his stomach had twisted itself into a knot by the end of his chat with Gram.

A little frustrated and a lot confused, he set down his drink and grabbed his Tarot deck from the drawer of his desk. He decided on a quick yes-or-no spread since his mind couldn't focus on much more than that. Just one question.

He closed his eyes and shuffled the deck while focusing on his simple but specific question: "Should I call Eric Austin tomorrow?" When his instincts told him to stop shuffling, he did, and he began to deal the first pile.

A smile twitched the corner of his mouth. This had been the first spread Gram had ever taught him once he was old enough to use the cards. Three piles dealt sequentially until you dealt an ace or hit thirteen cards in the pile. Aces equal yes, and the earlier they occurred in the spread, the stronger "yes" they indicated.

Jake started to flip cards into the first pile, and on the fourth flip, he stared down at the Ace of Cups. He sighed and started the second pile: third card, Ace of Wands. He shifted his hands to begin the third pile, pursed his lips and shook his head. Before the card hit the desk he knew what it would be, and he wasn't wrong: first card, Ace of Pentacles.

"Shit," he muttered and ran a hand through his hair. You couldn't get a much clearer "yes" than that. He scooped up the cards and slid them back into their pouch. He had a phone call to make tomorrow.

THROUGHOUT THE morning, Jake held on to the small hope that Eric might call one more time and Jake could just answer, playing off his absence the past few days with work obligations or an illness or… anything, really. It didn't happen. Eric had clearly lobbed the ball well into Jake's court, and now it was on him to pick up the phone and explain himself.

Jessie was due in the shop at noon, and Jake decided to wait until she got there so he would be free to head up to his apartment and call from there. She arrived about ten minutes early, as she often did, and Jake brought her up to speed on what needed to be done that afternoon, then excused himself upstairs under the pretense of lunch. He sat on his couch and stared at his phone like he could will it into another plane of existence with the power of his mind. He thought of ten reasons not to call, to just drop the whole thing, until he caught a glimpse of the picture of him and Gram on the end table. She didn't call like that for just anything. And his cards… they were like an extension of himself, and he couldn't think of a time when they'd led him in the wrong direction. With a deep breath in and a long, slow exhale he pulled himself together. He had to call.

He tapped on Eric's contact information and hit the call button. He waited through four rings and began to panic at the idea of leaving an unrehearsed voice mail when a familiar voice cut off the fifth ring.

"Hello?" Eric said. Jake thought he sounded a little out of breath.

"Hi, Eric? It's Jake." Silence. "Parker," he added for clarification since no response was forthcoming.

"That is so weird," Eric finally said.

"Come on, now. It hasn't been *that* long!" Jake huffed.

"What?" Eric asked, his tone confused. "No, I didn't mean—well, yes, it has, now that you mention it—but that's not what I meant."

"Oh," Jake said, unsure how to continue. "Well, what happened? What's weird? I mean besides me calling you back," he added with a touch of sarcasm.

Eric snickered on the other end of the line. "It's just that I'm working right now—writing—and I *never* leave my cell on while I'm working. In fact, I specifically recall turning it off about two hours ago when I sat down. It scared the shit out of me when it rang."

"Wow, that is weird," Jake said, knowing full well it wasn't weird at all, given their situation. He had half a mind to tell Eric to check the battery on his phone to see if it was close to drained as well, further proof of a spirit interloper, but he kept his ghost-thoughts to himself. "Well, I'll let you go; I don't want to interrupt if you're working. I feel like an ass. I should've thought of that."

Eric sighed. "No and yes," he said.

"Uh, what?" Jake asked.

"*No*, I'm not hanging up the phone now that I've actually got hold of you, and *yes*, you are an ass."

Jake laughed. "Okay, I guess I deserved that. I'm sorry. I don't really have a good excuse. I just got kind of freaked out."

Eric was quiet for a moment. "*You?*" he said incredulously. "You, the guy who sees dead people, got freaked out? By me?"

"No. Not by you, specifically. By the situation. You have to understand, my point of view is a little different here. It's more complicated, and I'm just not sure...." He trailed off, shaking his head, imagining how all this must sound to Eric, made-up at best, and completely insane at worst. "You know what? Never mind that for right now. What doesn't freak me out and what I am sure of is that I like you, Eric. I do want to see you again. That wasn't bullshit."

"Okay," Eric said.

"I'm sorry I disappeared for a bit. Let me make it up to you. Second date—you name it, and I'm there."

"Really?" Eric asked, a mix of smile and sinister in his voice.

Jake swallowed hard. "Yep."

"Anything?"

"Hey, don't make me regret this, okay?" Jake said with a laugh.

"All right. Friday night. An author friend of mine is having a party."

"Done," Jake said.

"A Halloween party," Eric added.

"Okay. I love Halloween," Jake said, a little less confident. He'd expected a movie or maybe another dinner, but this caught him off guard.

"Costumes mandatory," Eric said, the grin radiating through his voice as he threw down his trump card.

"Shit," Jake muttered and Eric laughed.

"Deal-breaker?" Eric asked.

Jake sighed. Despite his dislike for the typical parties full of people parading around in costumes with zero knowledge about the history of the holiday, he was not about to back out now.

"Not a chance," he said.

"Good. I'll pick you up at eight o'clock," Eric said. "And Jake?"

"Yeah?"

"I'm glad you called. Really," Eric said.

Jake smiled. "Me too," he said. "I'll see you Friday."

"Okay. Bye."

Jake hung up the phone and scrubbed a hand over his face as he flopped back on the couch. *A fucking Halloween party*, he thought. He imagined making idle chitchat with strangers dressed as God-knows-what for hours on end and a shiver ran up his spine. But before he could wallow too much, the voice in his head that always set him right reminded him of the most important part: he'd be with Eric.

"Better find a costume," he murmured as he headed back down to the shop.

FRIDAY SNUCK up on Jake more quickly than he anticipated, and late Friday afternoon found him sitting at his desk in the shop, his head in his hands, ranting to Jessie.

"I meant to come up with something, go out and pick something up, or whatever. But I couldn't decide, and I didn't want to just wander around aimlessly, so I put it off. And off. And then I thought maybe I'd call Laney and see if she had any ideas, but I immediately saw myself in some shirtless-policeman outfit, or naughty servant boy and that's not happening, so I didn't call her and now… well, now I'm here. Costumeless."

The torrent of giggles Jessie had been trying to hold back burst forth and she waved her hand in front of her face, trying to collect herself. "I'm sorry, really," she said. "But naughty servant-boy?" She dissolved into laughter again.

"Hey!" Jake said, pounding his fist on the table in mock-indignation. "I'd make a superhot naughty servant-boy!"

She nodded. "Yes, of course. Again, sorry." She dabbed at the corners of her eyes.

Jake smiled. "No, you're right. Totally not me. Ugh, I am so screwed!"

Jessie looked at him thoughtfully. "Maybe not," she said. Jake looked up at her. "Well, you're right—naughty servant-boy isn't you. But what you *are* is, like, the definition of Halloween," she said.

"And what am I, exactly?" Jake asked, his brows furrowed.

"A witch, duh!" she exclaimed.

Jake pursed his lips and thought for a few seconds. "Well, I haven't exactly explained it to him that way yet," he said.

Jessie waved a hand dismissively. "Oh, c'mon! It's Halloween—no explanations necessary."

Jessie ordered him upstairs to find a pair of black jeans and a black shirt—both preferably snug-fitting—and put them on. He came back down to the shop dressed as directed in a pair of black skinny jeans and a black T-shirt that had just a touch of spandex.

"Perfect!" she exclaimed. She glanced around and then said, "Storage room!" and pointed toward the door on the side wall of the shop. She grabbed the cloaks she had chosen, a moonstone on a cord, and her purse and followed Jake into the room. They left the door open in case any customers came in and Jessie went to work. She draped a deep purple cloak over his shoulders and discarded it almost immediately.

"What's wrong with that?" Jake asked.

"Nothing's 'wrong.' It's just not a great color for you," she said simply. Next came a forest green one that was also rejected. Finally, she settled a thick black velvet cloak around his shoulders and grinned. "That's the one," she declared. She set it aside while she went to work on his face, lining his eyes and spiking up his hair with some product. She took a bright red lipstick from her bag but Jake drew the line there.

"Whoa!" he said, backing away. "No drag, please."

She rolled her eyes and put it away. "Fine. But it's not drag; it's just… an accent." He shook his head and she let it drop. "So, let's check out the final product!" she said. She put the black cloak back on and arranged the pendant so it hung centered on his chest. "Close your eyes," she said and Jake complied. She led him to the back of the store where cloaks hung on a rack and stopped in front of the mirror beside them.

"Jesus," Jake whispered when he opened his eyes. "That's the last time I let *you* loose in the shop." Jessie stood behind him, a satisfied expression on her face.

"To be fair, the only thing from the shop is the cloak. Oh, and the charm," she added. Jake reached down and ran his fingers over the moonstone pendant, rounded and smoothed to resemble a crystal ball. Thanks to Jessie's imagination and some black leather cord, it hung from his neck like a mystical tool of the trade.

Jake nodded. "I think you deserve a raise," he said with a laugh. The black liner she'd used made his blue eyes stand out like he'd never seen, and whatever was in his hair had turned it nearly black. In contrast, his eyes looked even brighter.

"Not necessary," Jessie answered. "It was fun. Now, just a few instructions. Lose the Converse. Do you have any black boots or something like that?"

"Yeah, I think so," Jake said, recalling a beat-up pair of combat boots in the back of his closet.

"Okay, so put on those. Now, you'd better go grab something to eat and do… whatever else guys do before dates. He'll be here in less than an hour," she said.

"Okay," Jake said. "I'll be sure to eat something I can't spill on myself."

Jessie laughed. "Thank you. Oh, wait!" she said and zipped back to the storage room. She returned with something in her hand and said, "Wrist, please."

Jake stuck out his arm and watched as she snapped a black leather cuff with silver studs around his wrist. He looked it over and shook his head. "I don't even want to know why you're carrying this around."

Her face flushed a little. "Don't ask," she said. "Just trust me. It's hot."

"Thanks."

"No problem." She gave him a quick hug. "And have fun!"

"I'll do my best," he said and headed up to his apartment.

Jake made a sandwich and ate it standing up in the kitchen. He washed it down with a bottle of water and then moved into the living room to take care of the most important thing: a heavy-duty protection spell to block any spirits from coming through to him. He knew it might not work completely, especially this close to Halloween, but he gave it his best shot. He burned some sage, lit a white candle, and used a shorthand version of the best spell he knew: one of Gram's. He closed his eyes and focused his mind and began to repeat:

Third eye closed and silence be
Those in spirit shall not see;
I travel this night in disguise
Hidden from unearthly eyes.

He said the words over and over until he felt a change happen within him, his vibration lowered and his mind quiet. He would have liked to stay with the spell a little longer, but it was cut short when the buzzer rang.

"So mote it be," he whispered to close the spell. He tamped out the sage, snuffed out the candle, and went over to the intercom. "Hey, Eric?"

"Yeah, it's me," a voice crackled back.

"Come on up. I'm almost ready." Jake hit the buzzer to let Eric in, and in the time it took for Eric to enter and climb the stairs, Jake stored away his spell implements and put his cloak back on. He opened the door just as Eric was about to knock.

"Hi," Jake said and then his voice caught in his throat as he took in Eric's costume: a perfect replica of a Boston Red Sox uniform.

"Hey," Eric said. "Jesus, Jake, you look... *wow*. I don't even know what the word is." Eric stepped inside and shut the door behind him, his eyes roaming over Jake.

"I hope 'crazy' isn't the word," Jake joked, uncomfortable under Eric's steady gaze.

"No. Not crazy," Eric said. "Something more along the lines of... edible." Before Jake could process the compliment, Eric moved forward and covered Jake's lips with his own. Eric's mouth felt warm and soft and Jake let himself lean into the kiss. A quiet moan escaped him and he felt Eric smile against his mouth. "I'm glad to see you too," Eric said as he eased away from the kiss. "No offense but we have to stop or we're not going to this party."

Jake chuckled. "We can't have that," he said. "Not after all the work that went into this." He spread his arms and the cloak fanned out behind him. "Let's have a look at you." He spun his finger, motioning for Eric to give him a 360-degree view.

Eric tipped his baseball cap and obliged. Jake took notice of how the uniform pants hugged Eric's ass like a second skin and reached down to adjust himself.

"Pop quiz," Eric said as he came full circle to face Jake.

"What?" Jake asked.

"What number is on the jersey?" he asked, a mischievous glint in his eyes.

"Number nine," Jake answered with a serious expression. "Ted Williams, 'the Splendid Splinter.' Most famous Red Sox player of all time."

"Oh," Eric said, looking a little disappointed. "Exactly right."

Jake nodded. "It's awesome," he said. "You actually look a little like him, all tall and thin."

"Well, that's good, I guess," Eric said, fidgeting with his cap.

"But your ass is way better," Jake added.

Eric froze for a moment and then lunged at Jake, grabbing him around the waist. "You suck," he said, laughing.

"Maybe," Jake said with a wink and tilted his head up to plant a kiss on Eric's surprised mouth. "Let's get going."

CHAPTER 11

ONCE THEY were in the car, Eric took off in the same direction he had for the restaurant. They chatted as they drove, but for Jake it felt more like a reconnection of sorts. It seemed like everything in him lined up just right when he was with Eric, and he wasn't sure what to do with that. He also knew that now was not the time to figure it out. After they passed into the town of Newton, it wasn't long before Eric made a right and pulled into a development of townhouses. Jake missed the name on the sign—something Park—but he didn't miss the fact that most of the units could probably hold ten of his apartment.

"Damn," Jake said as they drove down the quiet lane lit by old-fashioned-looking streetlamps. "Must be one hell of an author."

Eric shook his head. "Nah, don't let it fool you. Family money. I mean, he does all right, but he's no Stephen King. Not yet, anyway."

Jake laughed. "Okay. I'll remember not to be too impressed."

Eric continued driving until they saw cars parked along one side of the street. He pulled up behind the last one.

"Jesus, looks like he's got quite a crowd," Eric murmured as he clicked his seat belt.

"So, what's this guy's name?" Jake asked as he did the same.

"Adrien. Adrien Bell. A pen name I'm sure, but it's the only one I know," said Eric.

"Adrien Bell," Jake said as he slid out of the vehicle. "That sounds familiar. Isn't he the one who wrote that book about a vampire who became president?"

Eric nodded as he came around the rear of the car, tucking the keys into his back pocket. "Yes. And it sold like a million copies. Everything he writes is vampire-something, so I can't even imagine what he's done for this party."

"I see," Jake said and leaned against the car. Eric now stood in front of him. "So, should I introduce myself to him? My *real* self, I mean, if he wants to know about things that go bump in the night?"

Eric moved closer, pressing himself lightly against Jake. "Are you kidding? No way. He'd probably hold you hostage in his basement for research purposes." Jake laughed. "Then I'd really never see you again." Jake grew quiet as Eric raised his hands to the sides of Jake's face. He ran his thumbs gently under Jake's eyes. "These eyes," Eric whispered and Jake reached up and hooked his hands over Eric's wrists. "I just…."

Eric trailed off and spoke so quietly it seemed that he was talking to himself, and Jake could almost see his brain working, reaching for some lost fragment that would help him understand what he felt. Jake gazed back at him for a few long seconds and then gently squeezed Eric's wrists. Eric shook his head and faint color flushed his cheeks in the dim streetlight.

"Sorry," Eric said. "I sound like such a freak."

Jake smiled and dropped a hand to Eric's waist. "Not to me," he said.

Eric's face still bore traces of the dazed expression, but he nodded, a smile playing at the corners of his mouth. "Good," he said. He leaned in and caught Jake's mouth in a kiss less chaste than the one they'd shared at Jake's apartment. Jake felt Eric's tongue brush over his lips and he parted them, paying no heed to the fact that they were once again on a residential street. He tangled both his hands in Eric's hair, knocking off his baseball cap, and pulled him as close as he could, teeth scraping and nipping all the way.

Jake was as hard as a rock, and Eric was pressed close enough that Jake knew he was too. He realized he either had to dial things down or they'd be climbing into the backseat in a matter of minutes, so he slowed his kisses and disentangled his fingers from Eric's hair. He settled his hands lightly on Eric's waist, and soon they stood forehead to forehead, breathing hard.

"One of these days we're not going to be in the middle of the street, you know," Eric said with a smile.

"I hope so," Jake said. Eric's eyes darkened with want and he leaned in again, but Jake dodged him. "Easy," he said with a hand on Eric's chest. "We still have a party to go to and, if I'm not mistaken, you have a… situation to deal with." Jake flicked his eyes down toward Eric's snug-fitting white uniform pants.

"I'm aware," Eric said, rolling his eyes skyward as he reached down to adjust himself. "Although I don't think I'm the only one." He brushed his knuckles over Jake's fly, and Jake sidestepped him.

"Oh, no, you don't!" he said. "Besides, I have the power of magic at my disposal." Eric lifted one eyebrow expectantly, and Jake flung his arms out full length, fanning his cloak, and then pulled them in dramatically, covering the front of his body.

"Ha-ha," Eric said, though his smile was genuine. "Well, I do not possess such powers, so you're going to have to give me a few minutes." Eric bent down and grabbed his displaced baseball cap.

"No problem," Jake said with a smile and leaned back against the car.

ONCE ERIC was presentable, they headed toward the last townhouse in the row, their shoulders and fingers brushing as they walked. When they got to the front door, a cheesy sign lettered in red to look like blood read "Enter If You DARE." Jake managed to keep from rolling his eyes as Eric opened the door and motioned him inside. They stood in the entryway and watched as creatures of all types paraded before them in varying states of sobriety: a pack of werewolves, Frankenstein, an evil-looking Little Red Riding Hood, a guy with an arm that looked like it had been chewed off, and groups of generic ghouls and ghosts.

Eric leaned over and spoke close to Jake's ear to be heard over the song "Monster Mash" booming in the background. "C'mon, we should go say hello to the host," he said. "You may need some kind of creep-away charm."

Jake laughed and followed Eric's lead through the crowd and into a spacious kitchen. The large granite island had been turned into a makeshift bar and at the end, perched on a stool, sat the only vampire Jake had seen since entering the house. Eric led them over and clapped Dracula on the shoulder.

"Hey, Adrien," he said with a smile. "You've really outdone yourself this time."

Adrien turned and smiled back, revealing fangs that looked to Jake to be actual teeth. "Eric! How good of you to come!" Adrien exclaimed and stood up from the stool. "Yes, it was a monumental effort, but everything fell into place just in time." His eyes flicked over to Jake, and Jake was fairly certain the predatory look in them had nothing to do with the guy's costume. "And who, may I ask, is this?" he asked, scanning Jake from head to foot. "An up-and-coming writer? Long-lost cousin, perhaps?" He reached out and ran a long yellow nail down the cord of Jake's moonstone pendant, and Jake swore he felt the stone get warm.

"This is Jake," Eric said.

"Jake," Adrien murmured. "I see. And what is it you do, Jake? Besides gaze at people with those inhumanly sapphire eyes?"

The yellow nail now brushed under Jake's chin, and he had to suppress a shudder. "I own a shop over in Brookline," Jake said, following his instinct and keeping his answer vague and short.

"A businessman. How impressive," Adrien said. "And how did you come to know Eric here?"

Jake furrowed his brows, unsure how to answer when Eric jumped in. "He's my date, Adrien," Eric said, slipping his hand under Jake's cloak and resting it on the small of his back.

Beneath the white makeup, blood red lips, and black wig, Adrien's face fell. "I see," he said, recovering quickly. "Well, there is a bar here, and food and another bar on the second floor. And venture up to the third floor, if you dare—the *haunted house*!" He clapped his white hands in a decidedly unvampiric way.

"Great. Thanks, Adrien," Eric said, directing them away.

"Enjoy, boys!" Adrien called and then turned back to whomever he'd been talking to before they arrived.

"Who—or what—the hell was that?" Jake asked. He picked up his moonstone and brushed it against the thick velvet of his cloak, trying to wipe off Adrien's weird vibes.

"*That* was Adrien Bell. The hottest thing in vampire lit," Eric said. "Let's go upstairs and get a drink."

Jake nodded and followed Eric to the stairs, taking in all the costumes as they passed. When they got to the top of the stairs, he grabbed Eric's wrist and tugged him close. "Is he the only one allowed to dress as a vampire? I don't see any others," he asked.

"That would be my guess—implicitly understood, of course," Eric answered. "Adrien is nothing if not an egomaniac." Eric twisted his wrist in Jake's grasp and laced their fingers together. "He was ready to pick you up right then and there," he murmured into Jake's ear.

"No kidding," Jake said with a shiver. He squeezed Eric's hand and let go. "I need a drink after that encounter."

"You got it. What are you drinking?" Eric asked.

"Scotch on the rocks," Jake said and Eric took off for the bar. Jake wandered around a bit, checking things out. Strategically placed tables offered a variety of hot and cold appetizers, as did the costumed staff who navigated the crowd with trays in hand. Farther down, he peered into a door where the music thumped the loudest and saw it had been cleared out for a dance floor. He made his way back toward where he had started and met Eric halfway. Eric held out a glass and Jake took it. "Thanks," he said.

Eric nodded and took a sip from his own glass. "Find anything good?" he asked.

Jake shook his head. "Food, dance floor," Jake said and took a healthy gulp from his glass. They stood in companionable silence, letting the alcohol wash away the remnants of Creepy Adrien until Jake saw an authentic-looking swashbuckler heading their way.

"Eric?" the man called as he approached, a surprised expression on his face.

Eric turned and his face broke into a smile. "Daniel! How are you?"

The two shook hands and Eric introduced Jake. "Jake, this is Daniel Shane. He's an editor who works with my publishing company. He gets stuck with a version or two of my manuscripts from time to time," said Eric.

"Always a pleasure, of course," Daniel said with a mock-sideways glance as he shook Jake's hand.

The small group moved to the fringe of the room where it was less noisy, and Eric and Daniel chatted about Eric's current project and some mutual acquaintances they had. Jake listened for a while, but eventually tuned them out and made his way to the bar for a refill. When he returned, it sounded like they were wrapping up.

"It's always good to see you, Daniel," Eric said.

"Likewise," Daniel said and clapped Eric on the shoulder. "And do remember to e-mail me that synopsis. I'd love to have a look at it."

"Will do," Eric said.

Daniel turned to Jake. "Jake, nice to meet you. Sorry if we bored you," Daniel said, his face genuinely contrite.

"Not at all. Nice to meet you too," Jake said with a smile.

Daniel stepped closer to Jake and set a hand on his shoulder. "And thanks for dragging this one out of hiding. It's been too long," he said with a thumb in Eric's direction.

"My pleasure," Jake said, snagging Eric's gaze over Daniel's head. Daniel patted Jake on the back and disappeared into the crowd. Eric moved to Jake's side as Jake sipped his drink. He wasn't much for alcohol, so he could feel a bit of a buzz already. And he could only imagine that Adrien Bell wouldn't be caught undead serving watered-down drinks. "So, what do you want to do now?" he asked Eric. "Food? Music? Haunted house?"

Eric shook his head. "Not hungry, really. Haunted house, I guess?"

Jake nodded and tossed back the remainder of his drink. He set his glass on the nearest table and offered his arm to Eric. "Lead the way."

THEY CLIMBED another staircase up to what Eric said was normally a large loft space, but when they reached the top it was dark with the exception of black lights and flashing strobe lights. Screams and moans rose up from every corner of the room courtesy of an overly loud soundtrack, and partitions created a maze-like pathway for guests to follow. A sign with an arrow pointed to the entrance and they stepped up.

"You first," Eric said and nudged Jake in front of him.

Jake laughed and elbowed him in the side. "You're kidding, right? Are you actually scared?"

"No," Eric said, his chin raised a bit. "You're just more used to this kind of stuff so you should go first."

Jake quirked an eyebrow at Eric. "I don't know what you think I do, exactly, but it has nothing to do with mummies or zombies."

"Shut up," Eric said and gave Jake a little push forward. "I just meant Halloween stuff. It's got to be a busy time for your work."

"It is. But this," Jake gestured to the space around them, "is *not* my Halloween."

"What's your Halloween, then?" Eric asked.

Jake sighed. "Now's not the time for a history lesson. I can explain it all to you later, but right now let's go be terrified in the haunted house. Or haunted loft space."

He held out his hand and Eric grabbed it. They walked down the corridor, and around the first corner, a man holding his own head reached out for them from an alcove.

"How the hell'd they do that?" Eric asked as they passed by just out of reach.

"No idea," Jake said. "But it's pretty creative."

They followed the maze, turning corners and running into mummies and zombies, as Jake had predicted, a freaky-looking magician sawing a woman in half, and a werewolf eating the last guest who'd walked through. Jake guessed they were nearing the end, and it wasn't a moment too soon. He felt a bit disoriented from the scotch, the strobe lights, and the screams. He squeezed his eyes shut for a moment as they rounded the final bend and came face-to-face with a towering man in a hockey mask waving a chainsaw as he approached.

"Holy shit!" Jake shouted and pressed himself back into Eric.

Eric slid an arm around Jake's waist and laughed. He put his lips to Jake's ear and said, "Easy, there. I've got you. C'mon." Eric kept his arm around Jake's waist and pulled them past the Jason wannabe and the "Happy Halloween" exit sign and out of the maze. Jake took a deep breath and closed his eyes, glad to be rid of the flashing lights. He broke away from Eric and leaned against the nearest wall.

"You okay?" Eric asked.

Jake nodded. "Yeah. The lights were just getting to me."

"Do you want some water or anything?"

"No, I'm okay," Jake said and then laughed. "You saved me from Jason."

"I did," Eric said, standing in front of Jake and stepping in close. "I'd do it again too."

Jake snagged a finger in Eric's waistband and pulled him closer. "My hero," he whispered. He reached up and palmed the back of Eric's head, crashing their lips together, tongues sliding alongside each other like they'd been matched for years. Eric gave back what he got, pressing Jake into the wall and sliding his hands inside his cloak and up the back of his shirt.

Jake couldn't help the moan that escaped him, and he reached down and grabbed a handful of Eric's ass. This time the moan came from Eric and Jake shifted his leg, fitting it in between Eric's and giving him something to grind against. Eric reached down and squeezed Jake's cock through his jeans, and that alone was almost too much.

"Shit, shit, shit," Jake said under his breath and Eric pulled away.

"Did I hurt you?" he asked, his eyes hazy with lust.

"No, no," Jake said and pulled him in for another kiss. "The show was almost over there for a second."

Eric pressed into Jake's thigh and groaned. "Yeah," he said. Eric scrubbed a hand over his face and looked at Jake with an expression he couldn't decipher.

"What is it?" Jake asked. He ran the back of his hand down Eric's cheek.

"It's just… I haven't done this in a while," Eric said.

"What are you talking about?" Jake asked. "We did this at the car before—"

Eric shook his head. "Not this," he said, gesturing between the two of them. "I mean…." He trailed off, bit his lip, and then spit it out all at once. "Will you come home with me?"

Jake stared at him for a moment while he double-checked that they didn't have any spirit tagalongs that he could sense. When he came up with none, he smiled at Eric. "Yes."

CHAPTER 12

"JESUS, IT'S hot in here," Jake grumbled as he yanked at his cloak, temporarily tangled as he tried to free himself from it in the car. With a final tug, it let go and he balled it up and tossed it into the backseat.

"Yeah," Eric agreed. He stopped the car for a red light and swiped a hand across his forehead. His foot tapped out an anxious rhythm while they waited. It was all Jake could do to keep himself in his seat; his muscles ached from the desire to rocket over the console and into Eric's lap. Eric glanced over at him, and Jake swallowed hard at the way the nighttime lighting had turned Eric's soft brown eyes to an inky black.

Jake turned away and rested his forehead against the window's cool glass. The light changed color but the car didn't move. "It's green," he said and flicked his gaze back to Eric.

"Thank God." Eric's eyes were still fixed on Jake, but he turned to face the road and hit the gas.

The ten minutes they spent in the car felt like a small eternity to Jake. He hadn't lived the life of a monk, but he couldn't recall ever wanting anyone the way he did Eric. He fidgeted and squirmed until he breathed a sigh of relief when Eric pulled the car to a stop in front of a monstrous structure. Jake's eyes grew wide as he took in what had to be at least a six-bedroom house. Eric caught Jake's expression as he unbuckled his seat belt and said, "Again, don't be too impressed. Condos. Only one's mine." Jake nodded as he stepped out onto the quiet suburban street and followed Eric up the walk and the short staircase to the porch. Before nerves or doubt could set in, Eric caught him as he crested the porch and pulled him in for a lingering kiss.

"One more out on the street," Eric said with a smile and Jake laughed. "You never know—we may have a following."

Jake didn't want to ruin the moment and give voice to his thought that a following of sorts was his exact concern, so he nipped Eric on the chin and said, "I'm ready to follow you inside if you open the door." Eric didn't need any further prompting; he had the keys already in hand. He unlocked the door and had them inside in ten seconds flat.

Jake had prepared himself for a large living space, and when he walked through the door, he wasn't disappointed. From the entryway he saw a spacious living room and stairs that curved upward. Eric toed off his shoes so Jake did the same and then wandered a few steps into the living room. Eric had left only one lamp lit, so the light was dim, but Jake could see the shadows of what looked like a formal dining room and an archway that he imagined led to the kitchen.

"Wow, this is a really nice place," Jake said as he looked around.

"Yes, well, it suits my needs. Suburban enough for peace and quiet, but close enough to the city for business and travel and all that." Eric turned the locks on the front door and moved over to where Jake stood. He put one arm around Jake and pulled him close and tossed his baseball cap at the couch. Jake wrapped his arms around Eric and they just stood, quiet for a moment. "I don't want to seem like a bad host or anything, but could I give you the grand tour later?" Eric asked, his voice a warm rumble in Jake's ear. Jake chuckled quietly and nodded. "Thank God," Eric said.

He held tight to Jake's hand and propelled them up the staircase and down the hall to the last room on the right. Eric pulled him through the doorway and cradled Jake's face with both hands as he brought them together in an open-mouthed kiss. Jake didn't miss a beat; it felt like the entire evening had been foreplay leading up to this. He kissed Eric back hard as he untucked the baseball jersey and ran his hands up the warm skin of Eric's back. Eric sighed at the contact. He tangled his fingers in Jake's hair and broke the kiss with a little laugh.

"Hmm?" Jake murmured as he nibbled his way along Eric's neck.

"I like your hair better soft," Eric whispered.

"What?" Jake brought a hand to his head. The spikes he felt reminded him of Jessie's Halloween transformation. "Oh, shit," Jake said with a laugh. "It's not usually like this. It was for the Halloween...." He trailed off as Eric tugged his shirt up and over his head.

"You know," Eric said thoughtfully, "I think I like you better without the whole costume."

"Really?" Jake's breath quickened as Eric slid his palms down Jake's chest, bumping his thumbs over nipples as he skimmed the smooth skin.

"Mm-hmm." Eric locked his lips on the curve where Jake's neck met his shoulder. "I'm sure of it," Eric said and continued his journey down Jake's chest with his mouth until his knees hit the floor. He made quick work of Jake's fly and peeled the tight jeans down his legs.

Jake stepped out of them, shook off his socks, and sucked in a breath at the sight of Eric on his knees. His hand went to his own hard cock and squeezed it through his boxer briefs. Eric tossed the jeans aside and looked up to meet Jake's eyes.

"Keep going," Eric whispered, and Jake dropped his head back and groaned. He continued with a few strokes outside his briefs and then slipped his hand inside. He looked down and saw Eric's hand working the front of his pants, moving up and down as he watched Jake. Jake thought he might lose it after only a few strokes.

"Shit," he whispered and his breath hitched as he slid his hand out of his shorts. He reached down and pulled the jersey over Eric's head and ran his fingers through the soft waves of his hair. Eric was fixated, though, and tugged Jake's shorts down his thighs until his cock sprung free. He trailed a finger along the hard length, and Jake shivered. His mouth dropped open as he watched Eric take the tip into his mouth, sliding it in and out, a little farther each time until he had swallowed Jake completely.

Jake fisted handfuls of Eric's hair and moaned. "Oh God! I'm not—I can't…," he panted, trying to hold off as long as he could but wanting to give Eric some warning too. "I'm… I…." Eric never broke his rhythm and didn't pull away when Jake let go and exploded into his mouth. Jake huffed out long, loud breaths until the tremors passed, and he ran a hand over Eric's head. Eric let Jake's cock fall from his lips and looked up at him.

"Sorry," Eric said with a lust-addled smile. "I couldn't wait."

"No complaints here," Jake said. "But now neither can I."

He tugged Eric up to a standing position and push-walked him backward until he fell onto the bed. He undid Eric's pants and slid them down his long legs along with his boxers. He took a lingering look at Eric, gorgeous and naked and waiting, then climbed up onto the bed and straddled him. He bent his head, locked their mouths, and found Eric's tongue still salty from his release. He felt Eric's hard cock pressing against him, demanding attention, but he couldn't tear his mouth away. He speared his fingers through Eric's hair and kissed deeper, his mind reeling from the new sensations and, at the same time, from that tingling familiarity that had veiled their very first kiss.

He finally came up for air and looked down at Eric, who smiled up at him. "You good?" Jake asked, brushing a lock of hair from Eric's forehead. Eric nodded, so Jake scooted down a little and started a trail of wet kisses across Eric's chest, pausing to run his teeth over a nipple.

Eric groaned and squirmed under him, and Jake smiled, taking time to lavish attention on both sides equally. By the time he moved farther down, Eric was thrusting against him, his body searching for friction. Jake settled himself between Eric's legs and took his cock into his mouth, swirling his tongue as he slid his lips slowly down to the base.

"Shit," Eric gasped and tried to push farther into Jake's mouth. Jake pulled back and began a steady up-and-down rhythm that had Eric writhing after only a few minutes.

"Jesus, Jake... I'm coming...," Eric choked out seconds before his orgasm hit, and Jake swallowed until the pulses subsided. He let Eric's softening cock slip from his lips and crawled back up the bed to lie next to him.

Eric had a hand over his eyes, breath still heavy. Jake waited until his breathing slowed and then lifted Eric's hand to lace their fingers together. He didn't want to sound like a mother hen, but he had no idea if Eric had even been with anyone since Andrew, thus making this possibly a big deal, and Eric wasn't talking.

"Okay?" he asked. He gave Eric's fingers a gentle squeeze.

Eric looked over at him with a smile. "Yes. Come here," he said and pulled Jake into the curve of his arm. Jake rested his head on Eric's shoulder and they lay there sideways on the bed with their feet hanging off, content not saying a word.

Jake had almost dozed off when he felt his skin prickle with goosebumps and the hair on his neck stand up. He couldn't suppress a shiver, and Eric looked over at him.

"Are you cold?" Eric asked.

"Yeah, a bit," Jake fibbed. He knew what the chill and the charge in the air around him meant. The quick spell he'd done earlier had actually lasted longer than he expected, but time was up, and he wasn't about to reunite Eric and Andrew while he and Eric were naked on the bed. He closed his eyes and used all the energy he could muster to push Andrew back and close himself off, halting any communication for the moment.

Eric bit his lip. "I don't want to assume anything but... do you want to get under the covers? Or I can drive you home if you prefer. If you can't stay just tell me."

Jake couldn't help but laugh at Eric's awkwardness. "Yeah, I've got a few other blow jobs to give tonight, so I better get home," he said.

Eric stared at him for a second and then jostled him off his shoulder. "Asshole."

"Covers are good," Jake said, still laughing.

Eric nodded and they stood up and pulled back the duvet and sheets and climbed in together. Out of habit, Jake curled up on his side and a moment later he felt the warmth of Eric surround him as he pulled Jake to his chest.

"Is this okay?" Eric asked into Jake's shoulder.

Jake craned his neck back and kissed Eric. "The best," Jake said and snuggled further into Eric. In their bedroom cocoon, and with unseen eyes watching from the Other Side, they fell asleep.

JAKE WOKE up from a fitful sleep a couple hours later. His rest had been peppered with images courtesy of Andrew, though they weren't angry or negative as Jake had feared. They were the same group of images he'd been showing Jake since Eric first turned up in the shop and, though Jake had put together more pieces of the story, he still had no idea what to do with them.

His eyes flickered open and he realized two things. First, he and Eric had switched places while they slept. Eric's back was now pressed snugly against Jake's chest, his arm draped over Eric's waist. Secondly, Jake was once again hard as a rock and ready to go. With Eric butted against him, he couldn't resist the urge to thrust his hips a little and ride along the cleft of Eric's ass. He kept his breathing quiet so he didn't wake Eric, but the next time he moved he felt Eric push back into him.

Jake let out a shuddering breath and held still, unsure if Eric had just shifted in his sleep or was inviting him to continue. He didn't wonder long; Eric reached a hand behind him and grabbed Jake's ass, drawing him forward again. Jake took the hint and grasped Eric's hip as he began to thrust more earnestly, his hard dick pressing against the crease of Eric's ass. Eric pressed back to meet him each time and they found a rhythm, their breathing becoming soft grunts of pleasure.

They carried on until Jake started to see that point of no return on the horizon and wondered what to do. Finish this way? Break the bubble-like silence that enveloped them and ask Eric what he wanted to do? He got caught up in his thoughts when suddenly Eric's warmth disappeared. A new moon had plunged the room into near-complete darkness, but Jake heard Eric moving in front of him, then the rattle of a metal handle and the slide of a wooden drawer. Eric rummaged around and a few seconds later his warmth returned and he lifted Jake's hand from his hip and pressed two items into it. Jake ran his fingers over them and realized that one was a condom. The second thing was a tube, which Jake assumed was lube.

Part of him wanted to press pause, turn on the light, and have a minitherapy session to make sure Eric was okay and that this was what he wanted. He kept his mouth shut, though. The voice in his head that he followed without question told him it wasn't time for a talk. Eric had made his intention clear, so Jake tore the foil package with his teeth and slid the condom over his cock. He tossed the wrapper aside and popped the top on the lube. He generously coated two fingers and slipped one into the cleft of Eric's ass. He stroked slowly and moved deeper each time until his finger brushed over Eric's entrance.

Eric pushed back and Jake let his finger slide past the firm muscle and inside. Eric let out a soft moan as Jake began an in-and-out movement, and soon he added a second finger, stretching Eric farther. Eric moaned for more, so Jake picked up the pace, brushing his prostate every few passes. Jake kept going until he couldn't hold off any longer. He gave Eric a final stretch and pulled out his fingers. He quickly covered the condom with lube and tossed the tube aside. He raised Eric's leg and held it up as he positioned himself at his entrance. As he pushed in, Eric tilted his hips and Jake slipped inside as smooth and silent as their coupling. He stayed still for a moment in part to let Eric get comfortable and partly to slow himself down.

The tight heat of being inside Eric was like nothing he had ever experienced. They fit together just right, with none of the fumbling awkwardness of first-time sex. They began to move together in time, and Jake buried his nose in the back of Eric's neck, breathing in his scent, which, to Jake, smelled like a rush of air just as summer gave herself up to fall. He pressed kisses to Eric's shoulder as they upped their pace, and Eric arched his neck to kiss Jake on the mouth. When their lips met, Jake felt joined to him in every possible way, like an invisible but unbreakable link ran between them and—his sixth sense told him—likely always would.

Eric turned back around and Jake heard the sound of Eric's hand skimming over hard flesh. Jake hit full speed, pushing hard and deep, and the moment he felt Eric's muscles clench around him as he came, Jake thrust one more time and followed him over the edge. They stayed still for a moment, and Jake felt his heart slowly return to its normal rate. When his cock started to soften, he reached down to hold the condom in place and pulled out. Eric let out a sharp breath.

"Sorry," Jake whispered. He took the condom off and got up. He vaguely remembered seeing a bathroom attached to Eric's bedroom when they came in so he went in that direction until he felt a door frame and tile floor at his feet. He didn't turn on the light until the door was shut behind him, and he made quick work of disposing of the condom and cleaning up. He shut off the light and went back out to the bedroom and found Eric had turned on a small reading lamp at his bedside. He had cleaned up too, and he lay in the bed waiting for Jake, his head propped on his hand.

Jake got back into bed and faced Eric, copying his position. Eric had a faraway look on his face, and Jake reached over and ran a hand through his hair.

"You all right?" Jake asked.

Eric focused his eyes on Jake and nodded but didn't say anything.

Jake knew he was taking a chance saying it out loud but he also knew he was right. "Was that the first time since Andrew?" he asked.

A startled expression took over Eric's face and he nodded slowly. "Yes," he said, his voice hoarse. "Did he tell you…?"

Jake shook his head. "No. He didn't need to. It's right here." He traced a gentle line under Eric's eye.

Eric flopped down on the pillow, and Jake reached out and pulled him over. Eric rested his head on Jake's chest, and Jake put an arm around his shoulder. They were silent until Eric spoke, his words muffled by Jake's chest.

"It's silly, really. I just didn't think it would be so…."

"So what?" Jake asked, encouraging Eric to continue.

Eric cleared his throat. "I don't know. Sad, I guess." He paused and added quickly, "I don't mean you, of course. You… I mean we… it was incredible."

Jake pressed a kiss into Eric's hair. "It's okay."

Eric sighed, ruffling Jake's chest hair. "It feels like it's been so long, you know? And everything was really messed up when he.... We were barely even together. But it still feels kind of like an ending. Like letting another part of him go."

Jake nodded. "There are all kinds of endings when we lose someone we love. It's not just the passing, though that's the big one. It's things we don't even think about or notice until a month, or a year, or even ten years later. And it hits us all over again."

Eric nodded into his chest and then huffed out a little laugh. "I'm sorry. I'm so fucking lame. I just had amazing sex with an equally amazing guy and I'm here whining about my ex. Jesus Christ."

Jake's chuckle was quiet. "You're not lame, and you're not whining. 'Firsts' of any kind are hard. But you know what also comes with endings?" Eric lifted his head and looked at Jake with glistening eyes. "Beginnings."

Eric gave him a small smile and nodded and then rested his head over Jake's heart.

CHAPTER 13

As HARD as he tried, sleep proved unwilling to cooperate with Jake. He lay with Eric and held him close until he fell asleep. He tried snuggling, which was usually a given, but gave up after twenty or so minutes. Never mind that snuggling was especially difficult when your snuggler was snoring softly beside you. Jake was wide awake.

He scooted away from Eric and flip-flopped a bit longer until he finally gave up. He blew out a breath in frustration and closed his eyes. When he opened them, however, he was mildly taken aback to see the faint image of an orb hovering around Eric and his side of the bed. Jake put out his feelers and felt fairly certain it wasn't Andrew. The energy didn't have the same intensity, the same male "you'll listen to me or else" quality he'd come to associate with Andrew. No, this spirit felt softer, gentler, and almost certainly female. She also felt older though Jake couldn't say exactly why.

Jake rose from the bed, and the orb zipped up the wall and disappeared. If he couldn't sleep, he could embark on a little ghost hunt under the guise of getting a glass of water. He spied a pair of flannel pants tossed over a chair in the corner of the room, snagged them, and pulled them on with his T-shirt from earlier. He padded out of the bedroom and downstairs on bare feet. His eyes had adjusted to the darkness so he made his way easily through the living room and to the archway, which, as he had guessed, led to the kitchen. He opened cabinet doors until he found the glasses and grabbed one. Eric didn't strike him as a tap water kind of guy, so he opened the fridge and located the pitcher of filtered water.

He poured a glass and headed back to the living room. The first traces of morning light had eked their way through the large front window and illuminated the room enough for Jake to look around. He was drawn to the fireplace mantle, where several framed photographs stood on display. From what he could make out, the first picture showed a younger Eric in college cap and gown, flanked on either side by people Jake assumed were his parents. He held out his hand and let it hover over the picture but picked up nothing. Eric hadn't specifically mentioned it either way, but Jake felt confident both of Eric's parents were still alive and well, and therefore not who he had seen up in the bedroom. Next were a few pictures of Eric at book signings and with official-looking people, followed by a framed scrawled signature on yellowing paper. *An autograph?* Jake wondered. He couldn't make out the name, but he touched the glass lightly and felt the icy cold of the long dead. But, again, there was no connection, no hum of activity.

He finally got to the last photograph of a very young Eric—maybe five or six years old—and an older woman. Eric sat on her lap and held up a paper full of childhood scrawl, and she was smiling and looking at it like it was the most wonderful thing she had ever seen. Jake raised his hand and before he even got near the picture, he felt warmth and comfort and—he sniffed the air—baking? In the air around him, he smelled the faint scent of cherries and chocolate and a warm oven. He smiled, closed his eyes, and invited the spirit to show him more, and she was happy to oblige.

He saw the same young Eric from the photo in a kitchen with the woman, stirring ingredients with a wooden spoon as she added them to a mixing bowl. She spoke, and when Eric looked up at her, she dabbed a spot of flour on his nose. Little Eric laughed, and the warm feeling Jake sensed grew. Next, Jake saw Eric—a little older—with the woman at a table working together to build a house of cards. They added cards, one by one, until Eric sneezed and sent the cards flying everywhere. He began to tear up, but she gave him a squeeze and swooped up the cards, and they started all over again.

Jake laughed quietly. "Hi, Grandma," he whispered. "Good to meet you."

"Jake?" Eric said.

Jake's eyes flew open and, startled, he fumbled, nearly sending his glass crashing to the floor.

"Holy shit," he gasped. "You scared me!"

"No kidding," Eric said, eyeing him warily from the bottom of the stairs. He had pulled on loose-fitting pajama pants and a white T-shirt. "What... uh, what's going on? I woke up and you were gone."

"Not gone," Jake said and tried to smile. "Just thirsty." He held up his glass and took a big gulp, willing his heart to stop hammering. "I borrowed some pants—hope you don't mind."

"No, it's fine," Eric said and descended the last few steps. He walked over to Jake and slipped his arms around his waist. "This probably sounds crazy, but were you talking to someone just now?"

Jake sighed. "Not as crazy as the answer is going to sound," he said.

"You were?" Eric asked, surprised. Jake glanced around for somewhere to set his glass. "Just put it anywhere. It's fine."

Jake set the glass on a nearby side table and looped his arms around Eric's neck. Eric pulled him in for a thorough kiss. When they separated, Jake looked him in the eye and said, "Yes, I was."

Eric looked equal parts amazed and confused. "What...? Who? What happened?"

"Can we sit down?" Jake asked, and Eric nodded and led them over to the couch. Eric kept their fingers laced together and hitched a knee up on the couch so he was facing Jake.

"So?" Eric prompted.

Jake was relieved to note that Eric seemed more curious than anything. He began to realize this had all likely happened for a reason. Eric's first real experience with Jake's abilities wasn't going to be the mess with Andrew. It was going to be something sweet and warm that made him smile.

"Well, I couldn't fall asleep. I was tossing and turning, and I looked over at your side of the bed, and I saw an orb hovering around you," Jake said.

"An orb? What exactly is an orb?" Eric asked.

"It's a kind of light from the spiritual plane, usually so faint most people don't notice them. Sometimes they're easier to catch with cameras. Anyway, it's one way spirits can manifest without draining themselves of too much energy," Jake explained.

"So, a spirit was hovering over me in our—I mean, my *bed*?" Jake nodded. Eric was quiet for a moment and then his expression turned dark. "Andrew?" he snapped. "Fucking Andrew was up there with us?"

Jake squeezed his hand. "No. That's what I thought at first but I realized pretty quick that it wasn't him at all. As soon as I got up the orb disappeared, and that's not Andrew's m.o. He has no problem getting in my face."

Eric's face grew darker but Jake brushed him off. "It's okay. Long story and nothing I can't handle. Anyway, I came down for a drink, and

I was kind of drawn to your pictures." Jake gestured at the fireplace. "They helped me figure out who it is. I think it's your grandmother."

Eric sat in stunned silence. Jake waited, allowing him to absorb what he'd just said.

"So, my grandma was in bed with us?" Eric asked, his voice confused.

Jake laughed. "Not like that! She was there, with *you*. She watches over you, I think."

"All the time?" Eric asked.

Jake shook his head. "No, probably not every second of every day. But she's here to check up on you, protect you. Maybe as a spirit guide."

Eric nodded slowly. "Wow. I haven't seen her since…. We were really close when I was young. She babysat me when I was little and then watched me after school. My dad's a dermatologist and mom's in real estate so they were both always really busy. Or they were before they retired.

"But when she was still fairly young—maybe when I was twelve or thirteen—she started developing some kind of dementia. It wasn't Alzheimer's but… it moved pretty fast. After another few years, most of the time she didn't know who I was."

Eric swallowed hard, and Jake scooted closer. "I'm sorry," Jake said.

Eric smiled. He sat, lost in his memories for a moment until he snapped to attention. "Is she still here?" he asked.

The question caught Jake off guard. "I don't know," he said. "Probably. Do you want me to…?" He tapped the side of his head.

Eric bit his lip and nodded. "Could you? I just… I want to know she's okay, if she's seen my work, what I've done. But it's okay if you can't. I don't exactly know how it works."

"Well, it's not always easy to read for someone you… you're close to, but I think I can handle this one." Jake smiled and leaned in to kiss him. "Any chance you have something that belonged to her? If you don't, that's all right. Sometimes if I hold an object that belonged to the person, I can make a better connection."

Eric thought for a moment and then leapt up. He darted upstairs and less than a minute later he returned and pressed a silver heart-shaped locket into Jake's hand. "Open it," Eric said.

Jake popped the clasp and opened the heart. On one side was a photo of the woman from the picture on the mantle. On the other side, a picture of young Eric. "It's beautiful," Jake said.

Eric sat back down. He flipped the locket over and showed Jake the engraving on the back: *To the best Grandma ever—Love, Eric.* "I got it for her before she really started going downhill, and she loved it. Later, even when I knew she didn't recognize me anymore, I guess I thought if she had this—a picture of how we were—she'd never really forget." This time, it was Jake who swallowed hard.

"It was kind of strange," Eric continued. "She never took it off. Even when she had a nurse with her 24-7, she never let anyone take it off. It was like somewhere inside she still knew it was special. When she died, my mom said it was in my grandma's will that I was to have it. I didn't really understand why; I thought they'd bury her with it. But maybe now I do." He looked up at Jake and placed a hand on the side of his neck.

The warm, fuzzy feelings came back to Jake and, as he had suspected, he didn't need to do much to connect with this spirit.

Jake took a deep breath. "I'm just going to close my eyes for a minute and make sure we have a connection. And that it's who we think it is." Eric furrowed his eyebrows. "You'd be amazed at how many spirits are out there, not necessarily bad, but looking to have fun at someone's expense. They'll tell you they're your grandmother, son, very first dog… whatever. And then load you up with a bunch of made-up crap. And, of course, there are the truly bad ones."

Eric's eyebrows rose in concern. "Maybe we should wait until we're at your shop or something to do this."

Jake put a hand on Eric's knee and felt his warmth through the cotton fabric. "It's okay, I promise. Like I said, I'm pretty sure it's her, but I'll ask. That's a big part of the reason I always try to get a name first."

"Oh, her name was—" Jake clamped his hand over Eric's mouth and shook his head.

"Do *not* tell me," he said firmly. "It has to come from them. That's the only way to know it's real." Eric nodded and Jake removed his hand. "Okay. Just give me a minute. I'll say as much out loud as I can. Sometimes they really get going in my head, and it's hard to keep up."

Jake clasped the locket in one hand and closed his eyes. He focused on the warm feelings the spirit brought and asked out loud, "Can you please tell me your name?"

He saw the letter *M* flash behind his closed eyes, so he sat and waited for more. When nothing else was forthcoming, he pursed his lips in confusion. He heard a female voice speaking at the usual spirit million-mile-an-hour speed saying, *that's it that's all just say it just say it.*

He took a deep breath and opened one eye to look at Eric. "This isn't going quite how I expected," he said.

"You mean it's not her?" Worry lines creased Eric's forehead.

Jake closed his eyes again but still saw and heard the same information. "Uh, I'm not sure. I'm getting something and I'm also being told to just hurry up and spit it out but…. Well, okay, here goes. M, like the letter M. Does that mean anything to you?" Jake asked. He felt a little embarrassed that what seemed like such a simple reading was off to a strange start, until he saw Eric's face. It was a combination of amazement and amusement.

"That's her," Eric said softly. "Emma. I called her Grandma Em."

Jake sighed and shook his head. The Other Side still never failed to surprise him. "Gotcha. Very creative, Grandma Em," he said.

Eric laughed. "She was nothing if not creative."

"*Is,*" Jake corrected. "*Is* creative. From her, not me."

"Sorry, Grandma Em," Eric said, directing his comment to the air around him. "Where is she?" His gaze panned the room.

Jake closed his eyes again. "Like I said, I don't often see them like some mediums can. But I can sense where the energy is…." He held out a hand and moved it slowly through the space around him until he felt a slight dip in the temperature and sensed the heightened vibrations. "Right about there," he said and opened his eyes to find he was pointing just over Eric's right shoulder.

Eric glanced at the space. "I don't see anything."

"That's why you have me," Jake said and smiled. He smelled the cherries and chocolate again. "Okay, now this might be some more information confirming who she is, but I'm getting the scent of baking, like in a warm kitchen. And chocolate and cherries. Does that mean anything in particular? I could smell it earlier at the picture."

Eric huffed out a laugh. "Yes. It was my favorite dessert that she made. Black Forest cupcakes—chocolate and cherries and whipped cream."

"Good. All right, I think we're safe in saying we have Grandma Em with us. Is there anything you want to ask her?"

"Is she okay? Where is she now?" Eric asked.

Jake felt momentarily imbued with warmth and strength and vitality. *Yes, yes, fine. I'm here, here, sometimes there, but here.* Jake caught the rapid-fire response and combined it all into an answer for Eric. "Yes, she's okay now. She's healthy again, and she's here. Not all the time, but she is here with you."

Next, she showed Jake a picture of books—what looked like hardcover novels—lined up on a shelf. "She's showing me books on a shelf. Novels. Did she like to read?" Before Eric could answer, he heard her whisper-soft voice say *No, no, his, his books!* "Sorry, my mistake— they're your books. I guess it's her way of letting you know she sees your work and the success you've had—what?" Jake interrupted himself and listened—*yes, yes, how many how many?*

"How many?" Jake repeated. He saw the shelf again and she repeated *how many how many.* Jake counted the books on the shelf and then said, "Fifteen." He puzzled for a moment and then, as often happened in readings, something clicked in his head and he got the message. "Oh! Okay, they're your books—so she has seen your writing and your success—and she wants you to know that there are fifteen books."

"Fifteen books? Where? I've only written three."

You will, you will. "Yes, but you have fifteen books in you. You'll write fifteen novels in the course of your career." Jake saw a gold sticker-star and laughed. "And she gave me a gold star for getting that right."

Eric sucked in a surprised breath. "I'd forgotten! She had sheets of gold stars! She had charts, and whenever I was especially good or helped her with a chore, I got a star. Ten stars equaled a treat."

"Wow. Thanks, Grandma Em," Jake said. He felt her energy waver and wane a bit. He knew spirits could only sustain this kind of interaction for a short time, and that was a signal it was time to wrap things up. "She's starting to pull back a little. Is there anything else you want to say?"

Eric cleared his throat but there was no mistaking the emotion that clogged it. "Just that I love her," he whispered.

Grandma Em sent warmth and hearts and sunshine from the Other Side. "She loves you, too," Jake said softly. "Anything else, Grandma Em?"

At that question, her energy surged once more and she showed Jake a picture of Andrew. Jake felt a shove on his chest and Grandma Em, her voice fading but frantic, said *keep away, keep away, too close, too close*. "Who, me?" Jake asked, desperate to clarify before she broke the connection. *No, him, him*—image of Andrew again—*I watch, I watch*.

"Okay, I understand," Jake said. "Thank you." The connection was fading rapidly as Em withdrew, but in her weakening voice Jake heard one last thing: *He loves you. Eric... loves... you.* With that, Grandma Em was gone.

CHAPTER 14

JAKE OPENED his eyes, his mind reeling from what he'd last heard. But before he had time to worry about it, he looked over at Eric and saw him sitting dazed and silent on the couch, a few tears trailing down his cheeks. Jake brought himself fully back to the present and turned toward Eric. He scooted forward and closed the space between them.

"Come here, baby," he said without giving it a thought. He pulled Eric toward him, and Eric went willingly. Jake held him close and ran a hand slowly up and down his back. They sat, tangled together, until Eric raised his head from Jake's chest and looked at him. "What?" Jake asked, tracing Eric's eyebrow with his thumb.

"You," Eric said. "It's incredible. I mean, the fact that you can… and you could never have known her name, or the dessert, or… I just think it's amazing."

Jake smiled. "It's no more amazing than what you do when you sit down to write. It's just different."

Eric shrugged and sat up but kept their legs draped over each other. "I can't even begin to imagine how you…." He trailed off and shook his head.

Jake smiled. "Well, you just wrote a best-seller about the occult. Are you telling me you didn't research it at all?" Jake gave Eric a gentle poke in the side.

Eric raised one skeptical eyebrow. "You haven't read it, have you?"

Jake felt his cheeks turn pink, and he shifted his gaze. "Umm, not exactly. Not yet. But I will," he added quickly.

"You don't *have* to read it," Eric said with a laugh. "It's just not about this kind of occult. It's actually a murder mystery more than anything, but there's a satanic cult that plays a role, so most of my 'occult research' focused on that. Nothing like what you do."

Jake nodded. "I see. Well, I'm definitely not in a satanic cult. And I *will* read the book."

"Okay," Eric said. "Anyway, I've come to realize the term 'occult' is broader than I originally thought. Or maybe narrower. Maybe this isn't occult at all."

"Yeah. Unfortunately, to a lot of people out there in mainstream America, what I do is only a few degrees away from satanic practices," said Jake.

Eric nodded and they sat quietly for a few moments until Eric broke the silence. "Hey, what was that last part about? The 'who, me?' and all that?"

"What?" Jake asked, confused.

"In the reading. At the very end, it was like... I don't know. You were having a conversation and I only heard half of it."

Jake sighed and laced his fingers through Eric's. He hadn't followed his usual protocol with this reading. If he had, he would've asked Eric if he wanted to know absolutely everything before they started. Some people weren't ready for all a spirit might have to say, and he felt it was his responsibility to give them that choice. He hadn't asked Eric, though, and he wasn't sure *he* was ready to share the very last bit he'd heard. He began by treading lightly.

"Well, Grandma Em isn't exactly a fan of Andrew," he said.

"What? They know each other?" Eric exclaimed.

"Yes, it seems so. They're both spirits attached to you, so they're bound to encounter one another. She tries to protect you from him. She thinks he's too close, around you too much."

"Is he?"

Jake paused, unsure how to answer. "I think he's very closely bound to you, yes. And he definitely has his own agenda. I don't think he's going anywhere until you talk to him." Eric's posture stiffened. "But I also think it has to be on your terms, when you're ready."

Eric nodded. He smiled and tugged on Jake's hand. "Boy, he must really hate you now, huh?"

Jake felt his face flush and laughed. "I don't think he's thrilled with me. But I also think he's not all bad—he's not going to try to off me because I slept with you. I think, mostly, he's like any other spirit. He wants to be heard." When Eric didn't respond, Jake moved close to him again, connecting them in as many places as he could. He felt Eric relax and he looked up into his eyes. "Will you tell me about him? What happened? I have his version, kind of, but I'd like to know what happened for you."

Eric pressed his lips to Jake's forehead and nodded. "Okay. I'll tell you. But how about we talk over breakfast?"

Jake smiled. "Sounds good."

THEY MADE their way into the kitchen, and Jake sat down at the table while Eric gathered cooking implements and ingredients from various cabinets.

"How about pancakes and sausage?" Eric asked.

"Sounds great," Jake said. "Do you cook a lot?"

Eric shrugged. "Some. When I have the time." He set a large mixing bowl on the counter. "And when I have the proper incentive," he added with a wink. Jake smiled. "But, yes, I do enjoy it. And I'm not too bad at it."

"I'll be the judge of that," Jake teased.

"Fair enough."

Jake shifted in his chair, unsure of how to get Eric started talking about Andrew, so he just dove in. "So. You and Andrew?"

Eric stilled for a moment and sighed. "Right. Me and Andrew." He started measuring flour and dumping it into the bowl. "Well, we met through my publisher. Andrew was an editor, and a good friend of the editor who worked on my book before *Trial by Fire*. It's called *Everyday Blue*. It needed a lot of work. I mean, *a lot*. I was staying in New York City temporarily, where Dark Days Books has their offices."

Jake made a mental note to carve out some reading time in his schedule.

"Anyway, I was there quite a bit—the recently-signed and totally freaked-out newbie author—and he was there... well, because he worked there. My editor at the time asked for Andrew's feedback on something—I don't even remember what—and we all met and talked and, as I was leaving, he caught me at the elevator and asked me to dinner."

"He didn't waste any time," Jake commented.

Eric laughed. "No, he didn't. And it's ironic because he was one hundred percent closeted. He had a girlfriend—Megan—and they'd been together a while. But I wasn't his first... distraction. I was the longest, though." Eric paused while he mixed the contents of the bowl and checked the heat on the griddle. "I said yes to dinner, obviously. I mean, he was a good-looking guy, and I was single and kind of awestruck. He was smart, had a senior position at my first larger-scale publisher, and he had this *presence* about him; when he was around, you couldn't help but look, notice."

"That hasn't changed," Jake said and Eric shot him a quizzical look. Jake shook his head. "Sorry. Continue."

"So, yeah, he pursued me quietly, and we became a regular thing pretty quickly. I broke every rule I ever made for myself. I told myself he just needed time and he'd come out. He'd dump the girlfriend and stay with me. I made excuses every time he blew me off and I knew he was with her. It's pretty sad now that I think about it."

"It's not sad," Jake said. "You wanted to be with him, and you had to believe certain things for that to happen. I think we've all done it at one time or another."

"Yeah, well, I did it for a *long* time. For nearly a year I was his little gay secret. He said all the right things—that he loved me, he didn't know what he would do without me, that it wasn't good with Meg, and he swore he'd leave her when the time was right. But I finally started to notice that the time was never right."

Eric ladled out pools of batter onto the griddle. "I started to lose my patience and make demands on him, on his time. We fought about him not being out because, if I was with him, it meant I couldn't really be out either and I wasn't used to that. I didn't want to live like that. I mean, I've never been one to run up and down the streets waving a rainbow flag, but I've always been honest about who I am. That created a lot of tension between us, a lot of fighting. *Jesus*, the fighting!" Eric flipped the pancakes one by one.

"Wow," Jake said. "That sounds like a tough spot."

"You have no idea. I mean, I was in love with him, or at least I thought I was. But after several months of all this... unhappiness and ugliness, I'd had it. He was becoming less and less available, probably because we just fought when we were together, but I took it as him choosing his fake life with Megan over me."

Eric sliced open the tube of sausage he'd taken from the fridge and set several patties frying in a pan on the stove.

"I can see how you'd think that," Jake said. He crossed his arms over his chest to temper the chill he felt. Somewhere around the time Eric had said Andrew loved him, Jake had become aware that they were not alone.

Eric glanced over at him from the pancakes that were accumulating rapidly on a plate. "Yeah. Well, I got this brainstorm that I was going to give him an ultimatum: a real, honest life with me or playing house with her. I really thought if he was faced with the idea of losing me—losing us—he'd get his shit together and pick me and we could still be okay." Eric flipped the last of the pancakes onto the serving plate and brought them to the table. He set a plate and fork in front of Jake and a place for himself opposite Jake.

Eric paused for a moment and shook his head. "It really was a perfect storm of events that night. Even *I* couldn't make this shit up." He retrieved the sausages from the pan and set two on each of their plates. "Dig in," he said, gesturing at the pancake tower. They filled their plates and syrupped the pancakes. Eric popped a forkful of pancake in his mouth and nodded slowly. "Not bad."

Jake swallowed, already on his second bite. "'Not bad'? They're great!"

"Thanks," Eric said with a smile. They ate in silence for a few minutes until Eric took a gulp of his orange juice and continued. "So that night. *The* night. Like I said, I'd decided to give him an ultimatum. But not just 'me or her—pick.' I went out and bought a ring. Nothing fancy, just a plain gold band. I cooked his favorite dinner."

Stuffed pork chops, Jake heard in his head.

"Stuffed pork chops," Eric said. "I lit candles, put on music—the whole nine. I was going to ask him to marry me."

"Shit," Jake said. The more Eric talked, the more the bits and pieces he'd gotten from Andrew made sense.

"Yeah. So, like I said, perfect storm. I tell him he has to have dinner with me, no arguments, and he agrees. Of course, he was an hour late and the food was ruined, but he showed up."

"Here?" Jake asked.

Eric shook his head. "No, he had this lake house that was out in the middle of nowhere. It was really nice, had a pool and everything. That's where we usually spent our time." Jake nodded his understanding. "He showed up drunk and looking all freaked out, and I was pissed because my plan was falling apart. So I lit into him about all of it: the hiding, the lying. Hell, I even defended *her* and told him he shouldn't be leading her on!"

"Damn," Jake murmured.

"I've got the ring burning a hole in my pocket, and he gets real quiet and sits down on the sofa. He looked so… *lost* that I shut up for a second and went to him. I thought something really bad had happened. I asked what was going on over and over, and finally he put his head in his hands and said, 'I asked Megan to marry me tonight. We're engaged.'"

Jake reached across the table and grabbed Eric's hand. "Jesus. I'm sorry."

Eric held on tight and kept going. "I was shocked. I just sat there, and then I started to panic. I went on autopilot with the plan I had, and I got down on one knee and asked him to marry me. To pick *me*. Well, he lost his shit and jumped up, started yelling about what the hell did I think we were doing, said he *wasn't gay*, and that I shouldn't have gotten so fucking obsessed. Obsessed!"

Eric took a few deep breaths. "Well, that's all I needed to hear, and I started yelling back about lies and broken promises and God knows what else. We were both crying by then, and I shoved the ring in his face and I told him it was his last fucking chance. Last chance to be with me, last chance to live a real life and not a lie. That just wound him up even more, and he knocked the ring out of my hand and told me he wasn't going to spend his life being a fucking faggot and took off."

"Oh my God," Jake whispered, his chin dropping down to his chest.

Eric's shoulders sagged as he concluded the story. "Apparently he went out and drank even more, got behind the wheel, and wrapped his car around a tree a few hours later. He died at the scene."

"The black BMW?" Jake asked.

Eric nodded. "Yes. And what made it worse was not only what had happened, but the fact that virtually no one knew about us. So there I was, grieving for this guy I'd loved—and I *know* he loved me—and everyone I knew fawned all over Megan and her personal tragedy." Eric paused, his fingers tracing random patterns on Jake's palm. "I know it wasn't her fault, and she lost him too. But she didn't even *know* him! Not really. Andrew and I, we were fucked up from the get-go, but at least I knew him. I saw all of him.

"I didn't begrudge Megan her grief, but to be totally sidelined when you just lost the one person who…. That was really fucking hard, you know?"

Jake nodded, at a loss for what to say.

"So I threw myself into my work, finished up my edits, and submitted *Trial by Fire*. I got picked up by a major publishing house and then here you are, beyond all reason, with Andrew in tow." Eric propped his elbows on the table and held his head in his hands.

Jake sighed. "That's quite the story, friend." Eric nodded wordlessly. "But I want you to know I'm not going to force you to connect with him. I mean, you did wander into my shop out of the blue, and I think that counts for something, but it's your call. It always has been. And I'm on your side, whatever you decide to do."

Eric looked up. "Won't he just haunt you forever if I don't talk to him?"

"Nah," Jake said easily. "One quick banishing spell and he's history."

"You can do that?" Eric asked incredulously.

Jake laughed quietly. "Well, yes, but it's typically for negative entities who need to go ASAP. Andrew… well, he's not negative. He's pushy and kind of pissy at times, but like I said, I think the bottom line is he just wants to be heard."

"I heard him loud and clear," Eric said.

"I know. And people don't often change when they pass over. I'm guessing he was pretty pushy and pissy in life too." Eric nodded. "But sometimes they do learn things or realize a mistake they've made, and they want to right it before they move on. I think that's where he's at."

Eric heaved a bone-deep sigh and sat back in his chair. "I get it. I do. I just don't know if I'm ready."

"That's okay. Truth be told, I'm glad you got to hear from Grandma Em first. At least that showed you it can be a positive experience."

Eric smiled. "Me too."

They fell silent, as though the saga of Eric and Andrew had exhausted them both. "How about we head back up to bed?" Eric asked.

Jake stood and stretched. "I could go for some more sleep," he said.

Eric rounded the table and looped his arm around Jake's waist. He pulled him in for a soft kiss. "Sure, that too," Eric said with a playful smile. They left the kitchen as it was, and Eric grabbed Jake's hand and led him back upstairs.

CHAPTER 15

AFTER SOME more fooling around and another hour or so of sleep, Jake peeled himself away from Eric and stood up.

"Shit, it's almost nine," he said through a yawn. "Have to call Jessie."

Eric flopped onto his back after unsuccessfully trying to drag Jake back into the bed.

"Who's Jessie?" Eric asked.

"She works at the shop. She's mostly there in the afternoons, but she minds it if she can when I can't be there. She's a grad student, so she's got a life too. Come to think of it, she's the one who was responsible for my costume last night." Jake rubbed a finger across his eyelid and it came away with a thick black smudge.

"Really? Well, please tell her I said thank you," Eric said with a wink.

Jake rolled his eyes. "She'll be thrilled, trust me."

He located his jeans on the floor and fished the phone out of the pocket. He tapped Jessie's number in his contacts and put the phone to his ear as he sat down on Eric's side of the bed. She picked up on the second ring.

"I'm getting on the train now," she said.

"Wait, what? You're not supposed to work this morning."

"That's why you're calling me, though, right?" Jessie countered, amusement in her voice.

"Well, yeah, but I had a…. I mean, I got tied up, so—"

Jessie laughed. "Please, spare me the details. Just tell Mr. Wonderful I said you're welcome."

Jake huffed into the phone. "Not tied up like that! But how did you know that I was going to—have you been practicing behind my back?"

"No need," she said. "I saw it coming a mile away. Who told you that you couldn't read it for yourself? I swear you have the biggest blind spot I've ever seen."

"Shut up," Jake said with a laugh. "So you'll be there to open up?"

"Yes, sir. Here comes the D line now. Just be in before noon if you can. I have class this afternoon."

"No problem. And thanks. Though you're starting to scare me a little."

"My pleasure," she said and hung up.

Jake tossed his phone onto the bed and shook his head.

"Can she cover for you for a little while?" Eric asked, scooting up behind him on the bed.

"Yes, she'll be there. On her way now," Jake said.

"Wow, she must've been already up and ready to go."

Jake sighed and leaned back against Eric's chest. "She was getting on the train heading to the shop. And she said to tell you 'You're welcome.'"

Eric paused and then craned his neck around to look at Jake. "But you didn't even tell her what I said."

Jake smiled. "I know. Welcome to my world."

A COUPLE of hours later, they had showered and dressed. Jake shimmied unhappily back into his skinny jeans and Eric tossed him a clean T-shirt to borrow.

"Are you sure you don't mind?" Jake asked as he pulled the heather gray shirt over his head.

"No," Eric answered. He ran a hand through his damp hair. "Now I'll have no choice but to stop by and pick it up." He grinned at Jake.

"Ulterior motive. I see." Jake smiled back and collected his phone and wallet and they headed downstairs.

Eric slipped on a fleece jacket and grabbed his car keys, but froze with his hand on the doorknob.

Jake waited a few seconds and then asked, "What is it?"

"I… don't know. I can't explain it, and it sounds crazy, but it's like I don't want to go out there. Here, it was just you and me and… I don't know. If we go out there…."

"The bubble will burst," Jake finished.

"Exactly! I mean, I've had good dates before, but with you it's just… different."

Jake shifted his gaze to the floor to hide his smile.

He always enjoyed seeing flashes of extrasensory ability in people for whom it was not an everyday occurrence.

Jake looked up and nodded. "Well, I was told for possibly the hundredth time this morning that I couldn't see my own future if my life depended on it. But I think I'm starting to get it. What if it's not me who's different? What if *we're* different—together?"

Eric let go of the door handle and paused, a thoughtful expression on his face. He turned to face Jake. "I'm not sure I get it at all... but I like that. It sure as hell feels different." He leaned in and kissed Jake thoroughly.

They separated, breathing hard, Jake's heart thundering in his chest. "Bubble or not, we've got to go now or Jessie's never going to make it to her class," Jake said and forced a little space between them.

Eric nodded and stepped back. He pulled the door open, and they made their way down the drive to his car. Twenty minutes later, Eric pulled up to the curb in front of the door that led up to Jake's apartment. They both sat there, unsure of what to do.

Eric broke the ice. "Well, this would be where I say I had a great time and I'll call you, but that doesn't seem quite adequate."

Jake laughed softly and reached across to grab Eric's hand. "Well, I *did* have great time and I *will* call you."

Eric started to return the smile but then his face fell. "Shit!" he muttered. "I completely forgot." He scrubbed a hand over his face.

"What?"

"I'm supposed to be in New York until Wednesday. Book stuff. I have an interview scheduled with some online crime-drama magazine at the asscrack of dawn tomorrow so I was going to take the train down today."

"Oh," Jake said, trying to ignore the tug he felt inside at the idea of being that far from Eric. "Well, it's all right. I mean, that's your job. And I'm not going anywhere."

Eric sighed. "I know, it's work. And I hope you're not going anywhere." He used their clasped hands to pull Jake in for another kiss.

"But I do have to go in there," Jake said with a nod toward his building. "You're leaving tonight?"

"Late this afternoon. I take the train when I can. I like it. It's a nice ride, and I can usually get a lot done."

"Okay. Travel safe and give me a call when you can." Jake had to forcibly swallow the sweetie-honey-baby that nearly tumbled from his lips at the end of the sentence.

"I'll call when I get there. I don't have anything scheduled tonight."

"All right."

They came together for one last kiss, and then Jake got out of the car and let himself in the side door. He gave Eric a final wave and shut the door behind him. He chuckled at his own silliness, the pull on his heart so strong it was like Eric was heading off to war rather than a city a couple hundred miles away.

He reached the top of the stairs, still smiling, but stopped cold at the entrance to his apartment. The space had an icy chill, and as he shifted his eyes from left to right, on every available surface, from floor to ceiling and any space in between, he saw one word.

FIX.

He felt panic well up inside him, but he took a breath and closed his eyes for several long seconds. When he opened them, his apartment looked as it always did, neat and clean and free of ghost graffiti. He exhaled his relief.

"Jesus," he muttered. He didn't often have waking visions, so when he did, it caught him by surprise. He stayed in place and closed his eyes again, opening himself up and sweeping the area for any identifiable energies that might have been responsible for what he'd seen. It didn't take long for the hair on his arms and neck to stand up, and he sensed an energy he now felt like he knew in both worlds.

"Hello, Andrew," he said.

JAKE SAILED down the steps and into the shop about thirty minutes later, changed into some usual work attire: a nice pair of jeans and a black button-down shirt. He strode into the shop and Jessie looked up from her psychology text.

"You are free, my child. Go toward the light!" he said with a dramatic wave of his hands.

Jessie laughed. "I don't think I'm ready for that quite yet, but I do need to get going. It's not like you to cut it so close," she said with a mischievous smile. "He must be someone worth being late for."

Jake felt his face get warm, and he knew he had a goofy smile spread across his face. "Yes, he is," he mumbled.

"So? Who is he?" Jake gave her a brief rundown of Eric's vital stats, and by the time he concluded, her mouth was hanging open. Jessie shook her head vigorously, her springy curls flying every which way. She took a deep breath. "Okay, so you're telling me you're dating someone famous?"

Jake pressed his lips together and thought for a moment. "No, not really. Well, I mean, I guess yes, maybe a little."

"Newsflash: a best-selling author who travels around for readings and interviews and whatever else qualifies as famous. At least in my book. No pun intended."

Jake laughed. "Okay, then, he's famous in his field. But it doesn't matter. He's still just a person."

"Do you like his stuff? His *books*," she added for emphasis.

Jake turned redder. "Uh, well, I haven't exactly read it."

"His new book?"

"Anything he's written," Jake admitted.

Jessie sighed and glanced at the clock. "I'm sorry, but I don't have the time right now for the lecture that response requires. I'll just say, 'Bad boyfriend!' and leave it at that." She stood up from the desk and began to pack up her books.

"I know. He's out of town for a few days so I'm heading over to the bookstore tonight after I close up. Don't worry."

"Good." She gave Jake a recap of what had happened in the shop that morning and slung her bag over her shoulder. She paused and looked at him and then at the space around him, a quizzical expression on her face. "Umm, you know you have a…." She waved her hand at the empty space beside him. "Right?"

Jake heaved a sigh. "Yes," he said, his tone clipped. "I know he's there. This is Andrew," Jake said. "Just in case you should ever run in to him. He likes to hang around, among other things."

Jessie shrugged and smiled. "Okay. Just checking. I'll be in tomorrow afternoon," she called as she headed out the door.

"See ya," Jake said and sat down at the desk. He took a moment to close his eyes and put as much space between himself and Andrew as he could, but Andrew didn't go far.

The afternoon and evening proved to be fairly busy. He did three short readings, two "Where is Mr. Right?"—it was all he could do not to answer "New York City"—and one for an older woman who had lost her husband. He talked a group of teenagers out of using their Ouija board in conjunction with a spell—he hoped—and helped a few other customers find the candles, crystals, and books they needed. Before he knew it, it was time to lock up, and he flipped the sign in the door as he headed out and up Harvard Street to the Brookline Booksmith.

Once inside, it didn't take him long to locate *Trial by Fire* on the first floor. It had a prominent display placed strategically between the best-seller and local authors sections. He grabbed a copy and then browsed their paranormal section for comparison purposes before checking out and heading home.

He had just changed into a sweatshirt and flannel sleep pants to take away the chill from his walk when the phone rang. He saw the caller ID and smiled.

"Hello?" he said.

"Hey," Eric responded, and Jake could hear the smile in his voice.

"How was the train ride?" Jake picked up his mug of herbal tea from where it had been steeping in the kitchen and carried it over to the couch.

"It was good. I didn't get as much done as I usually do. Seems I was kind of tired."

"Hmm. You should be more careful. Make sure you get enough rest and everything," Jake said with mock seriousness.

"I'd gladly walk around like a zombie for a repeat of last night," Eric said, his voice pitched low, warming Jake up a lot faster than the tea.

"I think that can be arranged."

"Good. I'm going to hold you to that. So, how was your day? Did Jessie give you a hard time for coming in late?"

Jake laughed. "It is my store, after all. But yeah, she tried. It could've been worse but she had to leave for class."

"How did she become… like you?" Eric asked after a short silence.

Jake's tea got sucked down the wrong pipe, and he started to cough. He was glad Eric asked questions about his world and work but the awkwardness was still kind of amusing. He caught his breath and said, "Oh my God, Jessie's a gay man?"

"Asshole," Eric grumbled but then started to laugh. "You know what I mean."

"I do. That's a hard question. I don't think any of us 'become' this way. I think we're all born with abilities like mine and hers, but if they're not nurtured or accepted, we just learn to shut them off. I don't think it's even a conscious decision."

"So, according to that, I could do what you do?"

"Yes, to a degree. With some study and practice. Kind of like how I can write… my name. But with some work, maybe I could write a short story. Probably not a best seller, though. Does that make sense?"

Eric sighed. "Yes, I think so. I feel like every time we talk about it, I understand a little more."

"The Other Side—spirits—they're not that different from us. It's like meeting someone who speaks a different language. You learn it, and then you can communicate. Jessie already had the basics when I met her. She'd been working on her own to develop her skills, and I just helped her along. She took a few classes at the shop, studied some with me, and now she gives her own readings."

"Damn. I feel like there's this whole other plane of the universe I never knew about."

"Don't feel bad. Most people aren't really aware of it. Besides, if everyone could do exactly what I do, I'd be out of a job," Jake joked.

"True enough," Eric said and then yawned.

Hearing the sound made Jake yawn too. "I'd better let you go. I know you've got to be up early."

"Yeah. Tomorrow's pretty full but I'll give you a call tomorrow night. If that's okay."

"Yes, it's fine. Perfect actually."

"All right, then. Good night, Jake."

"Night."

JAKE GOT settled in bed, slipped on his reading glasses, and opened to the first page of *Trial by Fire*. He'd only gotten to the end of chapter one when his phone rang again, vibrating against the wood of his bedside table. He glanced over at the caller ID: Gram. Even though it was nearly eleven o'clock, he wasn't surprised. Gram was a dedicated night owl. He set his book aside and picked up the phone.

"Hi, Gram," he said.

"Hi, sweetie!" she sang. "How have you been? I haven't heard from you in a while."

Jake smiled to himself. "A while" to Gram could be as little as forty-eight hours, depending on the day. This time it had actually been several days, though, so he couldn't tease her.

"I'm good. I'm keeping myself busy. You know, the shop, classes, Bobby… stuff." He had no intention of explaining the ways in which he'd been busy for the past twenty-four hours.

"That's good. And are you getting a lot of help from Jessie?"

"Yeah, she's great. Getting really good at reading, too. Like, scary good."

Gram laughed. "Well, good for her!"

"What have you been up to?" Jake asked.

Gram ran down a list of places she'd gone and things she'd done since they last spoke and, as usual, Jake was impressed. She'd barely slowed down at all as she aged, at least not that Jake noticed.

"Jeez, I'm tired just listening to you!" he said.

"Oh, stop! You know me. Anyway, the reason I called—I thought it might be a good time for you to come for dinner. Maybe tomorrow?"

Jake nodded his head. Tomorrow—when Eric was out of town and Jessie was coming in to cover the later part of the day at the shop. "Yes, I think that should work. Is this a special occasion of some kind?"

"No. No occasion. I'd just like to spend some time with you. How about seven o'clock?"

The same way Gram had probably known he'd be free, he knew there was a little more to this invitation than dinner. He also knew she'd never tell him on the phone.

"Seven sounds good. Now I know you're still going strong, but I'm winding down so I'll say good night and see you tomorrow, all right?"

"Of course, dear! I'm not even sure what time it is. I have a few more things to do before…. Well, I'll let you get some sleep. Bye, dear!"

"Good night, Gram." He clicked off the call and put his phone back on the table. His eyelids felt heavy, and he knew he wouldn't get any more reading done that night. He marked his place and put the book aside as he snuggled down under the covers, tugging the chain on his bedside lamp. He closed his eyes and unsuccessfully tried to push aside that persistent pull on his heart he'd felt since he left Eric that morning. As he slowed his thoughts and quieted his mind for sleep, that familiar guiding voice inside told him not only was the feeling not going anywhere, but it was *supposed* to be there, a strange, invisible cord that connected them for reasons he didn't totally understand but accepted willingly nonetheless.

CHAPTER 16

JAKE JOGGED up the porch steps to Gram's front door about ten minutes before seven o'clock. He had his messenger bag slung across his chest, *Trial by Fire* tucked inside. He'd made some good headway with it on the commuter train, and he had to admit he was feeling a little differently about Eric after reading some of his work. He'd known in an objective sense that Eric must be a good author or he wouldn't be having such success, though Jake had picked up a "best seller" from time to time that read like the author might have been better suited for the children's section. Not Eric, though; Eric was *good*. As soon as Jake had a solid stretch of time to sit down and really read, he was drawn into the story in that rare way when you simultaneously didn't want to stop reading but didn't want the story to end either. It was well-written, well-structured, and paced perfectly for the suspense of the crime/mystery genre.

He felt a bit in awe of Eric, that he could create a story and tell it in such a way that people all over the world wanted to read it. Probably not too far off from the feeling Eric had had after seeing Jake at work. He sighed and patted his bag, the book solid under his hand as he gave a quick knock and let himself into Gram's house.

"Hi, Gram, I'm—" Jake stopped dead in his tracks. There was no sign of Gram in the kitchen, but she had a couple of pots simmering on the stove and something in the oven. She'd set the table for two, so she couldn't be far, but the chill in the room put him on high alert. He felt the charge of a familiar energy and the hair on his arms and neck stood at attention. Before he could wonder about how or why, he thought of one thing: Gram.

"Oh, no, you fucking don't, Andrew," he muttered to himself. Andrew hadn't been around when he woke that morning, and Jake had been glad for it. He wasn't so glad that the prick had gone and tracked Gram down for God-knew-what reason. He lifted his bag over his head and tossed it on the floor as his quick steps took him through the living room and toward her reading room. The door was slightly ajar, so he peered inside.

"Gram, are you here? We need to do a cleansing. *Right now*." He stepped all the way into the room and was once again stopped in his tracks, this time by what he saw. Gram was seated at her reading table, white candles lit and lined up along both sides. She had an array of crystals scattered before her, and she smiled, her head tilted upward as though she was looking at someone. Jake stared hard at the space, and he could see the slightest shimmer of energy, like heat rising from the pavement in July.

"Holy shit," he said, and that got Gram's attention. She whipped around and just stared for a moment then leapt out of her seat, looking flustered to find him there.

"Jake! You're early!" she said. She waved a hand at the space where the spirit had been and every trace disappeared. The shimmer, the chill, the goosebumps, all gone in an instant. She blew out the candles. "I'm not quite ready for you. I guess I lost track of time."

"I can see that. I'm early, but what the hell's going on here? Do you know who that was?" he asked, his tone sharper than he ever took with Gram.

"Language! And of course I know who it is. You should know better than to ask me that. He just... well, he was supposed to be gone before you got here," she finished. She shifted her weight from one foot to the other and glanced down at the floor. She looked like a teenager who'd been caught sneaking her boyfriend into her bedroom.

"Sorry," he grumbled for the curse words. "But seriously, what's going on? I know that guy, and I can't even imagine what the... heck he's doing here!"

Gram sighed. "Jake, I'm going to ask something of you."

"Okay," he said, eyes narrowed.

"Can we start over? Pretend you found me in the kitchen, and then have a nice dinner? I promise I'll explain it all, but I just need a little time, maybe an hour or so. Can you do that for me?"

Jake ran a hand through his hair, exasperated. "Of course I can give you some time, but that guy—Andrew—how did he—"

She put a hand on his arm. "Just an hour. I'm tired and hungry. And you *know* I would never allow anyone or anything in this house who was a threat to you or me. Please."

Gram never asked him for much outright, so he felt he had little choice but to comply. "All right, fine. But you *will* explain?" She nodded. "And you're all right?" She nodded again. He shook his head. "Fine. I don't like it, but okay." He threw his hands up in a gesture of surrender.

"Thank you, sweetie. Trust me."

He put his arm around her and they headed for the kitchen. "I always have," he said and gave her shoulders a squeeze.

He did his best to put the Andrew incident aside and focus on Gram's chatter as she added the finishing touches to dinner, but it wasn't easy. His mind buzzed with unanswered questions, and he still had some anger on a low boil just beneath the surface. For the life of him, he couldn't figure out what Andrew could want with Gram. He turned it over and over in his mind but got nowhere. Gram, however, finally succeeded in distracting him when she seated herself across from him, their plates crowded with roast beef, mashed potatoes, green beans, and rolls, and said, "So. Tell me about this new man in your life."

Jake couldn't help but smile at the thought of Eric. He picked up his fork and started in on his meal. "His name's Eric. He's a writer, well, author, I guess."

Gram spent the meal drawing Eric-themed stories, thoughts, and details out of Jake, some things he didn't even realize he knew until she asked. By the time he pushed his plate away, his head was full of Eric—thoughts of how they'd come together, how they fit together, where he wanted to go with Eric, what Eric might be doing now. Jake was well and thoroughly distracted. Too distracted. He pressed his lips together, picked up his teacup, and took a whiff.

"What's in the tea, Gram?" he asked.

"Oh, nothing special. Just something I threw together." She waved her hand dismissively.

"A little heavy on the cinnamon, don't you think?" He raised his head and sniffed the air. Now that the meal was over, he picked up the distinct scent of incense. He'd known on some level that Gram had been burning something, but that was hardly unusual, so he hadn't given it a thought. Now he stood and followed the scent to the incense burner tucked in the corner on the kitchen counter. One good sniff and he knew. "Benzoin," he said.

She sat back in her chair with her hands in her lap. "Well, you know your herbs, dear."

"There's probably some coriander in that tea too, right? You were *trying* to distract me!" he exclaimed, knowing full well that all three herbs could have a powerful effect on the mind's ability to focus.

Gram shook her head. "Not distract—I wanted you to *concentrate*. On Eric. On who he is to you, who you are together. Focus on why you love him."

A flash of heat hit Jake's face. "Love? I never said I loved him! We've only known each other a few weeks!"

"You know as well as I do that time has nothing to do with it. Or maybe in this case, it has everything to do with it."

"What does *that* mean?"

Gram sighed. "I wasn't trying to trick you, honey. I just knew you were upset about Andrew, and I needed you to let that go for a bit. Let me explain."

Jake shrugged his shoulders. "Please do."

Gram picked up their plates from the table and deposited them in the sink. "Let's have a seat. In the reading room." Jake followed her into the reading room and Gram lit two white candles, as was her habit any time she was there. He took a seat on the settee along the back wall, and she sat beside him. "First of all, please don't be angry with me. I've just been trying to protect you, like I always have."

Jake nodded. "I'm not angry. I just want to know what you've been up to." He and Gram had a long-shared agreement, trusting the other to make the right call in any spiritual dealings that should arise between them, and this was no different. Jake was sure as hell confused, though.

"Yes, of course," Gram began. "Well, it started a few months ago. You were here for a visit, and I sensed something around you. A change of some kind coming your way. You seemed oblivious, so I went to my cards and my guides for more information. I thought if it was something you needed to know, I could help. Tell you, steer you in the right direction... whatever. But it turns out it was nothing like that."

Jake stood and went over to the small table where Gram always kept a pitcher of water and glasses for her clients. He poured a glass and sat back down. "So, what was it?" he finally asked.

"Love," she said simply.

"Love?" Jake repeated. "You sensed that love was coming for me so you went to your spirit guides for help? I'm sorry, Gram, but you're losing me."

"That's how I felt at the beginning. I noticed a shift in your aura, and I'd seen it before when people are about to enter a relationship. But this was different. Your vibration had changed, and I could sense *something* coming. It turns out that, yes, it was love, but I mean capital-L Love. A *big* one. The love of your life."

Jake stared at her, unable to speak for a moment. He took a deep breath and cleared his throat. "And that's… Eric?"

She nodded. "Let me ask you—does it feel different with him?"

"Different how?" Jake asked, starting to feel embarrassed about delving into his love life with Gram.

"From the very first time you saw him or touched him—shook his hand, let's say—did you feel something different? A connection?"

"Yes," Jake said. "It's only been a handful of weeks and I feel like I've known him my whole life. Like…." He hesitated for a moment but then plowed ahead. "I'm already bound to him."

Gram smiled and reached across to rest her hand over his. "That's because you are. There are a lot of people in this world we can be compatible with, build a life with, be happy with. But every so often—every few lifetimes, even, if you want to talk about reincarnation—something else happens. We find our soul mate."

Shit, Jake thought, though he didn't dare cuss again in front of Gram. "And that's what Andrew told you was going on?"

"No, he comes into it a bit later. Remember when I read for you a few months ago?" Jake nodded. "Well, those little changes I sensed are what brought about the reading. That's when I saw what was coming. That's when I knew."

Jake nodded. "So, why didn't you tell me this when we did the reading?" Jake asked.

"I couldn't, dear. Imagine it: you always on the lookout, knowing this important person could walk into your life at any time. It wouldn't work. It had to happen naturally, in whatever way the universe presented it to you. I think I did tell you that I saw you meeting someone special, but that's all I felt I could say."

Jake exhaled a long breath and looked at the floor. He couldn't argue. He knew he would've done the exact same thing if he were in Gram's place. He'd read for her about a year ago and had clearly seen her passing, but he certainly wasn't going to tell her even though it pained him to carry that knowledge. "Okay. So, Andrew?" he prompted.

"Right," Gram continued. "Well, my chief spirit guide, Avira, brought him to me. She knew I'd been seeking information about this person about to enter your life and Andrew had it. As well as problems of his own."

Jake jerked his head up and looked at Gram. "Andrew knew Eric and I were connected?" He couldn't quite bring himself to say "soul mates."

"He did, though only once he was on the Other Side, of course. Andrew is stuck. I don't know all of what happened, but he wronged Eric in some way, and he needs to make it right before he moves on. He needs to connect with him to fix things between them. Leading Eric to you was part of that because you can love him in a way Andrew never could in this life."

That idea turned Jake's mind upside down. Andrew as some kind of hero in the story of Jake and Eric? He'd never even considered it.

"He brought the two of you together," Gram continued. "He tried to put some distance between you, hoping you would stay in your role as medium long enough to help him, but it didn't work. Mostly because of me and my… encouragement, but never mind about that. Anyway, now that you've connected with Eric, Andrew can't get much further with what he needs to do. He said he tried to show you once. But now your feelings are too strong. You've taken a side."

Jake's mouth fell open as he recalled saying almost those exact words to Eric the last time they were together. "I have," he whispered. The image Andrew had shown him weeks ago of Jake and Eric kissing flickered through his mind. "And I guess he did try to show me."

"I know, sweetie, and that's okay. It's your natural instinct to want to protect Eric because of who he is to you."

Jake had no idea why he was still surprised by anything Gram said after all these years, but he was. "Wow. That's… big."

"It is. And he would do the same for you, whether he's realized it yet or not. *But*," she emphasized, "Eric can't fully move forward until he ends his chapter with Andrew. I mean *officially* ends it, not with negative feelings."

Jake sat, quiet for a long moment, piecing all the information together. "All right. So, you found out that Andrew had a connection to this… person who would be coming into my life. He kind of helped that along and started communicating with me, initially, about contacting

Eric. I listened for a while, but now I'm too involved, so I can't help them. Did I get it right?"

Gram laughed. "More or less. I know it's a lot. He did say you connected Eric with his grandmother—even though Andrew doesn't seem to like her—and that it went well."

Jake smiled at the memory. "It did go well. Great, actually."

"I'm glad. But you need to know that you can't do this one for him."

Jake nodded. "I understand. The last message I got from him was that something needed to be fixed, so I guess that makes sense. And it was visual, which is weird. I don't usually get that. I also saw... *something* when he was in here before."

"Like I told you, all of this has caused your vibration to change, to heighten, which was what I sensed first. It doesn't surprise me that you've noticed a change in some of your gifts." Jake nodded again. "But it's important to understand that Andrew isn't 'bad.' He's frustrated. He knows he did wrong, and he wants to fix it the best he can."

"So, am I supposed to bring Eric to you?" Jake asked, unable to fathom exactly how that might happen.

"No. I mean, yes, eventually. But Andrew has a request for you— well, you and Eric both. Earlier this evening, he asked over and over, 'Where is the ring?' I don't know what that means, but he's fixated on it. He can be very persistent. That's what he was telling me when you came in." Gram sighed. "I'm sorry I had to put you off like that, but I couldn't just give you that message without explaining *all* of it first. And as far as focusing you on Eric... well, I just wanted your heart and mind to be in the right place to hear all of this."

Jake leaned over and hugged her. "It was. I'm not upset. A little blown away, but not upset. And I know what he means about the ring."

"Oh, good," Gram said with relief. "I couldn't get any more than that out of him."

"Yeah, he's pretty stubborn," Jake said with a laugh. "I guess you'll be meeting him soon, then. Eric, not Andrew."

"Whenever he's ready. You'll know."

"Yes. I've been careful not to push him."

"Good," Gram said and patted his knee. Jake opened his mouth to speak, but the sound of his phone ringing in his pocket cut him off. He glanced down at the ID on the screen, but before he could say anything

Gram stood and headed out of the room. "I'm going to clean up the kitchen. I've got brownies waiting when you're done, though."

She disappeared into the living room, and Jake tapped the green button to take the call.

"Hi," he said.

"Hi," Eric answered. "Is this a good time?"

"Sure. I'm over at Gram's. We just had dinner."

"Oh, well, I don't want to bother you while you're visiting," Eric said.

"No, it's okay. She conveniently left the room when my phone rang," Jake said with a smile in his voice.

"I see. So, I guess she knows about me. Us."

Jake half laughed and half snorted into the phone. "You have no idea."

"Uh-oh. Don't tell me there's *another* person psychically spying on us," Eric said with exaggerated exasperation.

"I think the only way we could have more people spying on us is if we were closeted movie stars."

"Wow. That's some hard-core spying."

"Yeah. So how are things going in New York?" Jake was not about to tell Eric what he'd learned over the phone, so he opted for a distraction.

Eric told him about his early-morning interview, the reading and book signing he'd just returned from, and the meeting he had coming up the next day with his editor. Jake listened attentively, all the while feeling the pull of their connection, stretched by distance but not broken. And now he knew why.

When Eric wound down with his New York stories, Jake jumped in and said, "I went to the bookstore after I closed up last night. Bought a real page-turner."

"No kidding?" Jake could hear the smile in Eric's voice.

"Yep. I'm already about ten chapters into it." Jake's voice softened a bit. "It's great, Eric. You're really gifted."

"Thanks," Eric said, his tone modest. "I'm glad you like it. I know that sounds silly, but I really am."

"I believe you." They were silent for a short time, Jake swallowing the words he wanted to say for fear of sounding lonely and clingy. After a moment, though, and in light of what Gram had told him, he decided to just say it. "I miss you," he murmured.

He heard Eric let out a breath. "I miss you too," he said. He chuckled. "It hasn't even been two days. I'm not usually like this."

"Me either," Jake said.

Another beat of silence. "Well, I should let you get back to Gram."

"All right."

"Tell her hi for me, okay?"

"I will. She probably already knows, though."

Eric laughed softly. "I hope I can meet her one of these days."

"You will," Jake said. "And Eric?"

"Yeah?"

"Come home soon, okay?"

"I will. I'll call you tomorrow. Good night, Jake."

"Night, Eric."

Jake hung up and stared at his phone, everything Eric had said mixing with everything Gram had told him. He might be able to do a lot of things, but he couldn't make Eric manifest right here and now, which was all he wanted. He sighed and tucked his phone back into his pocket. At least he had some brownies waiting for him.

CHAPTER 17

WEDNESDAY EVENING arrived at last, and Jake felt restless and anxious at the thought of Eric's return to Boston. Eric had texted that afternoon saying he was heading for the train station and would be back that night. Jake had taken a few quiet moments throughout the day to close his eyes and do a quick meditation on Eric in light of everything he'd learned from Gram the other night.

Gram had long had an uncanny sense for where Jake was and what was going on with him. When he'd asked her about it as a teenager, her answer had always been the same: "I know because we're connected." Back then he'd assumed she meant they were family; as a young adult, he attributed it to the strength of her gifts. Now, however, he wondered if her answer hadn't been much more literal than he'd ever thought. He felt the binding connection to Eric as if it were a living thing. Perhaps the same kind of connection ran between him and Gram, and that was what she used to access his whereabouts from time to time. If Jake was right and the "connection" was a more literal one, it stood to reason that he should be able to do the same thing with Eric.

Early that afternoon, he slipped upstairs to his apartment once Jessie was in the shop. He sat in his favorite chair in the living room and slowed his mind so his sole focus was on Eric. Jake visualized the link between them as a cord and felt it pulled taut, the same as he had since Eric had left. Eric felt far, so Jake guessed he was still in New York. He stayed in that quiet place to see what else he could pick up and as he sat, the faint aroma of coffee filled his nostrils and he tasted phantom sweetness on his tongue. He felt cold, but not ghost-cold. It was chilly, end-of-October cold. Perhaps Eric was outdoors? He jotted down his impressions in a notebook he kept handy for these moments and went back down to the store.

Several hours later, just before Jessie had to leave for her night class, he went back upstairs and repeated the exercise. This time, when he visualized the cord, it felt shorter and had some slack in it. Was Eric closer now? He tried to pick up additional information but only got blackness. He sighed and stood up. It was an interesting exercise, but he knew he'd have to repeat it several more times before he could be sure he was getting actual information and not just images of things his subconscious already knew or could at least guess. *And* he'd have to try it on Gram.

Now that he had closed up shop for the night he lay sprawled on the couch, flipping through channels, his phone resting on his chest while he waited for Eric to ring and say he was finally home. He got halfway absorbed in a show on the Food Network and when he glanced up at the clock, he was surprised to see it was almost nine thirty. He'd thought he'd have heard from Eric by now for sure. He sat up and stared at his phone, debating if he should call or try his meditation exercise one more time, when the buzzer to his apartment shot its electric sound through the room and scared him into a standing position.

"Shit," he muttered and blew out a long breath. He set down his phone and crossed over to the intercom, the hardwood cool underneath his bare feet.

"Hello?" he said into the box.

"Jake." It wasn't a question or a greeting; it was a one-word request to be let in and Jake didn't have to think twice. He hit the button that opened the downstairs door. He heard feet take the stairs two at a time and within ten seconds Eric stood in the entryway to the apartment.

"Jake," he said again, this time with a smile and the sound of relief in his voice.

"Hi," Jake said as he closed the short distance between them. He barreled straight into Eric's arms and kept going, pressing his back against the wall. He spared a few seconds to flick his eyes over Eric's face, and then dove for his lips. Eric's hands came up and held both sides of Jake's head, thumbs running over his scratchy end-of-day stubble. Jake let his hands drop behind Eric and grabbed his ass to force their lower halves closer together.

They kissed, frantic and forceful, and Eric gasped into Jake's mouth, "Going to finish like this in about thirty seconds."

Jake smiled into the kiss. "No, wait," he said, but made no effort to slow down.

He felt Eric smile back against his lips. "Guess you missed me too?" he said into the space when their lips parted to change angles.

"God, yes," Jake answered. He felt pretty sure they were on the same page, but he pulled back from Eric to look in his eyes for a moment. "You want to slow down?" Jake asked, his chest heaving.

Eric's eyes looked nearly black in the dim light, and his hazy gaze quickly focused and softened. "Maybe a little. I wouldn't mind seeing more of you," he whispered.

"Can do." Jake grabbed Eric's hand and led him to the bedroom.

Once inside, they resumed the kiss and grappled with clothing, in a hurry to lose it. Jake had his T-shirt over his head and his jeans and boxers on the floor in no time. Eric, still dressed in business clothes, took a little more effort. He worked his belt free while Jake popped open buttons on his dress shirt. The clothes joined the pile on the floor, followed by an undershirt and boxer briefs, and they tumbled onto Jake's bed.

Eric fell on top of Jake and pinned him to the bed, lips picking up where they had left off. He straddled Jake's hips and thrust against him, hard cocks sliding alongside one another. Jake could already tell this was going to be a quickie, if for no other reason than they'd been apart and seemed unable to resist the pull they felt when skin met skin. He pressed his hips up to meet Eric's movements and felt the point of no return edging closer.

"Jesus," he groaned as Eric rubbed against him. "I'm almost there."

Eric didn't speak, just dragged his lips away from Jake's neck and nodded. He pushed himself up on an elbow and reached his other hand down between them. He wrapped his hand around both their cocks, pressing them together even tighter as his hand began to move up and down. Jake's eyes rolled back in his head at the sensation, and after a few seconds he glanced down to see Eric's hand working them simultaneously. In that moment, it was the hottest thing he'd ever seen, and it sent him careening over the edge. He felt himself tense as his release shot onto his stomach and over Eric's fist.

Eric followed right after, his hand speeding up briefly until Jake felt warmth spread across his midsection a second time. After the last shudder shook his body, Eric dropped down onto the bed, still halfway draped over Jake. Once their breathing slowed, Jake looked over to catch Eric's eye. Eric bit his lip and turned the faintest shade of pink.

"What?" Jake asked with a smile.

Eric shrugged. "I'm back."

Jake burst out laughing. "And I was just waiting for a phone call!"

"Sorry," Eric said and dropped his gaze downward.

Jake kissed his forehead and nudged his head back up. "Why sorry?"

"I don't know. I'm gone for a bunch of days and then I just show up here unannounced and practically maul you...."

Jake sighed. "Hand me some tissues?" he asked, gesturing at the night table behind Eric. Eric grabbed a handful and wiped them across Jake's stomach. "First of all, the last thing you should be saying after that is 'sorry.' Secondly, I believe *I'm* the one who began the mauling."

Eric snickered. "Let's call it a mutual mauling." He tossed the tissues into the trash behind him, then rolled onto his back and pulled Jake to his side. "All right, then I'm not sorry. And that was hot."

"It was." Jake dropped a kiss on Eric's shoulder.

"I just—" Eric stopped abruptly and shook his head like he'd thought better of what he was going to say.

"No, what?" Jake prodded.

Eric rolled to his side so they lay face-to-face and traced a line up Jake's arm with his finger. "I just... *had* to see you. I mean, I thought about calling, but I knew that wasn't what I wanted. I would've just been calling to tell you I was coming over, which, in hindsight, would've been polite but in the moment seemed like wasted time. So I took a cab home, talked myself into and out of it a hundred times, but by the time I got to my place, I just got out of the cab and into my car and drove here."

Jake smiled and brushed his hand across Eric's face. "I'm glad you came here."

"Yeah?" Eric leaned in and kissed him again.

"Yes."

Eric sighed. "I know I keep saying this, but I'm not usually like this. So... clingy or whatever."

"It's not clingy," Jake said. "I think... attached is a better word."

"Yes," Eric said. "I don't know what it is. Maybe it's just me. I don't know."

"Trust me. It's *not* just you."

Something in Jake's tone must have given Eric pause because he asked, "What do you mean?"

Jake decided the direct approach—"oh, by the way, we're soul mates and you're going to love me forever, no matter what"—was not the way to go, so he snuggled closer to Eric and said, "I was feeling the same thing, that's all. Ever since you left."

"Mmm." Eric hummed a nonresponse and kept his eyes fixed on Jake, like he knew there was more to it. He didn't push for more of an explanation, though. He just pulled Jake close and held him a little tighter.

THEY DOZED for a bit, tangled together, until Jake felt a kiss brush across his lips. His eyes flickered and opened, and he smiled when he saw Eric, his face just inches from Jake's, studying him intently.

"Are you watching me sleep?" Jake whispered.

Eric's lips quirked upward in a half smile. "Yes," he whispered back.

Jake laughed. "At least you're honest. And a little creepy."

Eric looped an arm around Jake's waist and pulled him in tight. "Oh, you don't know the half of it, babe," Eric said. "I've already got a good start on my Jake hair-doll."

Jake laughed and squirmed in Eric's arms. "Gross!" Eric shot him a mock-evil grin and seized his lips in a long, slow kiss.

When they separated Jake sighed and rolled onto his back. The level of comfort he felt bewildered him—the teasing, the laughing, a lovey little nickname thrown in. It felt so *normal*. It took most people months, at least, to get to that point, didn't it? Yet here they were, their second time in bed together, and it was all there. *Soul mates*, he thought. That must be part of the deal.

"What are you thinking about over there? It looks serious." Eric scooted closer to Jake.

"What makes you think it's serious?"

"These." Eric ran his finger over the two small ridges creased between Jake's eyebrows.

Jake grabbed Eric's hand and laced their fingers together. "So you can already recognize my serious face, huh?"

Eric shrugged. "Guess so. What's on your mind?"

Jake shook his head and pressed a kiss to the back of Eric's hand. "We're going to need some fuel before we go there. Are you hungry?"

Eric nodded, creases now lining his own forehead. "Yeah, but… is everything okay? That wasn't code for 'we need to talk,' was it?"

"No, it wasn't," Jake said, feeling a silly rush of relief at the reminder that they didn't know everything about one another yet. "I mean, we do need to talk, but not breakup talk." Eric looked only slightly less concerned. "C'mon, let's go to the kitchen and see what we can find."

Eric nodded and they got out of bed. Jake tossed him some sleep pants and a T-shirt, and then put some on himself. He snickered when he saw that the pants rode above Eric's ankles.

"Ha-ha," Eric said as he took a seat at the kitchen table. "It's not my fault you're short."

Jake spun around, a look of mock indignation on his face. "I'm not short! I'm nearly six foot!" He stood, towering over seated Eric for effect. "How tall are you?"

"Six two," Eric mumbled.

"So it's not my fault you're a beanpole!"

Eric pulled Jake down onto his lap. "I think we fit together pretty well, anyway," he murmured as he nipped a trail up Jake's neck.

Jake felt himself gearing up for round two and pried himself away. "Time out," he said. "Food, remember? When was the last time you ate?"

Eric let him go, and Jake headed for the fridge. He opened it and poked around at some containers. "Well, I stopped at a coffee shop before I got on the train and had a latte and a muffin. I guess that was it."

"See? So, you need to—wait, what?" Jake's head popped up from the fridge and he stared at Eric. "You... *when*?"

Eric shifted in his seat. "I don't know. Early afternoon. Are coffee shops a deal-breaker or something?" he asked, confused.

"No, no," Jake said, his mind reeling with the realization that what Eric had just described matched up very well with the impressions he'd gotten in his first meditation. "It's just that I...." His brain jumped ahead to the second meditation. "Did you sleep on the train coming back?"

"Yes, most of the way. Why? What's going on?"

Jake had only seen darkness in the second meditation because Eric had been asleep. Closer and asleep. "Holy shit," he whispered.

"Care to share with the class, Mr. Parker?" Eric asked, fingers drumming on the table.

"No. I mean, yes, I will. I just need a minute to.... Can we do the food first?" he asked, cringing inside at how much he sounded like Gram had the other night.

Eric put his hands up in surrender. "You're the boss."

"Okay. Thanks." Jake glanced back in the refrigerator. "Leftover lasagna all right?"

"Sure." Ten minutes later Jake set a plate of lasagna in front of Eric and sat down in the chair closest to him with his own plate. Eric took his first forkful and his eyebrows shot up. "You can cook too?"

Jake swallowed his mouthful. "A little. I had to learn some basic stuff with Bobby around."

"It's good," Eric said.

Jake rattled off a few of the other dishes he could make, thankful for the detour away from psychic talk. He just needed a few minutes to pull his thoughts together so he could explain his experience with the meditations to Eric.

Eric chitchatted about food until they were almost half finished with the lasagna, but when a moment of silence came, he steered the conversation right back to Jake. "So, what happened before? What was with the questions about the coffee shop and the train ride?"

Jake took a deep breath and sent out a silent request to the universe to please let him sound coherent as he attempted to explain it all to Eric. He spent the next twenty or so minutes describing the meditations he'd done and why what Eric had said about his day had caught Jake off guard. Jake even grabbed the notebook from the counter and showed Eric what he'd jotted down, the date and time precisely noted in his slanted scrawl. He went a little further and explained his connection with Gram and his theory that they both worked the same way. He decided to pause after that and give Eric a chance to say something.

"Wow," Eric said and ran a hand through his hair.

"Wow?" Jake repeated. "That's it?"

"Jesus, I don't know." Eric stretched his legs out so his feet rested under Jake's chair. "I mean, give me a minute here. I only understood about half of what you said, so…."

"I'm sorry. I forget everyone else's head doesn't work like mine sometimes."

Eric smiled. "It's okay. I'm getting it, like I said. It sounds… pretty big, I guess. I mean, you obviously have a very strong connection with your grandma, and if you're saying you think we have the same thing…. That's serious."

"It is," Jake agreed and rested his hand over Eric's. Eric squirmed a little and looked away. "What is it?"

Eric glanced back, discomfort clear in his eyes. "It just freaks me out a little. The idea that you can poke around and figure out where I am… it's a little unsettling."

Jake saw him watching their clasped hands and understood. "I'm not doing anything right now except holding your hand. I promise." Eric bit his lip and nodded. "And I'm not going to spy on your every move. Or any move. Honestly, I didn't even know I'd picked up anything real until just now. I'd never do it without your permission. That goes against everything I believe."

Eric visibly relaxed and nodded. "Okay. I'm not saying you can't work on it or test it or whatever. Just give me a heads-up."

"I will." He still sensed some unease around Eric so he picked up their plates, cups, and forks. "Let's move over to the couch." They dumped the dishes into the sink and headed to the living room. Jake flopped down into the corner of the couch and patted the open space between his legs. Eric sat, leaned into Jake, and Jake looped his arm around Eric's midsection and pressed a kiss into his hair. "What else is going on in here?" he asked with a tap to the side of Eric's head.

Eric was quiet for a few moments and then heaved a deep sigh. "Have you heard from him?" he asked, his voice pitched low.

Jake didn't need to ask who. "Not much. Once, right after you dropped me off the other morning. But I don't expect that I will now. Not since Gram's."

Eric sat upright and jerked his head around to look at Jake. "What do you mean? What happened at Gram's?"

Jake mentally smacked himself for letting that slip so casually, but there was no unsaying it. "A lot," he said.

Eric opened and closed his mouth a few times before he got words out. "Are you saying that he—Andrew—was there at your grandmother's house? What the fuck?"

"That was my reaction at first. Yes, he was there for a bit, but to communicate with Gram, not me."

"Communicate with…? Is this a family affair now or something?" Eric looked lost and confused, and Jake moved closer.

"Not like that," Jake said and rested a hand on Eric's knee. "All right. I don't know what's too crazy or too confusing for you, so I'll just explain it the best I can." Eric nodded. "Remember when I read for you at your place with Grandma Em?" Another nod. "And I told you that it's not always easy to read for someone you're close to?"

"Yes. But you didn't say why. And that reading was amazing."

"It was," Jake agreed. "But the reason it's not easy, depending on who comes through, is because I can't be objective. My feelings should never color the message, whatever the spirit is trying to get across. It wasn't a problem with Grandma Em. She's a great lady, and there were no sides to take."

"Sides?"

"Yes. See, with Andrew it's different because of my feelings for you. I can't read for someone you loved like that, and who loved you, and stay neutral."

Eric scoffed. "Yeah, right. He loved me a lot."

"He did. He just didn't know how to show you."

"So you can't read for me because you're on *his* side now?" Eric exclaimed.

Jake blew out a frustrated breath. He was not explaining this well. "No! I'm on *your* side! But it actually doesn't matter, because the fact that I've taken a side at all precludes me from being objective. I care about you and we're—" Jake stopped himself from going somewhere he wasn't sure they were ready to go. "Because of what I feel for you, I can't connect the two of you and sit here and tell you how sorry he is, or talk about what the two of you had, or whatever else he would say. It wouldn't be fair to any of us."

"Okay," Eric said slowly. "So he went and found your grandmother to talk to?"

"Not exactly." Jake could see Eric's frustration level rising, so he decided to hold off on that part of the story for now. "When he realized I couldn't help him, someone led him to Gram, and she's communicated with him a few times."

"Did this all go on the night I called and you were over there?"

"Yes. And don't even ask me why I didn't tell you then."

"No, I get it. Not a conversation for the phone."

"Right."

Eric sat silent for a long moment. "So, do I need to go see your Gram, then?" he asked in a tired voice.

"Not now. When you're ready. It'll always be when you're ready." Eric nodded and leaned back against Jake a little. "Besides, there's something we need to do first. Gram passed a message along from Andrew."

"What?"

"I'm sorry to bring this up—and that's exactly why I'm not objective—but do you still have the ring you bought for him?"

Eric shrugged. "Maybe. Remember how I told you he flipped out on me? He swatted the ring out of my hand and it went flying. I never bothered to look for it because a few hours later he was gone."

"So it's somewhere in your apartment?" Jake asked.

Eric shook his head. "No. We were at the lake house. It all happened there."

"Shit! Well, how the hell is that supposed to work?" Jake asked the space around him.

"What are you talking about?"

Jake sighed, frustrated. "The message from Gram was that you need to find that ring. I don't know why it's important or what you're supposed to do with it, but he was insistent about it from what she said. But I don't know how that's going to happen if it's at some lake house that's not even his anymore."

"I do," Eric said, his voice barely above a whisper.

"What? How?" Jake asked, resting a hand on the back of Eric's neck.

"We go there and we look for it… because it's mine. He left the lake house to me."

CHAPTER 18

JAKE SAT silent for a moment. He was pretty sure that if he listened closely, he could hear the sound of his mind being blown. He tamped down all the feelings that arose in him—shock, jealousy, amazement—and turned to Eric. Eric sat, elbows on his knees, his head hanging down. He looked sad and lost. Jake reached out a hand and ran it down his back.

"Eric... *what?*" He couldn't get his head around what he'd just heard.

Eric nodded. "The lake house—it's mine now. I haven't set foot there since that night, though."

Jake moved next to him and pressed his leg alongside Eric's, hand still traveling up and down his back. "How did that happen?" he asked.

Eric sighed and leaned back against the couch. Jake shifted to face him. "The lake house was our place, I guess. Because Andrew wasn't out, there weren't many places we could go, so after a few dates, he told me he had a place and gave me a key. We spent a lot of weekends there, and a weeknight on occasion when he could get away. Sometimes I went alone to work there too. It was so quiet. Peaceful."

Jake nodded and squeezed Eric's hand to let him know he was listening, though he didn't trust himself to speak just yet.

"Anyway," Eric continued, "you know what happened that night. I left and went back to my place, went through all the funeral stuff, and a couple weeks later I got a call from Andrew's lawyer. He said he needed to see me, so we made an appointment and I went. When I got there, he said he was handling Andrew's estate and he had left something to me. Andrew had given him specific instructions that I come by myself to the office should the need arise, so there I was. He handed me an envelope and left me alone to open it."

Eric pressed his lips together and just sat for a few moments, a faraway look on his face. "Hey," Jake said finally. "We don't have to talk about it now."

Eric looked up like he'd just remembered Jake was there. "No, no. It's okay. I've been... not dealing with the place, figuring I'd sell it someday." He took a deep breath. "So, it was a note from Andrew saying he was sorry if I was reading it, and that he'd bought the house right before we met, and I was the only one he ever brought there. One of the few who even knew about it. And if it couldn't be his, he wanted it to be mine."

"Shit," Jake whispered.

"Yeah. Try finding all that out in some stranger's office." Eric shook his head. "The lawyer came back in and explained his part—that the house was in the will as real estate held by a small company Andrew owned, and it was to be liquidated and the profits donated somewhere. Something people like Megan or his family would just assume the lawyer would handle. But Andrew had done the paperwork to have the deed transferred to me, paid in full. My very own lake house that I never wanted to see again."

"Eric, I… don't know what to say," Jake said. He wanted to tell Eric that they didn't have to go there, that they could just forget about the ring and the house, but he knew it would never really be over until Andrew moved on and, in the process, let go of Eric.

Eric stretched out his arm along the back of the couch and Jake slid alongside him. "There's nothing to say. It looks like I need to make a trip back there after all." Jake nodded, his stomach turning at the thought of Eric going back to the place he'd shared with Andrew. Eric pulled Jake close and buried his nose in his hair. "No way I can do it without you, though," he whispered.

Jake curled into him and nodded. "Of course. Whatever you need."

"I'm sorry for all this, you know." Jake gave him a quizzical look. "Well, it can't be easy being with someone and having their ex shoved in your face night and day. And this is weirder than your average ex situation."

"Weird is relative," Jake said. "I'm not going to say it's easy, especially now, hearing from all sides how much he loved you, how he still needs you, even though I know it's to help him move on. I admit I'm not a fan."

"Which is why you can't read for me about this," Eric supplied, and Jake nodded. "But what do you mean, 'especially now'?"

Jake thought back on how Gram had labeled his feelings for Eric without batting an eye, but he wasn't ready to say that out loud just yet. He shrugged. "You and I have definitely gotten a lot closer pretty quickly. The more I feel… yeah, it can all be hard to hear sometimes. But it's something you need to do, and I'll help you any way I can."

Eric wrapped his arms around Jake. "It's like you're not even real sometimes. You and your magic, all these things you see, even when it sucks beyond belief." Eric sighed. "I just—"

Jake pulled back to look at Eric, in a hurry to cut him off before he said what Jake thought he might say. "Hey! I'm not a prize 24-7. Ask Jessie, or Laney, or Gram. I can be a total pain in the ass."

Jake grinned and Eric gave him a tired smile in return. "I can't wait to find out," Eric said.

"You're exhausted," Jake said and ran his hand through Eric's hair. "Do you want to go back to bed? Or if you'd rather head to your place, that's okay too," he added as an afterthought.

Eric shook his head. "The only place I want to be right now is wherever you are."

Jake felt his face flush and he didn't even want to acknowledge the butterflies that fluttered in his chest at Eric's words. "Okay. Let's go to bed."

He stood and offered his hand and pulled Eric up off the couch. They headed to the bedroom and crawled into bed, arms and legs crisscrossed over and around each other as they fell asleep.

ERIC LEFT the next morning with a lingering kiss. They agreed to talk later that evening and went their separate ways, Eric out the apartment entrance and Jake down to open the shop. Jake checked his phone around lunchtime and saw he had missed a call from Eric but got sidetracked with a customer. He called back an hour later and got Eric's voice mail. He left a message but kept it short. He thought Eric might need some space after what they'd talked about the night before, and although Jake felt ready to crawl out of his skin with the need to be near Eric, he wanted to give him time if that's what he needed. The reasoning involved a lot of conjecture on Jake's part, but he had meant it when he told Eric that he wouldn't use any supernatural means to check in on him.

He finished off his day Eric-less and told himself that was okay as he closed up shop and went home. He decided a frozen pizza would pass for dinner since he didn't feel hungry anyway. He picked at his food while channel surfing as long as he could stand it until he gave up. Going to bed won out, and he shut off the TV and tossed away the remainder of his food. He brushed his teeth and was under the covers minutes later.

He tossed and turned for a while until he landed on his side, his face in the pillow that Eric had slept on the night before. It still held the faded scents of Eric's cologne and shampoo, and Jake sank into it. He felt himself drifting, the trace of Eric working better than any sleeping pill to relax and settle him. He was almost out when his cell phone vibrated against the bedside table. He groaned and rolled over to grab the phone. It could only be one person at this hour.

"What is it, Gram?" he mumbled.

"I've been called a lot of things, but 'Gram' is a new one," Eric said.

Jake sat up. "Eric?"

"Yeah. I'm sorry. I didn't mean to wake you. Why would your grandmother call you this late?"

Jake yawned. "She's a night owl, up till all hours. Sometimes she forgets how late it is and calls anyway." Jake pulled the phone away from his ear to glance at the time. "Is everything okay? I didn't expect you to call this late."

"Yes, I'm fine," Eric said with a sigh. "Well, that's not entirely true. My ego's taken a bit of a hit."

"What do you mean?" Jake asked and flopped back down on the pillows.

"I was under the impression I was a grown man and could pretty much handle myself in the world. But I've been lying here for over an hour staring at the ceiling and not sleeping because you're not here. Or I'm not there. Doesn't really matter. Either way, I should be able to sleep one night without my boyfriend."

Jake laughed. "Boyfriend? Is that what I am?"

He heard Eric breathing on the line for a few long seconds. "I don't know. It doesn't feel like the right word, but it's the only one I can come up with."

"I understand. It'll do for now." Jake sensed that Eric wasn't quite finished so he waited.

"So are you busy tomorrow night?" Eric asked.

"Are you trying to ensure a good night's sleep? Or do you need a date for a Halloween party that's actually on Halloween?" Jake asked, teasing.

Eric heaved a sigh. "Neither. I'm trying to get the balls to go down to the lake house and look for that goddamned ring."

"Oh," Jake said, his mind racing. Tomorrow. Halloween. He wasn't sure it was an ideal day to go poking around in a place where ghosts lay, when the veil between the worlds was at its thinnest.

"If you have something going on at the shop or whatever, it's okay. I can go myself."

Jake snorted. "Actually, I'm closing early tomorrow. I learned that my first year in business. A lot of strange people want to do strange shit on Halloween, and I don't want any part of it." Jake paused. "Are you sure you want to go tomorrow? It's a really active spirit day." That was an understatement but he hoped Eric would get the idea.

"Yes. I haven't even been aware of Andrew this whole time. Even if I were, I'm not afraid of him. I'm pissed and confused but not afraid. I really don't want to go without you, though," Eric added.

Jake realized that it likely had less to do with negotiating the Other Side and more to do with hand-holding through something that would be difficult. "Of course I'll go with you," he said.

He could hear the relief in Eric's voice. "Good. All right. What time are you closing?"

"Five o'clock," Jake said.

"Maybe I'll come by before you close?" Eric asked uncertainly. "I'd like to see the shop again."

"Sure. Come whenever you're ready, and then we can go after I close. Where is it?"

"It's down in Sharon. It'll probably take forty-five minutes to get there, maybe an hour depending on traffic."

Jake nodded. "Okay. I'll see you when you get to the shop."

"All right. Uh, Jake?"

"Yeah?"

"Is it too late for a sleepover tonight?" Eric asked.

Jake laughed. "It is almost midnight, and I don't think we'd get much sleep."

"You're probably right," Eric said with a sigh. "Back to staring at the ceiling, then."

"A least I have a pillow that smells like you. It's the only thing saving me from dragging you over here."

"Damn it. Lucky."

"How about I promise to leave one at your place tomorrow night?"

"Deal," Eric said with a smile in his voice. They lapsed into silence again for a moment until Eric spoke again. "Jake, I…. Thank you. For going with me tomorrow and everything. It's really… I mean, I—"

Jake cut off the fumbling words. "You're welcome. I want to be there."

"I'll see you tomorrow, then. Night," Eric said.

"Night." Jake disconnected before any unsaid words hung in the air too long. No matter what he knew or believed about himself and Eric, it was important to go slow and take things in the order they came. Next up was Eric and Andrew's lake house. He sighed and dropped his head back onto the Eric-scented pillow. He'd definitely need a decent night's sleep to face that.

"WAIT, SO what time is he coming?" Bobby asked for at least the fifth time.

"I still don't know. He just said he'd be by before I closed up." Jake left out that he'd forgotten that Bobby was coming to the shop after school when he told Eric to come. Not that Jake would have changed his mind; he just might have given Eric some advance warning. His last hope was that Laney would pick Bobby up before Eric got there, but he already knew that wasn't going to happen. So he dealt with Bobby bouncing off the walls until the bell over the door chimed around four thirty. Eric strode into the shop in jeans and a soft-looking black sweater. He spotted Jake at the desk and came over.

"Hey," Jake stood up, a goofy grin on his face.

"Hi." Eric wore a matching smile, and they just stood there staring for a few seconds.

Jake's brain kicked into gear, and he remembered Bobby, who'd run up to the apartment to get something. "I forgot to tell you—" Jake began but his words got swallowed up when Eric stepped around the desk and pulled him close for a kiss. Jake's mind blanked out at the feel of Eric's mouth on his, and he slid a hand up into Eric's hair. While they weren't making out, the kiss wasn't chaste either, and Jake lost himself in it until a familiar voice penetrated his brain.

"Oh. My. God," Bobby said from the foot of the stairs.

Eric jerked away and Jake started to laugh. "That's what I forgot to tell you," he said, gesturing toward Bobby.

Bobby's mouth still hung open, and he looked back and forth between the two men. He shook his head like a cartoon character and then stared at them some more. "Okay. First of all, *gross*." Jake rolled his eyes. "And second, oh my *God*! You're, like, *with* Uncle Jake?" he asked Eric with a shocked expression.

Eric looked to Jake for a cue on how to handle this, and Jake stepped in. "Yes, Bobby. We're seeing each other," he said simply. "And I'm sorry about what just happened. We should have been more careful."

Bobby glanced at Jake like he hadn't even spoken and turned all his attention to Eric as he approached them. "I met you at the book signing. You said I was your youngest fan."

Eric cleared his throat. "Yes, I remember. And as far as I know, you still are. Good to see you, Bobby." Eric offered a hand, and Bobby shook it.

Bobby was obviously a little starstruck, but that didn't keep his mouth in check. "I can't believe you came here... because you're going out with *Uncle Jake*?" Bobby emphasized Jake's name like you'd expect him to have a hump on his back and a couple of extra heads.

Eric snickered and visibly relaxed a bit. "Yep. I came all this way just to see him. He's a pretty great guy."

"Wow," Bobby said, nothing short of amazed.

"Hey, Bob, how about you show Eric around the store? He hasn't really seen it yet," Jake said. He stole a glance at Eric to get an okay, and Eric gave a quick nod.

"Sure!" Bobby said and proceeded to drag Eric toward the first aisle of books and crystals.

Jake sat back down in his chair with a thud. He watched as they wove their way up and down aisles until the bell chimed again.

Laney breezed in and over to Jake's desk. "Hey, Jake, where's Bobby? I've got to get him home and into his costume for the Halloween party at the rec center."

"He'll just be a minute. He's giving a tour of the shop." Jake nodded toward the back where Bobby was waving his hands at the cloaks and candles. Laney stared for a few seconds, and then her eyes grew wide.

"Holy shit!" she whispered. "Is that the book guy?"

Jake laughed. "Yes, that's Eric. I think he calls himself an author though."

Laney shot him an irritated look. "I guess when you look like that you can call yourself whatever you want."

"Yeah," Jake said with a smile and a sigh.

Laney swatted his arm. "Cut it out already! You look like a fourteen-year-old with his first crush."

"Shut up," Jake muttered, feeling his face get warm. "Well, you should probably know that Bobby walked in on us kissing. It was no big deal, but you might get an earful."

"I'm sure I will. Do you mean like peck-on-the-cheek kissing or do-me-on-the-desk kissing?"

Jake snorted. "Somewhere in between, I guess. Standing, fully clothed."

"Okay. As much as I'd like to stay and stare at that gorgeous man of yours, I do have to get Bobby home."

Jake nodded. "Hey, Bobby," Jake called. "Can you get your things together? Your mom's here."

Bobby said something to Eric and then bounded up to the apartment. Eric came to the front of the store.

"He's a real firecracker," Eric said with a smile.

"He is," Jake agreed. "And here's the woman who's responsible for it. This is Laney Gilbert, Bobby's mother. Laney, this is Eric Austin."

"Pleasure to meet you," Laney said and shook Eric's hand. "It's nice of you to get Jake out of this shop. He was a real hermit there for a while."

Eric laughed. "That's funny because my friends said Jake did the same for me."

"Well, I guess you two are perfect for each other," Laney said with a smile.

"I think so," Eric agreed and looked over at Jake with the goofy smile.

Laney watched them for a moment and then said, "Okay, I see you've got it just as bad as he does," jerking a thumb in Jake's direction.

Jake stood next to Eric, and Eric's arm slid behind his back like they'd stood side by side for years. "Afraid so," Jake said with a wink.

"Bobby's a great kid," Eric said as feet thundered down the stairs.

"Thanks," said Laney. "He can be a handful."

"Am not," Bobby said and slung his backpack over one shoulder.

"Thanks for the tour, Bobby," Eric said.

"No problem," Bobby said, back in cool mode.

"We've got to go. It was nice meeting you," Laney said as she herded Bobby toward the door.

"Same here. Hope to see you both again soon," said Eric.

With the jingle of the bell and a rush of cold air, Laney and Bobby were gone.

Eric turned to Jake. "Well, that was interesting. I guess he knows you're gay?"

"Yes, he knows. Laney and I have been honest with him about it since the beginning. Age-appropriate, of course."

"That's great."

Jake looked at his watch. "Hang on. I want to lock up before anyone else comes in." He locked the door and flipped the sign to "Closed," then returned to Eric. "So," he said, the reality of what they were about to do settling between them. Eric shifted his gaze to the floor. "Do you want something to eat before we go?"

Eric shook his head. "My stomach is in a knot. I can't eat right now."

"All right." Jake rubbed Eric's arm. "Let's head upstairs so I can change, and then we'll go."

Eric nodded and followed him up the interior stairs. Ten minutes later Jake was dressed and ready. He led Eric downstairs and out of the building into the cold Halloween night.

CHAPTER 19

THEY WERE both fairly quiet on the drive down to the lake house. Jake started out chattering away, asking questions and making small talk. He got minimal responses from Eric and eventually settled into his own uneasy silence. Eric reached over and took his hand after they got through the worst of the traffic, and Jake relaxed a bit. He tried to remember that however nervous or freaked out he felt, it was probably nothing compared to what Eric was going through.

He stared out the window and smiled at what he saw. A master horror movie director couldn't have created a more classic Halloween night: pitch dark, a misty rain falling, light from streetlamps and houses fading away the farther out they drove. Eric took an exit off the highway, and they passed through some small neighborhoods and then onto a more remote road. Jake could see lights from houses set far back from the road every mile or so, and he cracked his window and inhaled the scent of lake water. Just as he rolled up the window, Eric turned right into a long driveway that led up to one of the hidden houses. He pulled to a stop alongside a rolling stretch of grass that disappeared into the dark toward the road. A large white ranch-style house sat at the crest of the lawn, a huge bay window jutting out in front.

Eric's hands fell from the wheel, and he glanced at Jake. "We're here." He looked up at the house and Jake saw him swallow hard. "I guess we should go in. The sooner we start, the sooner we'll be done." Eric's flat tone unsettled Jake, but he reminded himself that Eric had to do whatever he needed to get through this.

"Okay. Let's go," Jake said. They got out of the car and Eric led them to a door on the side of the house. "Is this the back door?" Jake asked.

"No, this is actually the front door," Eric answered as he sorted through keys on his key ring. "The front of the house has that huge window, and the back is the same—windows that look out over the pool and then the lake. I guess this was the only place left for a door."

Jake nodded and Eric found the right key and slid it into the deadbolt. He moved to the next key, inserted it into the bottom lock and the door creaked its way open. Jake stepped inside behind Eric and was surprised to find the house was warm despite the stale air, which meant the utilities had been kept up. He heard Eric fumble around a bit and a light came on.

Eric took a deep breath and gestured for Jake to follow him. "This way," he said and led them down the short entryway hall and into a larger room. Another switch flipped and Jake saw they were in the great room, a large open space for both the living and dining rooms. The bay window he'd seen outside took up most of one living room wall. "Let me get a few more lights on," Eric said. He turned on lamps and flipped switches, and all the while Jake marveled at the beauty of the place. If anyone had asked him to describe a lake house before that night, he'd never have come up with this.

"It's a beautiful house," Jake said. "When you said 'lake house,' I guess I was thinking more along the lines of a one-room cottage."

Jake walked farther in and saw Eric standing in a large kitchen outfitted with top-of-the-line appliances and granite countertops. Eric smiled and shook his head. "It's big," he said. "Andrew never did anything small."

Eric came around the breakfast bar and stood next to Jake. He dropped an arm across his shoulders. "Do you mind if I just look around for a minute? Like I said, I haven't been here…." He trailed off but Jake knew how the sentence ended.

"Go ahead. It's fine," he said. Eric gave him a tight smile and squeezed his shoulder before he walked away, vanishing down a long hall. Jake wandered into the living room and ran his hand over the suede leather couch. He studied the huge wall-mounted TV, the hearth, and fireplace, and then checked out the oversized window up close. He peered out onto the lawn and felt a chill. For the briefest moment he thought how strange it was for such an updated house to have drafty windows but then he jerked back and froze in place. There was no draft, and the house was insulated just fine. He wasn't alone.

His hair stood on end, and the cold made him shudder. From the corner of his eye, he saw an orb sail past him and down the hall. "Fucking great," he muttered. He stood for a moment, weighing the pros and cons of what to do next. It was definitely questionable to open himself fully to the Other Side on this particular night. But if he didn't, whoever had just breezed by him would have free rein, and Jake would have no line of communication, no way to protect them. It wasn't much of a choice. He huffed out a breath, closed his eyes, and opened himself up.

He saw the swirling indigo of his Third Eye unwind itself, and once he had a clear channel, he politely told whoever he'd sensed to leave them alone. He suspected it was Andrew, but it wasn't worth taking the chance on a night when something bad could walk right in the door. He didn't know the history of the house—maybe Andrew had bought it from an ax murderer—so he went through the motions of letting the spirit know they meant no harm and wouldn't disturb anything. He explained they needed to find something and then they would leave. He was getting ready to put up his walls and close himself down when he heard the reply clearly in his head. "*Ring.*"

He'd thought it was Andrew and now he had confirmation. He had wanted to make an impersonal statement and close himself off to avoid this exact thing, but Andrew had grabbed a foothold just under the wire. They had an open line between them now, and he knew it wouldn't be easy to disconnect. Jake was on Andrew's turf, and Andrew felt strong. "Yes, ring," he muttered. They just had to find the ring and get the hell out of there before he was forced to tell Eric that Andrew had joined them. He doubted Eric would like it, and Jake didn't want to play referee.

"Everything looks all right," Eric said as he entered the room. Jake spun around and sucked in a sharp breath.

"Jesus!" he gasped.

Eric gave him a small smile. "Take it easy. It's just me."

Jake laughed. "Sorry. I guess I didn't hear you. I'm used to squeaky Boston brownstone floors."

"It's okay. But I can pretty much guarantee this place isn't haunted."

Wasn't, Jake thought and walked over to Eric. "So, where do we start? Wait. Maybe that's not the right question. I know this is hard, but… where did it happen?"

Eric took a deep breath and let it out in a rush. "Okay. I had dinner waiting there," he said, pointing at the dining area. "Andrew came in and sat down here." He tapped the couch next to them. "I sat with him, and he told me about the engagement. We talked, and then we yelled, and then I got up and started cleaning up the dishes."

"You *what?*" Jake asked. He had expected drama and grief, not household chores.

"I just had to *do* something. I couldn't sit there and listen to any more of his bullshit. I picked up the plates from the table and took them into the kitchen. He followed me, though. Wouldn't shut up, wouldn't even give me a minute to figure out what the fuck to say about the bomb he dropped. He just wouldn't… *stop.*" Eric pressed his fingers to his eyes for a few seconds and then walked to a spot between the living area and the kitchen. "I told him I needed to leave, I needed to get out of here, but he wouldn't let up. He grabbed my arm and just kept telling me to calm down and that it would be fine and nothing would change. That's when I lost it because I'd already decided something had to change. And he'd already made a choice for both of us."

Eric looked tired and worn out, his voice still flat as he recounted the night. "Do you want to sit down?" Jake asked.

Eric shook his head and continued. "So I was right about here,"— he moved a few steps away—"when I took the ring out of my pocket and shoved it in his face. More yelling, and he smacked the ring out of my hand and left."

Jake stepped toward Eric. "So he smacked it like this?" he asked and mimed swatting something with his right hand toward the kitchen.

Eric shook his head. "The other way. He was left-handed."

"Okay. So I guess we start in the living room. It could have rolled anywhere in there."

They moved the couch, loveseat, and several chairs and tables in search of small spaces where the ring could have landed. Eric grabbed a broom and dragged it behind a bookshelf and then into the small space underneath it. By the time they pushed a heavy oak sideboard back into its place along the wall, they were both sweating. Eric folded himself into one of the club chairs. "What the hell?" he said. "Where could it have gone?"

Jake shrugged. "I have no idea." His head was pounding because, as they worked, Andrew had grown louder and more insistent. Jake had done his best to just ignore him, but he knew that would be insufficient soon. "Can I use the restroom?"

"Sure. Down the hall, second door on the right."

Jake left Eric in the chair and headed down the hall. *I just need a minute*, he thought. Just sixty short seconds away from the house and the ring and the goddamned ghost who wouldn't get out of his head. He used the toilet and washed his hands and splashed some cool water on his face. There was no reprieve though; his temples continued to throb and he felt pressure building around him. He reached under his sweater and peeled his T-shirt away from his damp chest. He was sweating more than when he had been moving furniture, and he pleaded with Andrew in a whisper. "Stop! *Please*, just stop. I'll make sure he finds it. We'll come back another day. Just *back off*!"

He closed the lid to the toilet and sat down to collect himself. It felt like an invisible vacuum had sucked all the air from the room and his breath came harder. He buried his face in his hands, the mental stress making it impossible for him to figure out how to take back some control. He had just begun to think of ways to go back out and tell Eric they had to leave—*he* had to leave—when, in the blink of an eye, it all stopped. Andrew's voice, the pressure, the noise in his head—all gone.

"What the hell?" He patted himself down, checking he was still there, and he was. His next thought was Eric. Eric must have done something that got Andrew's attention. Jake was up like a shot, flying down the hall and back into the living room. "What happened?" he demanded.

Eric, now on the couch, sat motionless and stared at his open palm. He looked up at Jake. "I found it," he said, his voice clogged with emotion. He held up a gold band for Jake to inspect.

Jake sat down beside him. "Where?"

"In the fireplace. It rolled inside so we didn't see it."

"Shit," Jake said. He waited to take his cue from Eric as to what needed to happen next, until he saw a few tears escape Eric's eyes and roll down his cheeks. He wrapped an arm around him. "It's okay to be sad," he murmured.

Eric turned to look at Jake and wiped at the wet tracks on his face. "*Sad*? I'm not sad. I'm fucking *pissed*!" Eric held the ring out in front of him. "This thing... it represented a whole life!" he shouted. "A life I wanted with someone I gave everything to. *Fucking everything*!"

At that moment, Andrew's energy surged into Jake's head on overdrive. The mere presence of a spirit had never made Jake feel physically ill before.

"He didn't even consider it! He never considered *me*. After all the time we were together, and he just fucking threw it away! So he could live a fucking lie!" Eric continued to yell and Jake felt himself unraveling quickly. He tried responding to Andrew with his mind but Andrew was just as loud as Eric. Eric's voice became background noise and Jake's head filled with Andrew's booming demands. *Tell him to stop, tell him I'm sorry,* please *tell him I'm sorry! He's wrong, I love him, I couldn't do it I'm sorry!* It all came through in the fast-forward, hundred-mile-an-hour spirit frequency. Jake's head started to spin, and he worked hard to refocus his attention on Eric.

He saw that Eric had quieted and that there were fresh tear tracks on his cheeks. He pulled Eric toward him and Andrew pressed closer and harder and louder than ever. *Tell him, tell him! Why aren't you telling him? He has to know, I have to fix it! Why are you touching him? Don't touch him, don't touch him! Let him go, LET HIM GO!*

At that Jake leapt up from his seat and spun around to face the space where he sensed Andrew. "No, *YOU* let him go!" he shouted, his finger stabbing the air in front of him. He saw the same heat-wave-like image he'd seen in Gram's reading room just inches from his face. "I am sorry you died, okay? I'm sorry you fucked it up and you couldn't fix it! But it's *my* place to love him now!" The words were out before he could stop them. He turned toward Eric and took a few slow steps back.

"I'm sorry," Jake said, his hands raised in surrender. "I'm sorry. I need to get some air." He left a slack-jawed Eric on the couch and backtracked down the hall and out the door as fast as he could.

He walked in a slow circle in front of the car, fingers massaging his temples. The pressure and noise were all gone now, but he felt on the verge of collapse. Andrew's persistent presence and lightning-fast messages had drained Jake of everything he had. He didn't know if he had shut Andrew up or if he only felt relief because he'd left. Either way he embraced the silence and his body sagged against the frozen side of the car. The cold felt good this time—natural, wet, dewy cold—and he took slow breaths until they came normally and his heart stopped hammering.

He debated what to do next—attempt to go back inside or wait for Eric to come out? Before he could decide, though, he heard the front door open and shut. He looked up as Eric walked toward him.

"Are you all right?" Eric asked. He reached a hand out toward Jake but it stopped before it touched him, hovering in the air uncertainly until Eric let it fall to his side.

Jake nodded his head. "Yeah. I'm okay." With Eric standing there in front of him, the words he'd shouted at Andrew thundered through his mind. "Shit," he muttered. "I'm sorry about what happened. I shouldn't have let him get to me like that. Actually, I should never have opened myself up to begin with. And what I said—"

Eric held up a hand to cut him off. "Wait. Before you say anything else, I know this will sound like a beyond-stupid question but was Andrew in there? *Is* Andrew in there?"

"Yes, he was. I don't know if he still is or if he left after I…. He came in shortly after we got here. I did something stupid and opened myself up to talk to him, to make sure he'd leave us alone. Leave *you* alone. But it's Halloween and it's his place, so he was able to just take over. He got in my head and wouldn't shut up, not for a *second*. He pushed and pushed, and I couldn't stop him!" Jake felt himself getting wound up again at the memory.

Eric grasped Jake's shoulders and pulled him into his arms. "Shh. It's okay."

"No, it's not," Jake said into Eric's chest. "I know better. I should've never let it go that far. And what I said…."

Eric held him tighter. "We don't have to talk about that right now. You just… you scared me in there. I didn't know what was going on."

Jake pulled back to meet Eric's gaze. "I should have told you he was there. I just thought we could get in and out and I wouldn't have to. I know it's all still upsetting for you."

"You were trying to protect me from him." Jake shrugged and Eric pressed a kiss to his forehead. "I appreciate that. But as much as you don't want to see me upset over Andrew, I don't want you to have a brain hemorrhage trying to stop it. Okay?"

Jake nodded. "Okay. It was unprofessional for me to try to control it like that and to not tell you what was going on."

Eric smiled his first real smile of the night. "Correct me if I'm wrong, but I don't think you were there in a professional capacity."

"No," Jake said, dropping his gaze to the ground. "I wasn't. And that's why I can't be the one in between the two of you. That didn't just go badly; that was a spectacular fail."

Eric slid his hands down Jake's arms and took a step back. "Can you go back in with me so I can close up?" he asked.

Jake chewed on his bottom lip. "I don't know. I'm not sure what would happen. I don't know if he's gone or if I just can't sense him because I'm out here."

Eric was quiet for a second and then said, "Does it make me evil to kind of want you to go back in? I just wonder what other secrets will come flying out of here." He tapped the side of Jake's head.

Jake rolled his eyes. "I think that was enough spontaneous sharing for one night. I'll wait here."

"All right." Eric fished out the car keys from his pocket and handed them to Jake. "Get in the car. You're freezing."

Eric started back toward the house but Jake called to him. "Wait! Are you okay to go back in there? Ghosts aside, I know it's not an easy place for you to be."

Eric turned back to him. "Yeah, I'm okay. I'm more okay than I've been in a while. I don't know why. I feel like fucking Frodo on my quest for the ring, but finding it did something. Settled something."

"Okay," Jake said. "I'll be here when you're done."

Eric spent another ten minutes in the house while Jake thawed in the car with the heater on full blast. Then Eric got into the car with a small cardboard box.

"Just some things I wanted to grab," he said. Jake smiled and nodded. "Let's go." Eric put the car in gear and they left, the house swallowed up by the darkness as they drove farther away. Before they left the residential streets and merged onto the highway, Jake was sound asleep.

"HEY." JAKE heard a whisper and felt something warm and weighty on his leg as he willed himself back from the abyss of sleep. He cracked open one eye. "We're home," Eric said. Jake looked out the window, confused for a second, and then back at Eric. "Well, we're at my house. Would you rather I take you back to your apartment?"

Jake pushed himself up in the seat and rubbed a hand over his face. "No, this is good," he said.

They got out of the car and Eric let them into his condo. "Are you hungry?" he asked.

Jake shook his head. "Not really. Just dead tired. Could I get some water, though?"

He followed Eric into the kitchen and waited while Eric poured two glasses from the pitcher in the fridge. "Do you want to sit here or go upstairs?" Eric asked.

"I'd like to go upstairs if that's all right," Jake said through a yawn. "Tonight really wiped me out."

"I can imagine." Eric handed Jake a glass and they climbed the stairs to Eric's bedroom. Jake sat down on the edge of the bed and gulped the water. "Do you want a refill?"

"No, then I'll just have to pee all night."

Eric laughed. "All right. Pajamas?"

Jake shook his head and yawned again. "I don't think I'm up for much right now, but… can we not?"

Eric nodded. Jake began to tug his sweater and shirt over his head, but Eric stopped him. "Let me," he said. He pulled them off together and then hauled Jake up to a standing position. He undid Jake's jeans and tugged them off along with his boxers. Socks were the last to go, and he held the covers up for Jake to slide underneath.

Eric undressed quickly and got into bed. He shut off the bedside lamp and spooned behind Jake, pulling him tight to his chest. Jake sighed at the feel of warm, skin-to-skin contact. "Feels good," he murmured.

"Yeah, it does." Eric kissed Jake's head, shoulder, and neck, and Jake relaxed into the touch. He felt himself on the edge of sleep again when Eric's breath warmed his ear. "Jake?" he whispered.

"Yeah?"

"You know I don't love Andrew, right? I mean, maybe I love him in some way for what he was to me, but I'm not still *in love* with him."

Jake rolled over to face Eric and ran his finger along Eric's jawline. "I know."

"You and I are so different than it ever was with him. I never knew… I mean, I just wanted to make sure you know he doesn't stop me from… shit. However things go with us, I already know—"

Jake put a finger to Eric's lips to silence him. "I know," he said again. "And right now, we're exactly where we're supposed to be. And the only place we're going is to sleep. Together. Okay?" he said with a tired smile.

"Okay." Eric rolled onto his back and pulled Jake against his side. If Eric said anything else, Jake didn't hear it; he was out like a light in seconds.

CHAPTER 20

JAKE ROLLED over and reached his arm out toward the spot next to him. He felt a warm body buried under blankets, and he smiled as he turned toward it. He scooted up behind Eric and draped an arm over his waist. Eric stirred and shifted to face him and gave him a sleepy, closed-eyed kiss. When they separated, he looked at Jake, concern lining his forehead.

"How are you feeling?" Eric asked.

Jake smiled and slid his hand down between Eric's legs. "I feel pretty good. So do you." He let his fingers trail over Eric's morning wood and nipped at his lips.

"Jesus," Eric whispered. Jake leaned in for another kiss but Eric drew back. He stilled Jake's hand on him. "Wait a second."

"What's wrong?" Jake asked. His old self-doubt crept in, and he wondered if last night had tipped the scales of Eric's acceptance of Jake's odd world.

Eric cupped a hand to the side of Jake's face. "I'm really asking you: are you feeling okay?"

Jake did a quick inventory. Nothing hurt, he didn't feel sick, and his head was quiet. "Yes, I'm fine. Why?"

Eric glanced at the clock behind him. "Because you've been sleeping for almost fourteen hours," he said.

"Fourteen…?" Jake raised his head and saw it was nearly noon. "Fourteen hours! Shit! The shop! I've got to go! Why didn't you wake me?" He tried to roll away and out of the bed but Eric stopped him.

"Slow down. It's fine. Everything's fine," Eric said, urging Jake back toward him.

Jake went grudgingly and lay back down facing Eric. "Seriously, why didn't you wake me?" he repeated.

Eric pretended to think hard for a second. "Uh, because I'm not Superman?" Jake furrowed his brow. "Your phone rang at eight thirty, and I woke up. I saw that it was Jessie, and I tried to wake you. I mean I *really* tried to wake you. Shook you, called your name. You just mumbled something at me and rolled over so I answered it."

"That must've gone great," Jake grumbled.

"It was fine, actually. She was calling for me."

"What? What the hell are you talking about?"

Eric sighed. "I still don't get how all this works, how you all do what you do, but she said your grandmother called her this morning and asked her to go into the shop for you. She then told her to call your phone but to talk to me and tell me to let you sleep as long as you needed. She said you needed to 'charge your battery.' So I did."

"My God," Jake whispered. "Gram must have known something happened last night."

"Yes. A lot happened last night," Eric said in a matching whisper. He brushed his knuckles over the stubble on Jake's face. "Not all bad either."

"No?" Jake asked and dropped his gaze. He knew where Eric was going and there was no avoiding it.

"No. We found the ring, didn't we?" Jake nodded. "And I remember you saying something about loving me. Well, you didn't say it to me; you yelled it at a ghost." Jake felt his face heat up, and he looked up at Eric through his lashes.

"Sorry," he mumbled.

Eric pulled his head back to look at Jake. "Sorry for what? That you said it? Please tell me now if that's the case."

"No," Jake said, shaking his head. "I'm not sorry I said it. I'm sorry for *how* I said it. I shouldn't have lost it like that and yelled it at him. It wasn't fair to either of you. I should've handled it better."

"Was it true?" Eric asked, his gaze intense.

Jake took a deep breath and met Eric's eyes head-on this time. "Yes. It's true. I know we haven't been together that long, and there's more I need to tell you—some things Gram told me while you were away. But yes, I have... very strong feelings for you." Eric stared at him for a few seconds then dissolved into laughter. "What the hell?" Jake demanded and shoved him on the shoulder.

"I'm sorry," Eric said, snorting as he tried to get himself under control. "But that was the most unromantic declaration I've ever heard!" He started laughing again, and Jake pursed his lips.

"Excuse me," Jake said, all sarcasm. "I'm not the author who gets paid a million dollars for my words."

Eric got quiet and pulled Jake close. "You're right. That's my job. And I don't care how long we've been together. I've wanted to tell you for weeks that you're the most beautiful, gifted man I've ever met. And I'm falling for you so hard it scares me."

"Jesus," Jake said. "That's worth at least two million."

Eric grinned and climbed on top of him. Their mouths crashed together, the intimacy of what they'd shared driving them hard and fast. Eric slid down Jake's body and took him in his mouth, working his hard cock with his lips and tongue. Jake closed his eyes and let the feeling wash over him, but it wasn't long before he felt his orgasm start to build. He grabbed at Eric's hair to bring him back up. They kissed again, heads shifting to get them as close as possible. Jake looped one leg around Eric's waist and pulled him down so Eric's cock pressed against his ass. Eric slowed the kiss and looked at Jake.

"Do you want to?" he asked.

"Yes," Jake said and used his leg to push Eric closer. Eric draped his body over Jake as he reached for the bedside table. He yanked open the drawer and grabbed the K-Y and a condom. He wasted no time getting Jake ready and lubed up. Jake relaxed and opened his body to Eric and felt him slide all the way in. "Oh my God," he groaned.

"Are you okay?" Eric asked.

Jake could tell he was trying hard to restrain himself. He nodded and smiled. "Better than okay. Now *fuck me*."

He saw Eric's eyes glaze over at his words, and he propped Jake's legs on his shoulders and began to thrust. Jake took himself in hand and stroked in time with Eric's movements until Eric shifted his position a bit and hit the place inside Jake that made him see stars. He moaned and Eric picked up his speed, and after a few more thrusts Jake's release spilled over onto his stomach. He watched Eric watch him come, and a few seconds later, Eric tensed and cried out as his own climax hit.

He stayed put, panting for a minute, then slowly pulled out and let Jake's legs fall to the bed. He tossed the condom and flopped down on Jake's chest.

"Holy shit," Jake said as he wiped the sweat off his forehead.

Eric chuckled. "Yeah. Even I don't have any better words than that. But you can talk dirty to me any time."

Jake laughed and speared his fingers through Eric's hair. "I'll keep that in mind." They lay quietly until Jake broke the silence. "I hate to say this but I have to get going. I need to head back to the shop."

"Oh, right," Eric said, looking up at him. "That was the other part of the phone call this morning. You're off for the day. You're supposed to relax, preferably with me, and I quote, 'Have a life, already!'"

Jake laughed. "That had to be Jessie."

"It was. But she's got it covered, she said. So it looks like you're stuck with me today."

"I'm not complaining," Jake said and kissed the top of Eric's head.

"Good. Me neither."

"I do have one question, though."

Eric tilted his head up to look at Jake. "What?"

"When are you going to feed me?"

Eric smiled and kissed Jake's stomach. "Right now. Pancakes again?"

HALF AN hour later, Jake sat at the kitchen table, watching as Eric flipped golden brown pancakes onto a plate, much the same way he had after the first night they spent together. Eric set out syrup, butter, and orange juice, then returned with the platter of pancakes and sat down.

"Have at it," he said and slid the plate toward Jake.

Jake helped himself to a stack and inhaled his first bite. "These are so good," Jake said.

Eric smiled. "Thanks. They're not, actually. See, I wear you out with mind-blowing sex, and then I could feed you cardboard pancakes and you'd love it."

"Funny," Jake said and wrinkled his nose at Eric.

They ate in silence for a while until Jake started to slow down. "So what else do you have to tell me about?" Eric asked.

Jake gave him a blank look. "Huh?"

"When we were talking about what you said last night, you said you still had more to tell me. Something your grandmother told you? What is it?"

Jake felt his stomach clench around his pancakes. "Oh. Right." He tried to repress a sigh. He was getting really tired of the speak-before-you-think thing he'd apparently adopted. "It's not a big deal. We can talk about it later."

Eric shook his head. "Uh-uh. There is too much stuff in your world that I don't understand. I need all the help I can get." Jake shifted in his seat, stalling. Eric stood up and pulled his chair around to the other side of the table. He sat down facing Jake and took his hands. "Look, I know it hasn't worked out for you in the past—letting people you're with into your world—but Jake... you've got to know that I'm in. I'm not going to say some of it doesn't freak me out, but I trust you. I need you to trust me too. I'm not going to run."

Jake snorted out a laugh. "That's because you can't."

"Can't? What do you mean?" Eric asked, brows furrowed.

Jake sighed. "Do you remember the other night when we stayed at my place and I said I didn't know what was too crazy for you so I just went for it?"

"Yes. You told me about how Andrew had gone to your grandmother."

"Right. I'm going to have to just go for it again because I'm pretty sure none of this is everyday stuff for you."

Eric nodded. "Okay. So do it."

"All right. Well, the first thing you need to know is that Andrew led you to me," Jake said.

"I kind of figured that. He needed a way to communicate with me."

"Yes, but that's not all. In his own way, he was trying to make up for how things ended with you two. He put you in the path of someone who could love you the way he couldn't when he was here."

Eric swallowed hard and squeezed Jake's hand. "He always had good taste," Eric said, his voice soft.

"Better than you think," Jake said. He took a deep breath. "Here comes the hard part. When I was at Gram's that night, she told me she'd noticed some changes in me a couple months ago. Energy changes, aura... things like that. Gram had to be Gram so she went poking around to see what was up, and she found out I was going to meet my soul mate."

"Soul mate," Eric repeated.

"Yes, it's someone who—"

"I know what it means," Eric interrupted. "At least in a general sense. The person you're meant to be with. Like, fate."

"Exactly. Someone who is destined to be in your life. Sometimes it's your best friend or a sibling. Maybe even a teacher or something like that. But every so often, your soul mate is your partner in every way. And you're going to be together, come hell or high water. The universe won't have it any other way."

As Jake spoke, Eric had inched farther forward on his chair so their knees pressed together. "I see," he said.

Jake raised his eyebrows. "'I see'? That's it? No follow-up questions after that bombshell?"

Eric sat silent for a long moment, and then he said, "I do have a follow-up question."

"Okay. What is it?"

"Have you met them yet? The soul mate?"

Jake met Eric's steady gaze. "I have."

"Me?"

Jake nodded. "You."

With a sudden movement, Eric reached forward, scooped up Jake, and pulled him onto his lap. Jake laughed but Eric drew his head down to join their lips. They kissed long and slow, tongues sliding over and around one another until Jake pulled away. Eric studied him for a few seconds and said, "So I can't run, then? Not even if I wanted to?"

Jake shrugged. "You could. Nothing is physically preventing you. But I'd find you. Scratch that—*the universe* would find you and drag us back together one way or another. *We* are supposed to be." Eric nodded. "Have you ever heard about high-school sweethearts who break up, go on to have totally separate lives, and then meet up again later on? They're usually soul mates. Sometimes couples who get married, then divorced, and then marry each other again are soul mates. A lot of the time it's not easy. It's not an automatic perfect fit."

Eric rubbed his hands up and down Jake's back. "That's okay. I'm not a quitter. But why don't we agree to skip the part where we split up and find each other again in twenty years, okay?"

Jake laughed. "Agreed." Jake looked down at Eric, studying him closely. "You're really not freaked out by all this?"

"No," Eric said. "The opposite, actually. I feel less crazy because everything I've been feeling makes a little more sense now. After the first night you spent here, it seemed way too soon to know that I wanted to go to sleep next to you every night for the rest of my life. But I did. I thought it, anyway. And then I thought it was weird and creepy so I kept my mouth shut."

"Weird and creepy are kind of staples for me," Jake said, smiling.

"That's okay. Apparently, I fit right in," Eric said with a laugh.

"You do."

"I'd like to meet your grandmother sometime. You know, to kind of put things to rest with Andrew."

"You will. But not today. Today is my day off to relax and recharge my batteries or whatever they said this morning."

"That's right," said Eric. "What would you like to do?"

Jake thought for a few seconds. "I say we find something to binge-watch on Netflix for a while, and then we go back upstairs for some more quality time," he said with a wink.

"As you wish," Eric said with a mock bow. He pulled them both up from the chair and led Jake into the living room.

THAT EVENING, Eric drove Jake back to his apartment. Before they left, Eric had gotten squirrely and edgy, and Jake had finally grabbed his arm, spun him around, and asked him what the problem was.

Eric shrugged. "It's stupid," he mumbled.

"Try me," Jake said and leaned into him.

Eric sighed, "No, it's actually stupid but… I don't want to spend the night without you. After everything that's happened, I just want to be with you."

Jake shrugged. "So do it." Eric tilted his head in question. "Put some stuff in a bag and we'll stay at my place tonight. No big deal."

"I don't want to crowd you or anything. We just had the whole day together, so if you need some space, I want you to tell me. I don't want to suffocate you."

Jake smiled. "If I start to turn blue, then back off. Right now I'm good. I want you to stay with me."

They stopped at a Mexican place for carryout and got to Jake's apartment around eight thirty. They ate and crashed on the couch, Jake pressed tight to Eric's chest as they continued their marathon viewing of *Breaking Bad*. A couple hours later, Jake's cell phone rang and they both jumped.

"What the hell?" Eric said, and he hit Pause on the remote.

Jake reached over to the end table and grabbed his phone. He showed the caller ID to Eric and then clicked to answer. "Hi, Gram," he said. "No, I'm all right. Everything's fine."

Eric shifted behind him and Jake scooted forward. "I'm going to check my e-mail," Eric said, pointing toward his laptop on the kitchen table.

Jake nodded and turned his attention back to Gram.

"He's there with you?" she asked.

"Yeah, Eric is here. We hung out today, and he came back here with me."

"Did you tell him?"

Jake smiled. Gram didn't mince words. Ever. "Yes, I told him. Everything," he added before she could ask.

"Hmm. Good. I guess he's as open-minded as we hoped."

Jake laughed. "Yes, he is. I know he doesn't understand it all, but he's trying. And he's not going to bail."

"I know, sweetie," she said, affection clear in her voice. Then, just as quickly, the wind changed and her tone became sharp. "Now, do you mind telling me what the hell you were thinking conducting a one-man séance on Samhain?" she bit out.

Jake winced. She'd used the Wiccan name for "Halloween," which was a sacred holiday in their tradition, so he knew she was fired up.

"I'd love to tell you, Gram, but I don't really know. I wasn't thinking. It was dangerous and stupid, but"—he glanced over and saw Eric typing away on his laptop—"I had to try to protect him."

"A lot of good you'd have been to him if you let a demon in the door or if Andrew had tried to take your body for a spin!"

Jake had considered the possibility of letting a negative entity in. He had not, however, thought about how easily Andrew could have possessed him if he'd wanted. "Shit," he murmured. "Uh, sorry."

"No, this is one time I agree that 'shit' is right! I had alarm bells going off all over the place, and I had no way to help you! I understand what's between you and Eric, but you can't allow it to take away your common sense."

"Gram, I'm sorry, really." Jake sighed. "I was caught off guard and I made the wrong call. But I'm okay. We're okay."

Gram was silent for a moment and when she spoke, she eased up a bit. "Thank the goddess for that. And I can't say I've never made a bad call. It's how we learn, I suppose."

"I've learned," Jake said. "It won't happen again."

She laughed a little. "Oh, dear, yes, it will. And that's all right. I'm not angry with you. I was afraid for you. But you figured it out and got yourself out of it. I'm proud of you, sweetie."

"Thanks," he said. "So, I think Eric might be ready to come over and have a reading with you. Talk with Andrew."

"I thought so. I know Andrew is ready. And, for what it's worth, he's sorry for what happened too."

"Wow," Jake said. "That's surprising because he was pretty awful, honestly."

"I'm sure," Gram said with a sigh. "We can't change it now. But I think after he connects with Eric, he'll be ready to cross over. That's the peace he needs."

"I know," Jake agreed. Even though he agreed, he didn't like the idea of handing Eric over to Andrew, even for a short time.

"You need to come too, dear," Gram said.

"I do? I thought my presence might throw things off or confuse the reading."

"It could. But Andrew is very strong and very determined, so I should be able to connect with him just fine. Eric is going to need you there."

That was all Jake needed to know. "All right. When?"

"How about tomorrow night? All Soul's Day will have passed, but some of the energy will still be around. I think that should work out fine."

"Okay. We'll be there. And thanks for covering for me today, Gram. I needed it."

"It's fine, dear. Jessie and I worked it out. But don't you scare me like that again!"

"I'll try," Jake said with a smile. "See you tomorrow."

"Good night," Gram said and the call disconnected.

Jake tossed his phone onto the couch and headed over to the kitchen. He wrapped his arms around Eric from behind and kissed his ear.

Eric shifted in his chair, and Jake sat on his lap. "Everything okay?" Eric asked.

Jake nodded. "She was pretty pissed that I did what I did with Andrew but it's all right now. She would like to meet you, though. Tomorrow."

Eric blew out a breath. "To talk to Andrew?" he asked, and Jake nodded. Eric didn't say anything for a moment. When he finally spoke, he sounded resigned. "I guess I'm as ready as I'll ever be."

Jake bent down and kissed him. "I know you're nervous but, trust me, it's what needs to happen. Andrew will be able to move on after this."

"You're sure?" Eric asked, a skeptical look on his face.

"I'm sure. And if he doesn't, Gram and I will make him."

"You can do that?"

"Yes. It's not the best option. It's always better if they cross over on their own. And I think he will."

"Okay," Eric said. "But I want you with me."

Jake smiled at Gram's precognitive comment. "Of course. I wouldn't be anywhere else," he said.

CHAPTER 21

JAKE DECIDED early in the day that they would take the train to Salem instead of Eric's car. As soon as they awoke that morning, he could sense the uneasiness coming off Eric in waves. He tried to settle him down in all the earthly ways he knew—namely sex and food—but Eric wasn't up for either one.

"It's okay," Jake assured him as he pulled Eric's head down to rest on his chest. They had been fooling around in bed but Jake could feel Eric's distraction in the energy around him and in the waning erection pressed against his thigh.

"No, it's not," Eric grumbled and covered his face with his hand. "I don't know why I'm so freaked out. It's not like I've never had a reading before."

Jake smiled. "Eric, you've had exactly *one* reading. And it was a sweet, happy one with me and Grandma Em. This is a little bit different. It's okay to be nervous."

Eric sighed. "I'm sorry. Just as long as you know it's not you."

"I know. We'll have plenty of time to make up for it." Jake planted a kiss on his forehead. "How about breakfast? I make a mean bowl of Cheerios."

Eric gave a faint smile and shook his head. "I'm not hungry right now."

"Okay," Jake said and went back to running his fingers through Eric's hair.

"Fuck," Eric said with a groan and flopped onto his back. "I don't know how I'm going to get anything done today."

Jake propped himself up on his side. "What's on the agenda?"

"It's supposed to be a writing day," he said in a monotone.

Jake thought for a minute and then tugged Eric over to face him. "I promised you I would never do anything without your permission, so I'm going to ask. Do you want me to help you calm down?"

Eric smiled. "I think you just tried that and it didn't work out very well."

"Not sex," Jake said, his tone serious. "I mean I can use some of my abilities to help you relax."

"Really?"

"Yes. It would be a spell, and I know you're extra nervous so I can't say how long it would last, but it should buy you some time to relax. Maybe get some work done."

Eric paused for only a second before he said, "All right."

"You're sure?"

Eric nodded. "I trust you."

"Okay, then. Wait here." Jake got out of bed and pulled on sleep pants. He padded out to the kitchen and put water on to boil. While he waited, he searched the cupboard that held his herbs and found the valerian root. He ground up some of the dried herb and dropped it into a nylon teabag. When the water began to boil, he poured a cup and dropped in the bag to steep for a few minutes. He opened another small cupboard and grabbed his lavender essential oil.

When the tea was ready, he removed the bag and headed for the bedroom with the mug and the oil.

He handed the cup to Eric. "Drink this."

"What is it?" Eric asked.

"I thought you trusted me," Jake said, teasing.

Eric rolled his eyes. "I do. I was just curious."

"It's tea made with valerian root. It has calming and antianxiety properties."

Eric nodded and took a sip. He wrinkled his nose. "Well, I wouldn't order it out."

"Just drink," Jake said. He left the bottle on the bedside table and went to a cabinet in the corner of the bedroom. The top shelf held a rainbow of thin colored candles, and he selected a white one and a light blue one. He chose two candle holders, shut the cabinet, and returned to the bed. "How's it going?" he asked Eric, peering into the mug.

"Almost done," Eric said and swallowed the last gulp. Jake took the cup and set it on the dresser.

"Okay. We're ready to start." He sat down on the bed and twisted the cap off the lavender oil.

"What's that?" Eric asked.

Jake smiled. He knew Eric wasn't asking out of fear; it was his natural curiosity. "This is lavender oil. It also helps to promote calm. The same for the white and blue candles."

"Do the candles have a scent?"

"No, the colors are what's important. Every color has different properties, and is affiliated with a different element."

"Wow. So tea, oil, and candles are going to calm me down?"

"Partly. It's all part of the spell. Do you remember the first time you came here and I held your hands and did an energy reading?" Eric nodded. "I'm going to do the same thing, only this time I'm going to manipulate your energy a bit. Get rid of the nerves as best I can. I'll say some things too."

Eric held out his hands. "I'm ready."

Jake lit the two small candles and closed his eyes for a moment to center himself and to open his Third Eye to Eric's energy. He took a deep breath and dabbed some oil on his thumb. He brushed it over the pulse points on Eric's wrists and then the center of his forehead. He let his thumb rest on Eric's forehead and said softly,

"Once was there,
Now is banished,
Anxious, upset,
Now will vanish."

Jake made a circle with his thumb, spreading the oil, and said the words again. He continued until he felt Eric's vibration drop a little, then took hold of both of Eric's hands. Jake felt the swirling mix of anxiety and fear, and even traces of the sadness and loss Eric still harbored for Andrew. Jake knew Eric's chakras would be a jumbled mess, so he focused on surrounding Eric with a white light that would shield him from the full force of his feelings. In his mind's eye, he built a bubble of white light around Eric.

"White light come and soothe your head,
Calm prevails, anxiety dead.
This root and oil quiet your mind
So calm and focus you will find.
I bind this spell by the power of three
It harms you not, so mote it be."

He went through the verse three times, then drew back his own energy to assess the spell. White light shimmered around Eric and, while he knew it wouldn't last indefinitely, he felt confident that Eric would have more peace than he had had earlier. He let go of Eric's hands and opened his eyes. Eric sat with his eyes closed, his shoulders sagged in relaxation.

"It's done," Jake said softly.

Eric's eyes flickered open like he was waking from sleep. "Wow," he whispered.

"Are you all right?" Jake asked. He dipped his fingers into the glass of water by the bed and pinched out the candles.

Eric looked a little dazed but nodded. "I'm fine. I feel... okay."

"Good. 'Okay' is better than freaked out," Jake said with a smile.

Eric exhaled slowly. "Thank you."

"You're welcome. It's nothing heavy-duty, so I don't know how long it will last, but you should have a quiet few hours at least." Eric nodded, but his expression was far away. "Hello?" Jake waved a hand in front of him.

"What? Oh, sorry. This chapter I've been working on just popped into my head. I've been a little stuck, but I have an idea that might work."

"Well, then get to it!" Jake said.

Eric got out of bed and grabbed his jeans from the floor. "Can I stay here and work? I'm afraid if I drive all the way home I'll lose my train of thought."

"Of course," Jake said. "I'm going to jump in the shower and then head downstairs to the shop. I'll come up in a few hours to check in."

"Okay," Eric said. He pulled a T-shirt out of his bag and over his head. He headed for the door but turned on his heel and came back to where Jake sat on the bed. He brought his hands to the sides of Jake's face and bent down to kiss him. He pulled his lips back a fraction of an inch, just enough space to murmur, "Thank you, baby," then stood and disappeared through the door toward his laptop.

JAKE HAD a couple of readings scheduled throughout the morning, plus one walk-in close to lunch time. While he didn't often turn people away for readings, he considered it briefly when the last woman came into the shop.

The spell for Eric had depleted his energy some, though not terribly, and he'd used up more for the two readings he'd had on the books. When the woman came in, he sensed her sadness and loss from across the shop without much effort. He also saw the shimmer of a male figure following close behind her. He sighed. He knew this one would take quite a bit out of him, but he also realized that this woman had found her way to him at this particular time for a reason. He greeted her, they discussed her needs, and he ushered her back to the reading room just as Jessie waltzed in the door.

A half box of tissues and an hour later, Jake showed the woman out and then collapsed on the desk where Jessie sat.

"My God," he groaned.

"Long morning?" she asked as she pushed aside a notebook.

"Yeah. Well, normally not, but today I'd been hoping to hold back some. Eric is meeting Gram tonight to talk with Andrew."

Jessie nodded. "And you wanted to be able to kick his ass over to the Other Side?"

"No," Jake said with a roll of his eyes. "I just didn't want to be drained. In case Gram needs help, or Eric does. I don't know. It made sense in my head."

Jessie studied him for a moment. "Did you ever think that maybe the universe, or whoever, might be draining you for a reason?"

"No," Jake answered thoughtfully. "To what end? To give Andrew an upper hand or something?"

"Hmm. Could be, I guess. Though I think Gram would be all over that."

"True."

Jessie picked up her pen and doodled an infinity symbol in the margin of her page. "Maybe… you're just supposed to be *regular* tonight. Or as regular as you can be."

"Regular?"

"You know, you but without all the witchy bells and whistles. Well, with their volume on LOW, at least. Maybe you just need to be there tonight for Eric as his partner, not his psychic, you know?"

Jake stared, lost in thought for a moment, then hopped down off the desk. "You, my dear, are far more brilliant than I give you credit for." He pecked her on the cheek and turned to head up to the apartment but found Eric standing on the bottom step.

"Should I be jealous?" Eric joked as he descended the last step.

Jake met him halfway and slid an arm around his waist. "Never." He pecked Eric on the cheek and Eric laughed. "I'm sorry. I got tied up. I was just going to come up and check on you. How'd it go?"

"Good," Eric said. Jake could sense the apprehension working its way back, though it wasn't yet as bad as it had been in the morning. "I finished up a chapter and edited another. Sent some paperwork off to my editor."

"I'm glad," Jake said with a smile. "How about a late lunch?" Eric nodded, so he left the shop in Jessie's hands and they headed out to Jake's usual café a block away.

They ate, and Jake did his best to keep Eric distracted with food and talk, but by the time they made it back to the shop, Eric's nerves were back in full swing. He knew it would take a little longer to get to Gram's at rush hour so he decided they should take off. They said good night to Jessie and hopped on the T toward North Station and the commuter rail.

Once they were on the train to Salem, Eric sat without speaking, his leg pistoning up and down until Jake settled a hand on his knee. "It's okay," he said.

Eric sat up straighter in his seat and blew out a breath. "Sorry. I'm getting freaked out again."

"Is there anything you want to talk about? Something in particular that's worrying you?"

"No. Well, yes, but it's probably stupid," Eric mumbled.

"No stupid questions. What is it?"

Eric chewed his bottom lip for a moment and then blurted out, "What if he won't go? Does it make me a horrible person that I just want him to go… wherever you go when you're dead?"

Jake grabbed his hand. "No, it doesn't. The two of you are on different planes now. It's not good for either one of you the way things are now." Eric nodded. "And as for whether or not he'll go, I'd say yes. He's not here to do anything bad. He wants to fix things with you. I think that's all he needs." Eric nodded again. "Anything else?"

Eric cut his eyes sideways at Jake with a hint of a smile. "Yeah. What if Gram doesn't like me?"

"Not a chance," Jake said with a wink.

THEY TOOK their time walking to Gram's house despite the cool November air. Eric had visited the town a time or two growing up, but

Jake enjoyed pointing out landmarks, both historical and those from his own youth.

"See that building over there?" Jake asked, pointing at a storefront across the street. "It used to be a little restaurant. I had my first job there. Busboy."

"Really? You had a regular job?"

Jake bumped Eric's shoulder with his own. "Yes! What do you mean 'regular job'?"

Eric shrugged. "I don't know. I guess I just kind of figured you grew up doing what you do now."

Jake shook his head. "No. I grew up learning what I do now. God knows what havoc I would've caused if I tried to go out on my own as a teenager. Besides Gram never would have allowed it."

Eric nodded and they continued to walk in silence. They turned a corner, and before Jake knew it, they were climbing the porch stairs at Gram's house. He grabbed Eric's hand and laced their fingers together.

"Ready?" Jake asked.

Eric looked like he was about to be sick. "No," he whispered. Jake tugged him away from the door.

"Hey," Jake said softly, "it's going to be okay. I'll be with you the whole time."

"I know. But you'll be… working, won't you? I mean, if a reading is going on, you can't exactly tune out. Especially on your own grandmother."

Jake pulled Eric farther over until he felt the porch railing stop them. He slid his arms around Eric's waist and held him close. "Actually, that's not true."

"How do you mean?"

"Well, let me ask you this: could you write nonstop, all day long and never take a break?"

Eric shrugged. "I suppose I could. I doubt it would be very good though."

"Right. You'd run out of steam. So today, I started by doing your spell, and then I worked and had a bunch of readings, and I never took a break. I'm out of steam. I'm drained from all that, so I'm no good to Gram tonight no matter what happens. We can't work indefinitely either."

"So you're not going to be part of the reading?" Eric asked.

"I'll be there, right beside you. As your partner, not as a medium," Jake said, sending a mental thank-you to Jessie for her earlier observations.

"Oh," Eric said. He fell silent for a few seconds, then met Jake's gaze with a glint in his eye. "Partner, huh?"

"Yeah. Partner. I can think of a different word if you don't like that one. How about… boyfriend?"

Eric rolled his eyes. "We're not sixteen."

"This is true. What about… *lover*?" Jake pressed their lower halves together to emphasize the word.

Eric smiled. "I think we're a little more than that."

"Okay, paramour then! Concubine!"

Jake grinned when Eric laughed out loud. "Jesus. This is going downhill fast." Eric palmed the sides of Jake's face and drew him in for a kiss. "Partner is good," he whispered against Jake's lips. "For now."

Jake didn't have time to process what that might mean. They heard the click of the front door and light from the house spilled out onto the porch.

"Time to come in, boys," Gram's voice rang out. "Don't make me turn on the porch light!"

Jake snickered. "I think we just got caught making out."

Eric stepped back but held fast to Jake's hand. "Maybe we are sixteen after all," he said with a smile.

"Ready now?" Jake asked.

Eric shrugged.

They stepped out of the shadows, and Gram ushered them into the house. Jake kissed Gram on the cheek as they entered the kitchen.

"Gram, this is Eric. Eric, this is my grandmother, Rebecca Parker."

"Nice to meet you, ma'am," Eric said as he shook her hand.

She covered their clasped hands with her free hand and said, "It's wonderful to finally meet you, Eric. But that better be the last time you call me 'ma'am.' Call me Gram. Or Rebecca, if you must."

Eric nodded and smiled. "Okay, Gram."

"Good boy," she said and patted his cheek. "Now take off your coats and sit for a minute. I have tea on."

They draped their coats over the backs of kitchen chairs. Jake was just about to sit when another woman breezed in from the living room, her long gray skirt floating around her legs as she walked, hellfire red hair twisted up into an unruly bun.

"I think I have everything, Rebecca, but I couldn't find—Jake! You're here!"

"Anastasia? What are you doing here?" Jake stood and enveloped her in a hug.

"I'm here as second-in-command," she said with a wink. "Just in case your grandmother needs an extra set of hands. Or eyes. She didn't think you'd be up for it."

Jake laughed. "She got that right. Eric, this is Anastasia. I've known her… as long as I can remember, really."

Anastasia swatted Jake's arm. "Hush. I'm not that old. Lovely to meet you, Eric."

Eric stood and shook her hand. "Nice to meet you. So, you're a medium too?"

Gram placed four full mugs of tea on the table, and they all sat down. "I am," Anastasia said. "There are probably more of us around than you thought, right?"

Eric nodded. "That's for sure."

"Anastasia and Gram have worked together for years. They help each other out with readings and spells. Things like that." Jake felt a rush of relief when both women nodded.

The truth was that Gram and Anastasia had been in the same coven together for well over thirty years, where Gram was now the High Priestess. Tonight, though, Jake did not want them throwing words like "coven" at Eric. He was spooked enough already. Jake would find a way to explain it all to Eric in time. First, they had to get through the reading.

They drank tea and made getting-to-know-you talk until all their mugs were empty. At last Gram stood and stretched her arms overhead, her bracelets jangling a tune as they slid up and then down her arms. "I don't know about you," she said, "but I'm ready to get this show on the road."

"I'll go light the candles," Anastasia said and left the room.

Gram trailed behind her, Jake knew, to give him a moment alone with Eric.

"We'll go into Gram's reading room now," Jake explained. Eric just nodded, his face white as a sheet. "Hey," Jake said, placing himself in Eric's direct line of sight. He slid his hands up the sides of Eric's neck to cradle his face. "It's going to be okay. They'll take care of the reading, and I'm here with you. I'm not going anywhere. All right?"

Eric just stared at him for a moment and then scooped Jake up into a hug so tight he could hardly breathe. In that moment, Jake felt it all: Eric's sadness, anger, fear, regret. But stronger than all of those, he felt love. He squeezed Eric back. "Me too, baby," he whispered in Eric's ear.

Eric gave him one final squeeze and then loosened his hold and pulled back to look at Jake. He nodded. "Okay. I'm ready."

CHAPTER 22

JAKE LED Eric to the reading room. Gram dragged the chairs from her reading table into a semblance of a circle.

"I know four doesn't exactly make a circle, but we'll do the best we can," Gram said.

"We sit in a circle?" Eric whispered to Jake. "Why not at the table like at your shop?"

Jake bit his lip. He should have explained the difference between the other readings and what they were doing tonight, but he'd been so busy trying to hold Eric together he hadn't thought of it. Before he could say anything, Gram jumped in.

"It's easier for us to work this way, especially with the little group we have here. If we sit too close, sometimes energies can get jumbled and I don't know what belongs to who. It just makes things a little more clear when communicating with a spirit."

Eric nodded. "Okay. Where do I sit?"

Gram pointed at the chair in front of her. "Right here should do. I'll sit on your right and Jake on your left, if that's okay."

Eric nodded again and took his assigned seat. Jake took the seat next to him and shot Gram a grateful look. She'd managed to explain it without using the word séance—which was essentially what they were conducting—or any other technical terms that might push Eric even further out of his comfort zone. She smiled back and took her seat.

Anastasia joined them after she dimmed the lights, leaving the room bathed in the glow of the white candles surrounding the circle. Several more candles burned bright on the small table in the center of their group. Jake noted some of Gram's crystals scattered among them. Though they appeared to be tossed haphazardly on the table, he knew they had been set with care and purpose. He shifted his gaze to Eric, who sat silent, picking at a loose thread in his jeans. Jake reached over and grabbed his hand, and Eric gave him a strained smile.

"All right," Gram began, "we're going to start by taking a few seconds to close our eyes and center ourselves. Eric, try to focus on

Andrew—maybe a happy memory you have, or something about him you loved. Okay?"

Eric blew out a long breath and nodded. Jake waited until his eyes were closed, then closed his own. Despite the drain on his abilities, Jake scanned the circle with his mind's eye and picked up a flicker of energy hovering between Eric and Gram. The fifth participant in the circle was present.

Gram spoke and they all opened their eyes. "Before we begin, Eric, I want you to know that you're in control at all times. I'm going to ask for your permission to begin and, if at any time you want to stop, just say so." Eric nodded. "I understand this may be difficult, but please try to stay seated with us here. We've created a safe place for this communication to happen, and I need you to stay in that space until we're done."

Eric squeezed Jake's hand and cleared his throat. "Okay."

"I know you have some experience with how this works from Jake, so I won't waste time on what you already know. I'm taking lead this evening, but any one of us may get words, phrases, images, sounds... and we'll convey it all to you as best we can. You're free to ask questions, or speak to the spirit as well. Do you have any questions before we begin?"

"Don't you mean speak to Andrew?" Eric asked.

"Most likely, yes. But when we open ourselves for communication like this, it isn't ever for any one specific person. You could hear from your grandmother again, or a spirit guide. I doubt that will be the case, but we have to leave room for the possibility. It's like opening a door and seeing who walks in."

"I see," Eric said, his gaze fixed on the candles in the center of the circle.

"Good." Gram took a deep breath. "There is a spirit present with us. Eric, do you give us permission to connect you with this energy and facilitate communication between you?"

"Yes," Eric answered, his voice barely above a whisper.

"All right." Gram breathed in deep through her nose. "The energy here with us is a male. He passed at a young age." Gram closed her eyes. "I believe I'm seeing him as he was in this life when you knew him. And he's emphasizing... his hair." Eric raised his eyebrows as Gram smiled. "He flips it off his forehead. All the time." She mimed the action.

Jake jumped a bit when a chuckle rose from Eric's throat. "He never got it cut short enough to keep it out of his eyes," he murmured.

"I see," Gram said. "That's good. He's giving us details you recognize to identify himself." She paused. "Now he's showing me some images—oh! And a smell—burnt food? Black toast, charred hamburgers... maybe some kind of fish, or chicken that's dried out. Does this mean anything to you?"

Eric nodded. "Andrew couldn't cook for anything. He tried—a lot. I don't think he ever made us one meal that wasn't burned somehow."

"Good! Now I've spoken with this spirit before, and I know him as Andrew. So that's correct?"

"Yes. Andrew." Eric looked around the room. "Where is he?"

Gram turned to Anastasia who scanned the room with a raised hand. "He's by your side. To your right, behind you."

Eric glanced over his shoulder and nodded. "So, what does he want?" he asked.

Gram sat quietly, her head tilted upward in that way she had, like she was listening very carefully. After several long seconds, she responded with one word. "Forgiveness."

Eric huffed out a breath. "That's a tall order considering what he did before he... left."

"Died," Gram corrected. "He died. It's okay to say it. It's not a bad word. It's a natural part of our journey."

"Okay," Eric said. "Before he died."

"He's concerned about his words—what he said. He says 'the last thing.' It was bad, and he's giving me the feeling of weight right here," Gram said with a hand splayed across her chest. "It's still heavy on him."

"It should be," Eric said, his tone sharp.

"*Slow, slow,*" Gram whispered, her eyes closed again for a moment. Jake guessed Andrew had shifted into fifth gear at Eric's response, and Gram was trying to rein him in a bit. She furrowed her brow. "Okay. But he was *wrong*. And he knows he was wrong. He says, over and over, 'you knew better.' He's very insistent on that. You saw what he couldn't."

Eric swallowed hard and nodded.

"Now he's moved on to an image of a girl—thin, blonde, big smile. He says... *she* was wrong too?" Gram said with a question in her voice.

"That's Megan. His girlfriend while we were together."

"Ah, I see. He did wrong by her as well."

"He did," Eric said.

"Yes. He knows that too." Gram paused. "Give me a moment, please. He changes like the wind," she murmured.

Eric shifted in his chair and let go of Jake's hand in the process. He leaned forward, elbows on his knees. Though the gesture seemed unconscious, Jake knew it was necessary. Eric had to be alone in a spiritual sense to deal directly with Andrew. Jake's energy, even depleted, could still cast a shadow over Eric's, and he was glad that Eric, either subconsciously or with help from the Other Side, had separated himself for now.

"The energy has shifted," Anastasia said while Gram worked through whatever came next. "It feels warmer, almost happy."

Gram smiled. "Yes, it does. All right, Eric—my goodness, Andrew does like pictures."

"He always did. I always told him he was missing out on things because he spent so much time behind the lens. Cameras, his phone... whatever he had, snapping away."

"It makes sense, then, that he favors images for communication," Gram said. Jake hadn't known that bit of information about Andrew, but in hindsight, it made sense. "Now, I'm not 100 percent sure where he's going with this but now I've got lobsters."

"Lobsters?" Eric asked.

"Yes. Two lobsters and, like Anastasia said, warmth—like sunshine on your skin." Gram turned her nose upward a bit and sniffed. "And sea air. Salt water."

"Oh my God," Eric whispered.

"Does this mean anything to you?"

Eric nodded. "Yes. When we first got together, one morning I said I wanted lobster for dinner." Eric laughed. "Andrew showed up that afternoon on a motorcycle. We rode up the coast, found this little out-of-the-way lobster place.... It was so good. I'd completely forgotten about that."

"Good, good. Now, we're not stopping. He's moved right on to a swimming pool. A kind of kidney shape, red brick all around it, a two-seater raft. And now he's soaked and as mad as a wet cat!"

Eric laughed again, this time louder, one Jake recognized as a happy Eric sound. "That's the pool at the lake house. Andrew worked a lot. We'd go out and get on the raft, and I'd have a book to read and he'd bring work. One day I warned him not to do it, to pick something relaxing to do—read, listen to his iPod. He just rolled his eyes at me and brought along a chapter he was editing. After about five minutes I tossed the chapter onto the patio and flipped the whole raft over." Eric grinned and shook his head. "He was so pissed. I mean, not really, not for long. We… uh, we made up pretty quickly." Eric shot a look at Jake. "Sorry," he murmured.

"It's okay," Jake said and, while he meant it, he couldn't erase from his mind the image of Andrew fucking Eric's brains out in the pool. He crossed his arms and swallowed the bubble of jealousy that rose up in him. Of course Eric was bound to have good memories of Andrew; he couldn't have been all bad. Still, Jake could live without a replay of Eric and Andrew's hottest moments.

Gram cleared her throat and continued. "He's moving on again. Now I see a birthday cake. It's beautifully done. But there's a kind of sad-happy feel to it, if that makes any sense." Gram squeezed her already closed eyes. "I'm trying to read the writing… I see 'AJ,' and I think it says—"

"It says 'Happy 45th birthday AJ,'" Eric supplied. "I made the cake. But when I went to do the writing, I didn't have enough space for his whole name so I used AJ. It was a nickname I gave him—his first and middle initials—since he insisted everyone call him Andrew. Always so serious. I surprised him with it for his forty-fifth birthday," Eric finished quietly.

"I see. But why does it feel a little sad?"

Eric sighed. "Andrew's family had money. Has money, I guess. As a kid he had these really fancy birthdays—professionally decorated, catered… the works. Then, after he was sixteen or so, his family decided his birthday wasn't such a big deal and pretty much ignored it. That was the first time anyone *made* him a birthday cake. I surprised him with it and I thought he'd say thanks, tell me it was good but… he *cried*. I had no idea what to do." Eric bit his lip and Jake saw the shimmer of unshed tears in his eyes. It took all of Jake's self-control not to reach over and put an arm around him.

Eric drew in a shuddering breath and continued. "After he explained why a stupid cake hit him so hard, well, that made *me* cry." Eric laughed softly and a tear escaped down his cheek. "Damn you, Andrew. That was the first time he told me he loved me," Eric whispered.

"Did he mean it?" Gram asked.

Eric nodded, tears streaming steadily down his cheeks. "Yes. He did. I know that." Eric turned to Jake and reached for his hand. "I'm sorry," he choked out. "I didn't know he was going to…." Eric wiped his face with his free hand. "I'm sorry."

Jake squeezed his hand and brushed away a stray tear with his thumb. "It's all right. I'm not going anywhere, remember?"

Eric nodded and kept his death grip on Jake's hand.

"So all of these things Andrew just shared—they're happy memories. And that's what he wants you to hold on to. That's how he wants you to remember him." The room fell silent for a long moment until Gram burst out with, "Language! That's my grandson you're talking about."

"What?" Eric and Jake asked in unison.

Gram cleared her throat and tugged at a wrinkle in her skirt. "Well, the message is the last gift he gave you was Jake. He brought you to him because he can be what Andrew never could."

"What's with the 'language!' comment?" Jake asked. He'd heard the same thing from Gram more times than he could count.

"Well. It seems Andrew finds Jake quite attractive. I'll censor myself, if you don't mind, and say 'flipping hot.'"

"Jesus," Jake grumbled as his cheeks took on their usual flush.

Eric laughed and used their clasped hands to pull Jake close. "He's right," Eric said and planted a kiss on Jake's temple.

Gram sighed. "Eric, I'm sorry, but Andrew's energy is starting to fade. I'm impressed he's held on so long. Is there anything you want to say to him before we close?"

"Uh, wow. Well, I never thought I'd say this," Eric began, his voice quavering, "but I'm not angry at you. I understand now, at least some. Thank you for those times we had together… even the bad ones. They're part of who I am now, I guess. And thank you…." Eric paused and swallowed hard. "Thank you for bringing me to Jake. It's where I belong."

Jake felt his own eyes fill as he sat witness to Eric letting go.

"I want you to go," Eric continued. "Not because I hate you, but because it's time. And I hope, wherever that is, you find the peace you didn't have here." Eric dropped his chin to his chest.

"He's pulling back now, getting ready to go," Gram said. "We bless you and thank you, Andrew, for sharing this time with us. Find your light and go toward it. Your work here is done."

Eric looked up as the candles on the table flickered. A moment later, Jake saw a large orb shoot up from the middle of the circle and out of sight.

"What the hell was that?" Eric exclaimed and jerked back in his seat.

"What?" Jake asked.

"That light that came out of nowhere! It went from those candles and then straight up!"

"You *saw* that?" Jake asked.

Eric nodded, still shaken.

"That was an orb," Jake said. "It was Andrew leaving."

Eric scrubbed a hand over his face. "Holy fuck."

"Language!" Gram snapped.

Jake snickered at Gram's exclamation while Eric turned nearly purple.

"Sorry, Gram," Eric muttered as Jake had done a thousand times before. Gram eyed him with a stern glare, but Jake doubted she was serious. He bumped his knee against Eric's and smiled when Eric looked up. The corner of Eric's mouth quirked up and Jake felt the pressure returned on his knee. He nodded and they turned their attention back to Gram as the ritual came to a close.

GRAM AND Anastasia closed the circle. "Why don't you wait in the kitchen?" Jake said to Gram. He didn't need to see the pallor of her skin to know the reading had taken a lot out of her. "We'll get the room back in order."

She smiled and patted his arm. "Thank you, dear."

The three of them extinguished the candles and set the room back to its original layout in just a few minutes. Anastasia led the way to the kitchen where Gram sat at the table.

"You need to get some rest, so we're going to head out," Jake said. "You'll make sure she gets some tea and gets to bed?" he asked Anastasia.

"Of course, dear. Don't worry."

Jake bent down and kissed Gram on the cheek. "Thank you. You're still the best there is," he said with a smile.

Gram laughed. "Go on. Flattery won't get you anywhere."

Eric stood in front of Gram and hesitated for a moment before he bent down and pecked Gram on the cheek like Jake had. "Thank you. I can't tell you what this meant to me."

She squeezed his hand. "I know. How about I make us dinner in a few days and we can talk about it?"

"I'd love that."

Jake handed Eric his coat, and they slipped out the door into the nighttime chill. They walked in silence for a while until Jake looped his arm through Eric's and asked, "You okay?"

Eric nodded. "Yes. Better than I've been in a while." He took a quick glance around them then pulled Jake into the doorway of a closed shop. In the shadows, he drew Jake toward him and kissed him, lips brushing softly at first, and then with more force as he slid his tongue against Jake's. Jake felt his head spin and wondered briefly if kissing Eric would always do this to him. He let the thought go and lost himself in the feel of Eric's warmth against him and around him. Eric pulled back but kept his forehead pressed against Jake's.

"Wow," he whispered.

Jake smiled. "Yeah. Wow."

Eric pulled back further to look Jake in the eyes. "Thank you," he said. "For waiting until I was ready for this, for being there for me tonight as my partner."

"No thanks necessary. I've always felt it was a privilege to be there when a soul passes on."

Eric pressed his lips together. "It couldn't have been easy this time, though. Hearing about what Andrew and I did, how we felt. I'm sorry for that."

Jake shook his head. "Don't be sorry. It was an important thing for you to do. Honestly, yes, I felt a little jealous for a minute. Maybe two," he said with a wink. "But then I realized how silly that was. Yes, you have your memories of Andrew, but I have you here and now. And we have the rest of our lives to make *our* memories."

Eric stared at him for a few seconds then kissed him again. "Every time I think I can't be more amazed by you, you prove me wrong."

Jake shrugged. "I'm not trying to be amazing. I think, maybe, seeing things from the Other Side gives you a little more perspective. How short a time we're here. I've seen so many clients tied up in knots over someone they lost, what they should've said, should've done. I don't want that to be me."

Eric nodded. "Well, I'm allowed to think you're amazing if I want. And flippin' hot."

Jake rolled his eyes and gave Eric a shove. "Shut up," he said, trying not to laugh.

Eric held up his hands in mock surrender. "Hey, I speak the truth. I'm not dumb enough to lie to a psychic."

Jake grabbed his hand and dragged him out of the doorway. "All right, that's enough out of you," he said as he turned them toward the train station. "Let's go home."

"Yours or mine?"

Jake shrugged and smiled. "You pick."

CHAPTER 23

JAKE LOCKED the deadbolt on his apartment door and turned to Eric.

"Not that I mind, but why did you pick to stay here?" he asked.

Eric shrugged. "It just seems to make more sense, I guess. I don't have to show up anywhere in the morning. At least this way you're close to the shop."

Jake nodded and studied him with a narrowed gaze. His gut told him Eric was leaving something out. "And?"

Eric maintained his neutral look for about five seconds and then flopped onto the couch. "God! Is this always how it's going to be? I can't keep one single thing to myself?"

The smile playing at the corner of his mouth told Jake he was mostly kidding, but he guessed there was probably a genuine question buried in there too. "No. You can keep things to yourself," Jake said as he entered the living room and sat down next to Eric. "But there are three possible outcomes: number one, if it involves us, it may fall smack into my blind spot and I'll have no idea. Number two, I'll know you're not telling the whole story but I'll just let it be. And number three, I'll know you're not telling the whole story and I'll call you on it."

"So why call me on this?" Eric asked. "It's hardly life or death."

"Because I asked you a direct question and you're withholding," Jake said simply. "So? Why here?"

Eric shot him a mock dirty look. "I'm never playing poker with you." He sighed. "It's stupid, really."

Jake grabbed his hand and laced their fingers together. "It's not, I'm sure. If you don't want to say, you don't have to."

"No, it's okay. It's just hard to explain. It feels different here. I don't know if it's you, or the apartment itself, or something you do to the place but it just feels… good. My mind feels clearer. It's comfortable and homey. Safe."

Jake leaned in and kissed him. "I'm glad it feels that way. And I can promise you it's safe. Wait—let me rephrase that. It's safe in a spiritual sense. I'm no black belt. If a serial murderer decides to come busting through the door, we're probably toast."

Eric laughed. "We'll just have to hope you see him coming." Jake nodded, covering his yawn with his hand. "Tired?"

"Yes. Even though I wasn't doing the reading tonight I'm still exhausted."

"Me, too. C'mon." Eric stood, held out his hand and pulled Jake up from the couch. "Let's go to bed."

JAKE AWOKE the next morning to the feel of warm wetness surrounding his cock. He groaned and opened his eyes to see Eric's feet sticking out from the covers next to him. He smiled and ducked under the blankets, happy to find Eric just as hard as he was. He maneuvered a bit to compensate for their height difference and took Eric's cock all the way into his mouth. Eric hummed, the sound vibrating around Jake's length, and picked up his speed. Since Eric had a head start, it wasn't long before he had Jake gasping and thrusting. Jake slid his lips off Eric as he felt his orgasm building. He pushed deep into Eric's mouth and grabbed a handful of his ass as he let go and tremors shook his body.

As soon as he could breathe again, he turned his attention back to Eric and swallowed him down to the base. Jake knew watching him come was a huge turn-on for Eric, so he thought Eric had to be close. He smoothed his lips up and down his cock, pausing to twine his tongue around the tip every so often. He felt Eric's hips begin to move and Jake egged him on, pulling him faster and deeper into his mouth. He heard Eric gasp, "Oh God!" just seconds before he came with one long, hard thrust.

Eric twisted around and popped his head up from the covers, his face flushed and his hair wild. "Good morning," Jake said as he grinned and wiped his chin with the back of his hand.

Eric's response was little more than a growl, and he lunged at Jake and fused their mouths together in a deep kiss.

"Good morning," Eric said when they pulled apart.

Jake smiled. "You could make me late for work every morning, couldn't you?"

Eric grinned. "Only if I'm doing my job right."

Jake kissed him once more and then rolled out of bed. "I have a reading scheduled for nine o'clock, and I still have a small chance of making it down there on time so I'm going to jump in the shower."

"Okay. I'll be good and stay here," Eric said.

"Thank you!" Jake called from across the hall and started the water running.

ONCE HE was dressed, Jake headed out into the kitchen and found a still-messy-haired Eric setting out two bowls of Cheerios. "Before you tell me how late you are, you have to eat," Eric said.

"No, this is great. I usually skip breakfast. Thanks." He pecked Eric on the cheek and sat down. He dug in but after a minute or so he noticed Eric only playing with his breakfast, dragging his spoon through the sea of Os, pressing it down to drown some of them in milk. "Everything all right?" he asked.

Eric looked up. "Yes, fine. Why?" Jake gestured at his bowl and Eric sat back in his chair. "Sorry. I guess I'm not hungry."

"Okay," Jake said warily. A lot had happened the night before and he could easily see how Eric could be upset or freaked out by it. "Not hungry why?"

Eric ignored the question and asked one of his own. "What time do you finish work today?"

Jake shrugged. "Well, I absolutely have to be there until one o'clock when Jessie comes in. After that, I don't know. Why?"

Eric sat quiet for a moment, then looked up and met Jake's gaze. "Will you go somewhere with me? This afternoon?"

"Of course," Jake said without hesitation, following the guiding voice inside him that said *yes, yes, yes*. "What time?"

"Maybe two? Before it's dark."

"All right. Just come by any time after one and I'm all yours."

Eric got up from the table and walked around to hug Jake from behind. "Thanks," he whispered.

AT ONE thirty on the dot, the bell over the door chimed and Eric walked into the shop. Jake was in the back of the store so he had a few seconds to study Eric as he walked up to the counter and said hello to Jessie. He looked a little tense, but nothing like he'd been before the reading at Gram's. He decided not to speculate anymore and made his way up to the front counter.

"Be careful. She may be putting a love spell on you," Jake said as he came up beside Eric.

Eric laughed and gave Jake a quick kiss while Jessie rolled her eyes. "Please. He's so far gone I don't think there's a spell on earth that could save him," she said with a smile.

"That and he doesn't *want* to be saved," Eric added with a wink.

"Okay. Now that I feel like a single crazy cat lady next to you two, where are you going? Hot date?"

Jake looked at Eric and then at Jessie. "I... don't know, actually."

"I asked Jake if he could come with me this afternoon. There's something I need some help with. I hope you don't mind," Eric said.

Jessie shrugged and tossed her curls. "He's the boss. I can hold down the fort, no problem."

"Thanks," Jake said. "Are we taking your car?" he asked Eric.

"Yes. I'm parked around the corner at the entrance to the apartment."

"Okay. Let me run upstairs and grab a coat, and I'll meet you there."

Eric nodded and Jake jogged up to his apartment. He hesitated for a moment over what kind of coat he needed considering he had no idea where they were headed. He closed his eyes and held his hand out in front of the open closet. He moved it slowly over the contents until his sixth sense stopped him. He opened his eyes to find his hand hovering above his winter jacket. It seemed an odd choice but Jake grabbed it and made his way downstairs and out the door.

He slid into the passenger seat of Eric's car, but before he could say anything, he inhaled a nose-full of perfumed air. He sniffed again and looked at Eric, puzzled. "Is that"—he inhaled once more—"gardenia?"

Eric nodded and pointed toward the back seat where a stocky blue vase packed full of white blossoms sat tucked in an open box. "That was a good guess," Eric said. "You didn't even look."

"It wasn't a guess. My work uses lots of herbs, as you know, and flowers too. Gardenia is hard to miss."

Eric nodded. "Well, we should go. Like I said, I want to get there before dark." He turned the key in the ignition, but Jake rested a hand on his arm.

"Eric, what's going on? It won't be dark for a few hours. Where are we going?"

Eric drew his lips into a tight line and swallowed hard. "Cemetery."

Jake nodded and faced forward. Enough said.

THIRTY MINUTES later, they passed through the entrance to Mount Auburn Cemetery in Cambridge, Massachusetts. Jake had heard of it before, and he knew it was a place with historical significance and the resting place of many well-known figures. But he'd had no idea it was still an active cemetery.

"This is where Andrew is buried?" Jake asked as Eric steered the car along the winding road. If not for the monuments jutting up from the earth, the place could easily have been mistaken for a park. They passed gardens and benches, and a large marble-edged reflecting pool.

Eric sighed. "Yes. This is the place. I've only been here one other time and…. Let's just say I didn't stay long. I hope you don't mind I brought you with me."

"No, not at all," Jake said, reaching over to rest his hand on Eric's knee. "But why didn't you just tell me?"

Eric pulled to the side of the road and stopped the car. He rested a hand over Jake's. "I guess because I wasn't really sure I was going to come. But I thought about it most of today and I knew. It was the right thing to do."

Jake nodded and slipped his jacket on as he followed Eric out of the car. He zipped his coat against the November chill while Eric took the flowers from the back seat. They walked side by side among headstones and monuments until they approached a low granite wall that bordered an overlook. Eric walked a few feet down the row in front of the wall and came to a stop. Jake stopped beside him and looked down to see Andrew's name and the dates of his birth and death carved into gray speckled stone. Below that it read "Beloved Son" next to an intricately carved stack of books.

Eric held up the vase of flowers. "Gardenias were his favorite. I never knew why, but any time he had the chance, he'd have them at the lake house or his office. Sometimes just the blossoms floating in a bowl of water."

"Gardenia can be used to reduce stress, encourage harmony and peace," Jake said. "It's a very tranquil flower, and it sounds like Andrew was anything but tranquil." Eric laughed and nodded. "Maybe that was his way of trying to bring a little peace into his space, even if he didn't realize it. He was drawn to it for a reason."

"Maybe," Eric whispered. He took the flowers from the vase and laid them at the foot of the stone. "You're only supposed to leave natural materials at the graves," Eric explained. "No plastic or glass."

Jake nodded. "Do you want a few minutes alone? I can head back to the car—"

Eric shook his head. "No. If I've learned anything from last night, from seeing your work, it's that Andrew isn't under this ground. Who he was—is, I guess—is someplace else, still going, still existing." Jake grabbed Eric's hand and squeezed. "I hope it's somewhere filled with light and the peace he didn't have here. And books." Eric smiled and Jake laughed softly.

"You're a wise man and a quick learner, Eric Austin," Jake said. "I feel certain he has all of those things now."

Eric sucked in a deep breath. "All right. Just one more thing." He fished around in his pocket and produced the ring they had found at the lake house. He set it carefully on the flat peak of the headstone. "This is yours, Andrew. It was meant for you, and I want you to have it. Even though it's not the way we went, I loved you. That's why I bought it, and that's why it's yours."

Eric took a step back and looked at Jake. Jake saw traces of sadness in his eyes but nothing like the confused, aggrieved man who'd walked into his shop that first night. He wrapped his arms around Eric and hugged him tight. "That was perfect," he whispered.

Jake linked his arm through Eric's and they made their way back to the car, Jake taking in the impeccably kept grounds as they walked. Eric's gaze stayed fixed on the ground and Jake sensed some tension rolling in again. He wanted to make sure Eric had gotten to do and say everything he needed to before they left, so he asked, "Is everything okay?"

Eric stopped and leaned against the car, still reluctant to meet Jake's eyes. "I don't know how to say it. I mean, it's weird, and I don't even think it matters…." He trailed off.

Jake lifted Eric's chin and forced him to make eye contact. "Hey. It's me. I can handle weird. And it matters to me. What's bothering you?"

After a moment of silence, Eric said, "The ring."

"Okay. Do you want it back? You don't have to leave it if—"

"No, no. It's not that. I just want you to know… I never would have given that ring to you."

Jake stared at him, unsure if he should be insulted. "Wait, I don't mean it like that," Eric continued. "It's just that that ring was for Andrew and from the past and that's where it belongs. And if I got one for you, I'd want it to be yours. I mean, just for you. Oh God, never mind," Eric said with a groan and let his chin drop to his chest.

Jake smiled. "Eric?"

Eric glanced up with one squinted eye. "Yeah?"

"You're not proposing to me in a graveyard, are you?"

Eric's eyes grew wide, a horrified expression on his face. "No! God, no!"

"Okay, good. I'm not that into my work." Jake leaned in and kissed him. "Let's not worry about any other rings right now, all right? I'm looking forward to just having you to myself for a while. Just us, no ghosts. Well, none that want to join us, anyway."

Eric exhaled and nodded, his shoulders relaxing as he let go of some of the tension.

"Good," Jake said. "Now, how about an early dinner?"

Eric smiled. "That sounds perfect."

They got back into the car. As Eric pulled carefully back onto the cemetery road, Jake looked out the window. For a fleeting moment, he saw a familiar shimmer several yards away, where they'd just walked. He smiled. *Good-bye, Andrew,* he thought. *And thank you.* The shimmer vanished as quickly as it had appeared. Jake reached over and linked his fingers with Eric's, certain, perhaps for the first time, that they had only the future to face. And, whatever that future might hold, he knew they would face it together.

Stay tuned for an excerpt from

Once Upon a Spring Break

By Jillian Snyder

A bar hookup and a spring-break fling—it's not supposed to last, right?

But when party boy Justin Covelli meets Greg Waterman on his spring trip to Hawaii, hooking up is only the beginning. Greg's a grad student, serious to the bone, who has put his partying days behind him. Justin's just looking to blow off steam and get away from an oppressive family while checking out the graduate program at Hawaii Pacific University. But when these two young men start spending time together, they discover that what was supposed to be a random meeting of bodies may truly have the seeds of happily ever after.

www.dreamspinnerpress.com

"*THE GOAL of the project was to evaluate management approaches to prevent and reverse coral reef ecosystem degradation, focusing specifically on the effectiveness of point and non-point source pollution management plans in reducing impacts to coral reef ecosystems. The methodologies employed took into consideration the standard water quality thresholds and the potential adverse affects of disturbances in the....*"

Greg Waterman shook his head and started the passage from the beginning for the fifth time. He got as far as the second line and then gave up, pushing the article away and resting his head on his arms atop his desk. He knew what the article was talking about, or he should, anyway. As a first-year graduate student in the Marine Science program at Hawai`i Pacific University, he'd spent the better part of the last five years—first as an undergrad and now working toward his master's thesis—living and breathing that kind of research. So why, then, did he suddenly feel like he was looking at some kind of abstract shorthand for documenting dolphin clicks and whistles? He didn't have to pick apart a journal article to figure out the answer to that.

Greg pushed his chair away from his desk with his heels and stretched his tanned legs out in front of him, crossing them at his ankles. He scrubbed a hand over his face and willed himself to concentrate on his work, all the while knowing it was a losing battle. Finally he gave up and padded barefoot down the hall to the kitchen where he grabbed a beer, popped the cap, and headed through the living room and out onto the small balcony. He slid the door shut behind him and scanned the horizon. He could see Kaneohe Bay in the distance, still dotted with people soaking up the last of the sun's rays for the day.

He raised the beer bottle to his lips and took a long sip, then leaned his elbows on the railing and sighed. A week ago, everything was different. Actually, a week ago, everything had been the same. The same as it had been throughout most of Greg's time in the Marine Science program. He had been single-minded in his studies, his passion for the reefs and their inhabitants driving him day after day to choose work over play, dry research journals over actual human conversation. But now, everything was different. How his whole life could have been derailed in a week, he had no clue. As he thought back on it, he realized that, no, it hadn't happened in a week. It had happened in an instant: the moment he met Justin Covelli.

One Week Earlier, Saturday

ANNALISE EVANS breezed into the lab and set her books down at the station next to Greg's. He didn't even have to look up from his laptop to know who it was; he'd figured she'd find him eventually, like she'd threatened to do. She pulled up a stool and scooted it closer so she could look over his shoulder.

"Whatcha doing?" she asked, her naturally cheery demeanor coming through loud and clear.

"Entering the data from the latest batch of water samples I took," Greg answered, thankful that her cheeriness didn't often cross the line into annoying.

"Hmm. Anything interesting?" Annalise had been in the program with Greg from the beginning, and even though her research focused on finfish populations, sometimes they found the more general data collected could be useful to them both.

"Nope. No change since the last group of samples so far."

"Well, good!" she said, standing up and putting her hands on his shoulders. "That means the ocean will still be there after you take a night off!"

Greg groaned. "I'd really like to finish this up. If I can just get all these values entered, then I'll be able to graph the—"

"Blah, blah, blah," she said with a dismissive wave and a flick of her long auburn hair. "I knew you were going to try to back out, and I won't let you! Look around here, Greg! It's dead. There's nobody here. Do you know why? Because it's spring break! You're allowed to go out and have fun, you know."

He clicked a button on his laptop to save his work and then closed the computer with a sigh, knowing it was futile to argue with her. "All right, fine. I'll go. But I don't want to be out late. I was hoping to do a dive early tomorrow morning and get some more photographs of that potential bleaching I spotted last time."

Annalise rolled her eyes as he packed up his laptop and notes. Then she leaned close and said mischievously, "We're going to Hula's, so maybe if we can find you a cute guy to wake up next to, you won't give a crap about diving in the morning!"

Greg shot her a look and growled as he stood and slung his bag over his shoulder. While he was out at school, at least among his friends, he made sure they knew his views on how distracting relationships, even casual ones, could be, and that he had no intention of getting involved with anyone until he finished his degree and secured a decent job. A job over at the Oceanic Institute, if he had his way.

He had screwed around a lot when he first arrived at HPU, enjoying that first bit of freedom out from under the watchful eye of his parents. He'd learned the hard way where his energies should be directed, though, after almost failing his second semester and risking his scholarship. "Please don't make me say it again," he moaned as they left the lab. "I'm not picking anyone up, there's not going to be a one-night stand, and you"—he fixed her with a pointed stare—"better not try playing matchmaker. I'll come and hang out with you and… whoever for a while, and then I'm going home and going to bed."

They pushed through the main doors of the building and stepped out into the warm spring air and sunshine. Annalise gave Greg a quick once-over and shook her head. "It's such a waste, though."

"What is?"

"Your…." She waved a hand as she searched for the words. "Monastic lifestyle! Look at you, all tall and blond and tan and muscle-y. You should spread that around! You could make some equally hot guy really happy."

Greg blushed a little at the compliment. "Yeah, well… I'm not saying never. Just not now."

She cast a thoughtful look his way. "You don't always get to pick when it happens, you know. Sometimes it just… finds you."

"'It'?" he questioned, furrowing his brow at her.

"You know, true love! The one," she answered with a wink. "C'mon, wikiwiki!" She laughed and picked up her pace. Greg smiled and sped up, surrendering himself to the upcoming night of "fun".

Two hours later, after a stop at his apartment to shower and change at Annalise's insistence, Greg found himself stationed at the bar at Hula's Bar & Lei Stand. Hula's was the most popular gay bar in Waikiki, and it was more crowded than usual that night due to the influx of people that came with spring break. While the Hawai'ian Islands weren't the most popular destination for spring-break travelers, usually due to the expense, a good number of college students still flocked there every year to party in the crystal waters under the golden sun. The music boomed and the dance floor vibrated with the movement of all the bodies pressed together, gyrating to the beat.

It hadn't escaped Greg's notice that some of those bodies, the male ones in particular, were shirtless and looked like they'd been chiseled out of granite. No harm in window shopping, he told himself as he took a sip of his gin and tonic and scanned the crowd again. This time, though, he spotted a head of wavy, reddish hair bopping toward him. Annalise stopped in front of him and fanned herself with both hands.

"Woo! It's hot out there!" she shouted.

Greg nodded. "I bet."

"Can I?" she asked, pointing at the drink in his hand.

He handed it over, and she took a healthy gulp. Annalise could definitely hold her liquor and, though she wasn't drunk yet, Greg could tell she was well on her way by the goofy grin on her face and the slightly glassy look in her eyes.

"Pace yourself, or you'll be home before I will."

She rolled her eyes, set the drink on the bar, and grabbed his hand. "Come dance with me!" she said, giving his arm a tug in the direction of the dance floor.

"What happened to Kai and Kevin and Halia?"

She picked up the drink again and took another sip. "Kai and Kevin are probably screwing in some dark corner. Halia is...." She skimmed the crowd, but then gave up, saying, "Over there somewhere, I guess."

When she set the glass back down, Greg picked it up and drained it. "Let me have a couple more of these, then maybe I'll dance." He motioned to the bartender for another drink.

"Okay, fine. I'll respect your tight-ass ways and let you get good and drunk before I make you do anything embarrassing."

"Thanks. I appreciate it," he said wryly.

She dropped his hand, popped up on her toes to kiss his cheek, and then bopped away and disappeared into the mass of people.

Greg was halfway through his next gin and tonic, still people-watching, when he felt a light tap on his shoulder from behind. Greg turned and found himself staring straight into a pair of stunning blue eyes, as clear and calm as the waters in which he spent his days. The shock of dark hair above them made them stand out even more. His heart sped up a little as the guy leaned in to say something.

"Do you know what time it is?" he asked, close to Greg's ear so he didn't have to shout.

Greg took one more look at the stranger and then glanced down at his watch. He leaned in to give his answer. "Ten forty-five."

The guy nodded and took a swig from the beer bottle in his hand, making no move to leave. They stood facing each other, not saying anything more, and Greg waited to see what he was going to do with the information.

After about a minute of silence and furtive glances, the guy moved toward him to speak again, and this time, Greg met him halfway.

"I don't really care what time it is," he said. When Greg turned his head slightly and shot him a questioning look, he added, "I just wanted to talk to you."

Greg moved back slightly to look at him head-on, a little taken aback by his directness. "Oh," was all he managed to say.

The stranger smiled and stuck out his hand. "I'm Justin," he said, loud enough to be heard over the din of the music.

"Greg." Greg slid his hand into Justin's, and he felt a tingling sensation pass through his fingers as they moved over smooth skin and into a firm grasp. They held on a little longer than necessary, and Justin leaned in toward Greg a third time.

"Wanna go out on the balcony?" Justin asked.

Greg nodded, vaguely surprised at himself but intrigued enough by the handsome stranger that he wasn't willing to stop and think about it. He followed Justin through the crowd and out onto the much quieter balcony. Justin spotted by the railing a recently vacated table overlooking the beach and zipped over to claim it. Greg caught up to him and they sat down as Justin waved over a waitress and ordered another beer and a gin and tonic for Greg. A brief, awkward silence descended, but Justin soon broke it, repeating his introduction in the quieter outdoor setting.

"Justin Covelli," he said. "Just in case you couldn't hear me in there."

"Greg Waterman."

"Waterman, huh?" Justin said with a smile. "That's interesting, considering…." He gestured toward the beach that was visible across the road.

"Yeah. I guess it's kind of weird that I ended up here with a name like that."

"So you're not a local?"

"Well, I suppose maybe I am now, after five years. Moved from Connecticut for school, but I'm not planning on leaving any time soon."

"Where d'you go to school?"

"HPU. Hawai'i Pacific University. I'm a first-year grad student in Marine Science." Greg nodded his thanks as the waitress set their drinks on the table.

"No shit!" Justin said with a laugh. "Part of the reason I came down here was to check out that school!"

"Really? Where're you from? Aren't you here on spring break?" Greg took a drink and shifted his position, propping his elbows on the table, already interested in learning more about Justin.

"I'm from upstate New York. I go to Cornell; I'm a junior in the Natural Resource Management Program. HPU caught my eye because of their grad program in sustainability, and because it's pretty fucking far from New York."

"So, you don't like it there?"

"Cornell's great. But I grew up right in the same area, plus my dad and I don't really get along. Just want something different, I guess."

"Well, it's different here, that's for sure. When did you get here?"

"Yesterday afternoon. I figured I'd kill two birds with one stone. Have a kickass spring break, and come check out the school," Justin said with a smile.

"Good plan."

Justin asked some more questions about Oahu, HPU, and what Greg was studying, and Greg found himself genuinely enjoying the conversation. He couldn't ever remember meeting someone from outside his program who was actually interested in the details of what he did. And Justin had his own views on a lot of topics when it came to preservation and protecting the environment, which made it even better. As the school talk wound down, Greg tipped his glass back and drained the last of his drink. When he set the empty glass down on the table, he noticed that Justin was looking at him with a devilish glint in his eyes.

"So, do you think you've had enough now?" Justin asked.

"Enough what?"

"Enough drinks so you'll dance with me."

Greg's mouth fell open slightly as it sank in that Justin must have been watching him at the bar for longer than he realized. Instead of making him feel weird and uncomfortable, though, the idea made him feel warm and a little nervous. Good nervous. But he kept all that to himself, and he looked at Justin with a straight face and said, "No." A look of surprise followed closely by disappointment flashed across Justin's pale features. He opened his mouth to say something, but before he could, Greg added, "But I'll dance with you anyway."

A grin bright enough to rival the island's summer sun spread across Justin's face and he laughed. As they started to make their way back inside, Justin came up close behind Greg and put a hand on his waist. "You're gonna pay for that," he murmured in Greg's ear.

JILLIAN SNYDER lives outside of Rochester, NY, with her lovely wife and their herd of rescued critters, which includes a blind Chihuahua, a Pomeranian, bunnies, and a chinchilla. She has a longtime love of languages and works with words every day in her job as an interpreter. She is fluent in American Sign Language and also has over a decade of French under her belt. She listens to all types of music, but has a special love for the music of the late Freddie Mercury.

She is the epitome of a Gemini personality, and she often speaks well before she thinks. She has been a vegetarian for seventeen years and is a fan of earth-friendly and fair trade products and clothing. Her wardrobe is as eclectic as her personality, with the exception of her devotion to her growing collection of Kate Spade handbags. She is an avid reader, loves improv comedy, and movies of any genre, all of which are engaging ways to tell stories. And there's nothing Jillian loves more than a good story.